Finding Papa's Shining Star

by

Judy Nickles

Finding Papa's Shining Star

Cover Art by *Rae Monet*

The Wild Rose Press
PO Box 706
Adams Basin, NY 14410-0706
Visit us at www.thewildrosepress.com

Publishing History
First Vintage Rose Edition, 2010
Print ISBN 1-60154-695-5

Published in the United States of America

Portions of the Burial Service are from the 1979 U.S. *Book of Common Prayer of the Episcopal Church.*

He stopped and looked away from her, then back. "I wasn't sure you'd wait for me."

She felt her face flame. "I'm your wife, David."

"We didn't have much of a marriage. Ten days, and from what I remember, we spent most of that time in bed. We can't spend the rest of our lives there."

"I always wondered if that's why you married me," she said before she thought. "Because you couldn't get me any other way."

"Is that what you thought?"

"Well, you said..."

"I know what I said, but you had a choice, didn't you?"

"I guess so. Yes."

"Well, assuming that I married you because I wanted you, why did *you* marry *me*?"

Her mind raced frantically for some kind of answer that would be honest but not heartless. David would know if she was telling the truth.

Taking a deep breath and expelling it slowly to buy time, she said, "I don't know, David."

"I didn't think you did. Do you want a divorce?"

"You haven't been home but a few hours. I don't think this is the time to discuss anything so...so final."

"When do you think it will be time?"

"What do you want, David?"

"You, Annie. Just you. I was in love with you. I still am."

"We hardly knew each other."

"I remember telling you once that love can't be explained. It just happens."

Dedication

To Donna, Leona, and Linda,
my good and true writing friends,
with affection and appreciation

Prologue

"When you adopt me tomorrow, will my name be Ashley?"

The child edged closer to the man in the pine-green wing chair, her eyes fixed on his as if he could see her.

"Yes, it will, unless you would rather not."

"I want to be an Ashley. I want to be Annette Lenore Ashley. Girls should be named for their mothers, you see."

"You were named for your mother, weren't you? Roberta?"

"Alan, please..." The woman in the matching chair twisted her hands in her lap.

"Answer the question, Bobbie."

The delicate face paled. "She's dead, and she didn't want me anyway."

"You are very much wanted here with Lenore and me."

The child knew he spoke the truth. From the moment he'd found her hiding in one of the confessionals at the church in Greenfield, she'd known she could trust him. "So can I?"

"I'll speak with Mr. Bernard before the hearing tomorrow."

She smiled then. "And you can call me Annie, and I'll...I'll call you Pa." She leaned against his knee. "Mum and Pa sounds nice together."

Chapter One
New York, 1941

Annie Ashley woke with a start. The dream had come more often of late and left her feeling fragmented and a little afraid. She sat up, scanning the dormitory room which appeared unfamiliar now with all her things packed.

She switched on the lamp and glanced at the clock. Six-thirty, still four hours before the commencement exercises and almost two until she could meet her parents for breakfast at their hotel. She was aware of a sudden desperate need to see them and feel their arms around her, to reassure herself that their love was still the one unchanged thing in her life.

Though she'd been Annie for ten years, Bobbie remained alive in the recesses of her mind. No matter how hard *Annie* tried, *Bobbie* couldn't forget that, as a child, she'd been abandoned twice by the very person she'd loved and trusted above all others.

Where are you now, Papa? Do you know that I'm twenty-one and about to graduate Vassar? Do you ever think of me, your best little girl...your shining star?

She turned off the lamp and lay down again. The light filtering through the drawn blinds cast shadows that undulated across the floor and danced eerily in the corners of the room she'd occupied for four years. She pulled the sheet over her head and squeezed her eyes shut.

Oh, Papa, you promised you'd come for me, and you came twice, but you didn't take me. Why, Papa? I wanted to go with you so much. Why did you take Rebekah and leave me? I waited and waited for you, Papa. I'm still waiting, only now I couldn't go. It would hurt Mum and Pa, and I couldn't do that.

Annie threw back the covers and swung her feet over the side of the bed, shivering in the chill of the early May morning. She remembered the winter mornings she'd waked in the long, icy room at the Home when the furnace wasn't working, her exposed face stinging with cold. Even on good days there was no hot water upstairs, so she and the other girls always skimped on washing and rushed to the dining room where they could warm themselves in front of the cavernous wood-burning fireplace.

The chill of June mornings in Maine, where she'd spent two weeks every summer after her adoption, was a happier memory. She'd hurried to wash and dress just so she could be waiting on the stairs when her parents emerged from their own room.

Pa always took the same house every summer, the one he said his parents had brought him to as a child. It sat right on the beach, and after breakfast Annie would run to the water's edge and let the waves nibble her toes while she waited for Mum and Pa to come down.

Despite being blind, Pa was a fearless swimmer, and he'd insisted that she learn also. Mum was content to wade a little, although sometimes Pa could coax her farther from the beach. Sometimes they would stand holding each other while the waves rolled in around them, and Annie would watch them kiss. They were so very much in love, but she never felt left out. The three of them were, as Pa had promised, a very special family.

No trip to Maine awaited her this summer. Instead, she would be entering the world of business now, earning her own way. The job at Ashley

Enterprises, if Uncle Trent hired her as his assistant, would mean that she could live at home, and she was counting on going home to stay.

She shook her head. She couldn't think of him as *Uncle Trent* anymore, but rather as Mr. Young, vice-president of Ashley Enterprises, who wouldn't hire her unless she was the best applicant. He did his job independently of Pa, who owned the company, which was how Pa wanted it. The fact that he'd watched her grow up, that she'd spent weekends with Aunt Jean and him on their wonderful farm, would mean nothing when it came to making the choice of his new assistant.

She tried to tell herself that was how she wanted it. Ashley Enterprises didn't deal in granting favors. Everyone was treated the same. She knew that from experience.

When she was fourteen, she'd begged to go to work with her parents in the summers, and they started her out with Mr. Sheeley in maintenance. He set her to mopping floors and scouring employee bathrooms and lounges, but she knew how to work, because she'd done the same things at the Home.

The next summer, Pa arranged for her to work in the employee lunchroom. When she declared that she'd made enough sandwiches and salads and washed enough dishes to last her a lifetime, he merely laughed before sending her to the kitchen to hunt up the butter cookies that their housekeeper, Mrs. Swane, hid in a different place every week.

The third summer she graduated to the mailroom where Rod—Mr. Rodman, Pa's chauffeur before Mum came—ran her legs off. Then came the metal shop and the secretarial pool, and finally, the year she finished Arlington Hall, Pa let her work in his office. He was the hardest taskmaster of all.

She knew Ashley Enterprises well, loved it and wanted to be part of it, so she had to give a good account of herself in the interview next week. There were other jobs, of course. She had appointments scheduled with three businesses in towns around Rumers Crossing, but any one of them might mean living alone in an apartment.

The vision of her room at home elicited a visceral ache. It had been Pa's when he was growing up, and he'd had it remodeled just for her. Within its cool, dove-gray walls, books strained against the glass doors of built-in bookshelves, which had been expanded more than once. The morning sun coming through the white sheers on a wide bank of windows made the roses that spilled over the upholstered window seat seem so alive she was sure she could smell their delicate scent.

Over the light maple headboard, *The Pink Lady* looked down on a four-poster bed spread with a coverlet as white as winter snow on the lawn. The pink satin comforter spread across the bottom of the bed just matched the flowing dress of the picture's subject. A chaise, two wicker chairs with overstuffed cushions that matched the window seat, and a spacious writing desk shared space on the thick silver-gray carpet.

Annie closed her eyes. She'd taken jealous and meticulous care of the room she considered her castle tower, running the carpet sweeper daily and scrubbing the adjoining white tile bath every Saturday until it gleamed like sunlit snow.

She'd taken particular care of her castle knight, too, the shaggy, lumbering black dog rescued, like herself, from a dumping ground for the unwanted. Actually, he'd chosen her, with thumping tail and eyes full of love and devotion. Mrs. Swane called him a small horse, but she came under his spell, too. It would be good to drift off again at night with one hand stroking his massive head.

Sighing, Annie stretched and got out of bed. *I'll*

be home tonight, home to stay. Don't come with me, Papa. You left me behind, now leave me alone.
****

Just before eight o'clock, she went downstairs. *Pa said he wanted to give me back my childhood, but it lasted such a little time. I don't want to be an adult, not yet, but I can't say that to him. He'd be disappointed in me.*

She glanced at her watch, then out the window for the cab she'd ordered and saw it waiting at the curb. In the back, after telling the driver where she wanted to go, she leaned her head against the seat and closed her eyes.

Mum wouldn't care if I never grew up. She'd let me stay her little girl forever. We've been through so much together, just trying to survive. Pa doesn't really understand what it was like for us living the way we did. He only knows that he forged ahead despite his circumstances, and he expects me to do the same. I know he's right, but...if only time had gone a little slower...if only...
****

Alan Ashley lifted his wife's glossy black waist-length hair out of the way so that he could kiss the back of her slender neck. "Almost ready, my love?"

Lenore reached back to touch his smooth-shaven cheek. "Almost, Alan dearest."

"I don't believe you slept well after we finally ended our marathon conversation. Weighty matters shouldn't be discussed before retiring."

"It was something of a debate, wasn't it?" She turned to face him.

"I believe it ended up that way, and we didn't actually settle anything. In a few hours, Annette Lenore Ashley is graduating *magna cum laude*, but last night at dinner I glimpsed Bobbie again. She's not ready to move on."

"That's what worries me, Alan." Lenore sat

down at the dressing table and began to twist her hair into its accustomed coil.

"Does it? Sometimes I almost believe that you'd keep her a child forever if you could."

"Oh, Alan, of course I wouldn't!"

"Her reluctance to embrace her new status concerns me also, but she's stronger than you think. The end of her schooldays means taking her place fully in the adult world, and that in itself is often frightening to some extent, even to a well-balanced young woman like our Annie."

"I suppose I was apprehensive when I finished business school and began work in Judge Sutherland's office, but I was excited, too. What did you feel when you first came home to take over Ashley Enterprises?"

"Despite my arrogance, I was filled with self-doubt."

He moved closer behind her and put his lips against her neck again. "I don't suppose I gained a full measure of courage as a whole man until we were married. Then, despite my lack of sight, I suddenly gained a vision of the future. You were that vision."

"Perhaps we should have a talk with her when we get home," Lenore said. She rose and folded her arms around his neck.

"Tell her everything about her father, you mean? Insist that she put it behind her once and for all?"

"Perhaps not everything."

Alan sighed. "We're back to that."

"I know you felt we should tell her when she finished high school and that I disagreed. Perhaps I was wrong."

"I thought then that we were only putting off the inevitable, but we can't go back."

"I'm still afraid he'll want her."

"Do you think he's ever stopped wanting her? Wanting his daughter? Still, all his contact is through Emory Roth, who won't tell me exactly where Albert Rycroft is. 'Somewhere in Palestine' is all he'll say."

"I'd like to believe she'll feel happier when she's home again to stay. She's missed Mrs. Swane's attention and Prince's companionship."

"The old fellow is getting on. She won't have him forever."

"And that will break her heart, Alan. She's lost so much."

"No more than many others, including the two of us. You might consider instead that the world is before her with all its thrilling possibilities."

"That would be the better way to look at things, wouldn't it?"

"Infinitely." He opened the glass on his wristwatch. "It's almost eight. Annie will be waiting for breakfast." He felt his way to the chair where he'd placed the new cashmere sweater he'd bought for Lenore despite her usual protest that she didn't need anything. "You'll want this in case the dining room is chilly." He held it so she could slip her arms into the sleeves.

"Really, Alan, you hover over me more every day."

"I suppose you become more precious to me every day."

Lenore's eyes filled. "What a lovely thing to say!"

Sensing her emotion, Alan drew her into his arms. "Your health has been a concern for me since what you experienced last year."

"Dr. Sims assured you I was all right and that it wouldn't happen again."

"We didn't expect it to happen at all, and after eight years..."

"We agreed to let nature take its course," she

murmured.

"Unfortunately, it did."

"I wanted so much to give you a son."

"It wasn't meant to be, darling Lenore."

"I prayed for a miracle, and I was so happy when I thought it was granted."

"It just wasn't a viable pregnancy, given your age and, more especially, in view of my circumstances."

"*It* was our baby, Alan."

"And you are my life."

She sighed. "If it had to end, I'm glad it happened early and that Annie was away at school."

"You're still protecting her."

"I know." She lifted her face and received the expected kiss. "Perhaps, in a sense, I'm still running away from the past, too, but I was helpless to protect her once, and now..."

"You can't shield her from life."

"Is that what I'm trying to do?"

"I believe so."

"Be patient with me awhile longer, please, Alan."

"This is a day for celebration, not introspection." He offered her his arm. "Shall we go?"

****

"Didn't you sleep well, Annie dear?" Lenore inspected the dark circles under the younger woman's eyes.

"Oh, Mum, I'm just excited about graduation, I suppose." Annie kissed Lenore's cheek, then Alan's. "And starving for breakfast!"

In the hotel dining room, Alan removed a small box from his pocket. "We decided to give you your graduation gift now," he said, sliding the box along the table toward Annie.

"I don't need a single thing, Pa, and you know it."

"You're tearing the wrappings as if you do," he teased.

Annie rolled her eyes. "Your ears are like an amplifying system." She gasped as she lifted the lid and saw a key nestled in cotton. "A car?"

"There's a picture in there also," Lenore said. "It's still in the show room, so if you don't like it..."

"It's...wonderful...gorgeous! Thank you both so much!" She jumped up and hugged them, eliciting polite stares from the other hotel guests. "I can't believe it!"

"You'll need transportation wherever you find employment," Alan said, then added, "All your friends have had their own automobiles for years."

"So I've never lacked for a ride," Annie replied.

"You've shown a singular lack of interest in the things you might have had," Alan observed, feeling the rim of his cup before tipping the tiny glass bottle of cream into it.

"I've had everything. What else could I have wanted?"

"I'm speaking of material things."

"I didn't need those either."

Alan laughed. "I've failed miserably in all attempts to spoil you and Lenore."

"I think you've made up for it now in one grand gesture," Annie said. "Thank you. Thank you so very much!"

****

After breakfast, Annie left her parents at the college auditorium and returned to her dormitory room for her commencement regalia. She switched on the lamp so she could see to adjust her cap in the mirror. The face looking back at her was almost haggard.

Excitement about graduation hadn't made her look like this, and she was sure that Mum knew that. But she couldn't confess to the recurrent

10

dreams about Papa. *Mum always knew that I never gave him up, even after he left me behind the second time. She knew I loved her completely, but she always believed that, given the choice, I'd go with Papa. I could tell she didn't believe me when I said that I hated him after what happened that night.*

Annie remembered how, a few weeks after Alan and Lenore were married, Alan had presented her with several options, including legal guardianship, but she'd chosen adoption. *"Please, I want you and Mum to adopt me. I want to belong here forever."*

He'd turned those cloudy, slightly unfocused eyes on her, and she felt he was seeing into her very soul. "If you're quite sure that's what you want, Bobbie."

"You said we'd be a very special family."

He nodded. "We will indeed."

Seeing the invitation of his open hand, she placed hers inside, feeling the warmth and strength of his fingers around hers. The tangled scarring on the backs of his hands, like bursting, dying stars spiraling to earth, fascinated her. Mum said they were part of the war injury that also blinded him.

"I want you to understand, Bobbie," Alan said, "that you may change your name, but you are still yourself. You can't run away from the past. I would do you no favor to let you try."

Annie could hear her own reply as clearly as if the little girl she'd once been stood beside her now. *"But bad things happened to Bobbie. I don't want to be her anymore."*

****

"Isn't a compartment rather extravagant for a six-hour trip?" Annie asked as she shoved her hand luggage into the overhead rack.

"After the excitement, I thought we might enjoy some quiet time together," Alan said.

Annie settled herself into the seat across from Alan and Lenore. "Honestly, Pa, I'm going to be a poor working girl soon. I'll do well to travel coach instead of riding in the coal car."

"Surely your circumstances won't be so dire. Tell me, what are your plans for the next few weeks?"

"Sleep until noon, take long walks with Prince, and have cinnamon buns twice a day."

He chuckled. "An epic endeavor."

"Actually, I have four interviews scheduled." Annie removed a piece of paper from her purse. "Two are with banks in Canon City, one is a manufacturing company in Bissel, and then the one with Uncle Trent...that is, Mr. Young."

"I spoke with him earlier this week. He understands that if he hires you, it must be on merit alone. I wanted to be sure that he understood my position." Alan reached for Lenore's hand. "The only impulsive hiring decision I ever made was deciding to take on Lenore as my personal assistant, and you can see the result. I lost my heart forever."

"And the peace and quiet of your bachelor digs," Annie said.

"Yes, you and Prince livened things up a bit."

Lenore took off her hat and laid it aside. "We're so proud of you, Annie dear. Are you glad to be going home?"

"So you've said several times, Mum." Annie reached across to pat Lenore's knee. "And, yes, I'm glad and would be gladder if I knew I could stay. It all depends on which job I get. I could possibly commute to Bissel, but I'd have to take a room in Canon City and only come home on weekends."

"If you live and work in Canon City, you must put down roots there," Alan said. "Become a part of the community in which you live and work. Make friends, involve yourself in activities that young people pursue."

"Like finding a man to marry?"

"I'm sure that will happen someday."

"Not until I find someone just like you, Pa."

Lenore smiled. "There's only one Alan Ashley."

"Billing and cooing," Annie said.

Alan laughed. "One day you will leave the nest, and that's as it should be." He felt the numbers on his Braille watch as the train lurched forward. "Right on time."

"I like my nest," Annie insisted. "Four years away at school were enough."

"I remember how you always cried when you had to go back after a holiday," Lenore said. "It broke my heart."

"And then she'd call to tell us that she'd arrived safely but didn't have time to talk because she was going to do this or that with her friends," Alan added.

"I suppose I just like things the way they are, and before you say it, Pa, I know that things don't stay the same forever."

"You should know before we get home that Mrs. Swane is thinking of retiring," Lenore said. "Her sister needs her more and more often. She regretted missing your graduation, but she had to go to her sister."

"I thought you were going to talk to her about having the third floor remodeled to suit her, Pa."

"She knows the option is there, but her sister is family, after all."

"Well, so are we!"

"Things are going to change more drastically than just losing Mrs. Swane," Alan said. "The news from Europe grows worse each day."

"Do you really think there'll be another war, Pa?"

"No one likes to think so, but it seems inevitable. I suppose you know your friend Bea has moved up her wedding date because Patrick is considering enlisting as a chaplain."

"Yes, she wrote me. She'll stay in Kentucky even if Patrick goes into the service. She said she can't leave the school."

"A small, poor school like that has difficulty getting teachers, especially those of Bea's caliber," Alan said. "Her mother knows the problem first hand."

"But Ellen and Sam supported Bea's choice," Lenore reminded him. "And they adore Patrick."

"A penniless young minister with no prospects except for a lifetime of satisfying service to others," Alan said. "Bea chose well."

"So that's why you're trying to match me up now?" Annie teased.

Lenore patted her purse. "Why, I have a list here of half a dozen potential husbands."

Alan produced the tickets from his pocket when the conductor tapped on the door. "First things first," he said as the man moved on. "If war comes, Ashley Enterprises like every other company must gear up to meet production quotas. We've acquired a shipyard on the coast, but the executive offices are in Canon City. Would you like to accompany Lenore and me there next week? It would be a good opportunity for you to see how these mergers happen."

"I'd love to go, but I'm not an A-E employee yet and may not be, at least not in the foreseeable future. "

"Still, it will provide you with some experience and insight about things to come."

"You make it sound as if the war's already begun."

"Oh, it's begun," Annie," Alan said. "It has indeed begun."

Chapter Two

"I've never seen anything like it." Annie pressed her face against the window as Lenore drove through the huge iron gates of the shipyard's Canon City facility. "It's enormous."

"This place and others like it have an enormous responsibility for the country's defense," Alan said. "I'm sorry that you won't be able to attend the meeting with us, but I've arranged for you to tour the establishment."

"We may be a long time, Annie," Lenore said. "There's a lunchroom where you can get something to eat if we're not finished by noon."

"I'll be fine, Mum. Who's going to take me on this tour?"

"A young man named David Levinson, the chief draftsman."

"You *are* setting me up at every opportunity."

Alan frowned. "Not at all, Annie. When I mentioned that you were coming with us and learned that you couldn't attend the meeting, I asked about the availability of someone to..."

"Entertain me?"

"David Levinson is a very knowledgeable person," Alan said.

"You know him?"

"I've met him."

Annie sat back in the seat. "Eligible, too, I'm sure."

Lenore laughed. "As a matter of fact, he is."

"Oh, Mum!"

****

15

Annie settled down in the outer office after Alan and Lenore went into the boardroom. "Mr. Levinson will be here shortly," the secretary said.

Annie glanced around. "He needn't bother with me if he has other things to do."

"I'm sure it's no bother to spend some time with an attractive young lady."

Annie smiled at the middle-aged secretary. "Thank you." She picked up the latest issue of *Look*. A few minutes later, the door opened and a man strode into the office. "These need to go out today, Mrs. Bradshaw," he said, dropping a sheaf of papers on her desk. "I'd do it myself, but I'm supposed to show some little debutante around the yard."

Before Mrs. Bradshaw could reply, Annie lifted her chin. "I'm the little debutante, but it's quite all right if you haven't time. I can amuse myself."

The man looked at her so intently that she grew uncomfortable under his scrutiny. She stood up, dropping the magazine back onto the side table. "I'm Annie Ashley," she said, extending a gloved hand as she took in his tall, muscular build and the face that she and her college friends would have called *movie-star handsome.*

"Ashley?" his eyebrows went to his hairline.

"Alan Ashley is my father."

His eyes traveled from her face to the ceiling and back again.

"He didn't mention a daughter."

"Why should he?"

"Are you part of Ashley Enterprises, too?"

"I hope to be. I'm interviewing next week."

"Why would the boss's daughter have to interview at all?"

Annie resisted the temptation to counter his sarcasm. "Because that's the way things are done at Ashley Enterprises. Hiring is done independently by the head of each department and is by merit alone."

"You don't say."

Mrs. Bradshaw cleared her throat. "Mr. Levinson, perhaps you'd like to attend to these papers yourself while I conduct Miss Ashley around."

For a moment, he appeared to consider the idea before he said, "No...no, I'll do it. It might be interesting." He held the door for Annie. "I'm David Levinson, by the way. Shall we go?"

Annie strode to the door confidently, the way Bea had taught her. *You're Annie Ashley, not Little Orphan Annie. Act like it.*

"Certainly, Mr. Levinson." For a moment, her tongue tripped over the name even as it seemed suddenly familiar.

"Are you just along for the ride today?" David asked as he pointed her toward the elevator.

"My father thought I should become familiar with this new branch."

"It sounds like you're already hired."

"Not at all, but I am his heir. Someday I'll be responsible for Ashley Enterprises."

"Like I said."

Annie stepped past him into the elevator, ignoring the gibe. "How long have you been here, Mr. Levinson?"

"Six years, since I finished college."

"I just graduated last week."

"From where?"

"Vassar."

"Naturally."

She ignored the intended slight, although her irritation was growing. "Where did you attend college?"

"The University of Texas."

"Really? I was born in Texas." She regretted the words as soon as they were out of her mouth.

"I see. If you don't mind my asking, why would

an attractive young woman who doesn't have to work for a living choose a business career?"

"Everyone is obligated to earn his living," Annie said, biting off the words without caring if they sounded rude. "I've always been interested in Ashley Enterprises, and I believe I explained that I'm the only one to take it over someday."

"No brothers or sisters interested?"

"No brothers or sisters, period."

"And you're really interested in running a business like Ashley Enterprises?"

"Someday."

"It's convenient to be the daughter of the company president, then."

Annie's chin came up again, this time with a definite haughtiness that she knew the man noticed. "No, Mr. Levinson, I told you that we don't do things that way at Ashley Enterprises."

He grinned, irritating her further. "So what will you do if you aren't hired as..."

"Administrative assistant to Trent Young, the vice-president."

"Yes, well, what will you do *if* he hires someone else?"

Annie was tempted to tell him that it was a good thing he wasn't applying, because his arrogance would be the first thing Trent Young noticed and the only thing he remembered.

"I have other interviews scheduled...two banks and a manufacturing company. The other option is the secretarial pool at Ashley Enterprises."

"I'm sure that won't happen."

The elevator ground to a halt, and she waited until they'd both stepped out before she turned to face him. "I could work in maintenance or the mailroom or any other department of Ashley Enterprises, as I have every summer from the time I was fourteen. I started out mopping floors."

"No offense, Miss Ashley."

"Offense accepted, Mr. Levinson."

She let the silence hang between them until they reached the drafting department. "This is where the plans are made," David said. "I studied architecture, actually."

"Why did you decide to design ships instead of houses?"

"It's good experience. The architectural firms I applied to wanted experience, and the shipyard was more interesting than anything else available to me at the time. We were still in an economic depression, you know."

"I know all about hard times, Mr. Levinson. I lived through it, too." She paused beside the man sitting at the nearest drafting desk and peered over his shoulder. "Ships are quite different from buildings, I imagine."

"And more needed right now."

As they moved on through the room, she waited for him to ask how she'd experienced hard times, but he didn't. "More needed because of the war in Europe," she added, to fill the break in conversation.

"The war that's coming to us."

Annie frowned. "Pa says it's inevitable, but I can't help hoping..."

"We'd all like to hope, Miss Ashley."

****

At noon, Alan and Lenore were still closeted with the manager of the shipyard, so David invited Annie to lunch. "There's an employee lunchroom downstairs. Nothing fancy, but the ham salad is always fresh, and there's iced tea."

They carried their trays to a corner table. "I'm still trying to see you in the role of a business executive," David said as he spooned sugar into his tea.

"Administrative assistant to the vice-president

is by no means an executive position." Annie took a bite of her sandwich. "I made enough ham salad to feed an army the summer I worked in the lunchroom."

"That was after you mopped floors?"

"And cleaned employee restrooms and the break room. Yes, the very next summer."

"What happened after that?"

"Oh, I worked my way through the mailroom, the metal shop, and the secretarial pool. The summer I finished high school, Pa let me work in his office. He taught me a great deal."

"So what does an administrative assistant do?"

"Anything that's needed. Mum works with Pa in his office and uses the Braille writer to transcribe notes for him. Mr. Young's assistant travels a great deal as a liaison between Ashley Enterprises and its subsidiaries here in New York and in Pennsylvania, New Jersey, and Massachusetts."

"I had no idea that it was such a large company."

"The subsidiaries are more or less independent, with their own executives, although they have to adhere to certain standards of ethical business practice."

"Such as?"

"I'm sure you know what ethical business practices are, Mr. Levinson."

"So those will be in place here, too."

"I'd think that they already are." Annie toyed with the pickle on her plate. "Actually, my mother became engaged to my father a few months after she began work as his assistant. They've worked together for almost a dozen years now."

"A *dozen* years?"

Annie allowed herself a smile at David's surprise. "My mother was my step-aunt, and after she married Alan Ashley, they adopted me."

"You look like her. Same height, dark hair and eyes."

"No one realized that we weren't really mother and daughter until she became ill and was hospitalized. The state took me away from her then, and I ended up in an orphanage for almost two years. Before that we lived in a third-story room with no hot water, and I swept the first floor and sidewalk and did some babysitting to help earn money for groceries. I was nine."

David stared at her. "I apologize, Miss Ashley."

"I accept the apology, and I do understand how you might think of me as privileged. In a way, I am. I've had every advantage since I was eleven, but Mum has always been quite strict about an over-abundance of material possessions. Pa would have indulged me, but he also set high educational and personal standards for me. Gram—that's Mrs. Swane, our housekeeper—took up any slack. I had chores and responsibilities, unlike most of the girls at Arlington Hall. That's the private school I attended in Rumers Crossing."

"Oh."

Annie smiled at David over the rim of her glass. It was easier to be pleasant to this abrasive person now that she had the upper hand. "And while I was offered the opportunity to make my debut, I declined."

"I've been out of line. I'm sorry."

"Yes, you have, so with that out of the way, perhaps we might move on to more pleasant topics."

He nodded. "What else are you interested in, besides business?"

"I love history and once thought of becoming an archaeologist."

David sat back in his chair. "We have something in common then, because I thought of that career choice also. Then I decided that architecture would earn me a better living. But I went on several digs during my college days."

"Really? Where?"

"I've been to Peru twice and to Egypt once."

"I envy you. I've only read about such things. We were going to Europe two years ago, but we had to cancel our plans because of the uncertain political situation."

"I haven't been totally honest with you, Miss Ashley. My condescending attitude is uncalled for, as I, too, came from an affluent family."

"So you were never hungry or had to put cardboard in your shoes?" She couldn't resist the opportunity to put him more firmly in his place. She hid her smile when he squirmed.

"No."

"I was never hungry. Mum ate less, so that I could have more, which is why she got sick. But replacing the cardboard in our shoes was a weekly event. I remember how we made it almost like a party. I always saved a nickel from what I earned so I could buy day-old pastries at the bakery down the street. Mum would make cocoa if we had milk. We called it our hard times holiday."

A look of honest distress passed over his face. "I feel worse and worse."

And you deserve to, Annie thought, but she said, "Don't, Mr. Levinson. As Pa says, the bad times build character. His own was certainly forged in the fires after he became blind during the last war."

"I've only met him once, but he impressed me as someone who was in complete control and knew what he was doing."

"Yes, he does, not only as a businessman, but as a husband and a father as well."

"Obviously. May I offer you dessert, Miss Ashley? I saw a chocolate pie on the counter."

****

"I'm glad that you were occupied this morning," Alan said as Annie drove them home. "I didn't anticipate being so long, and they were adamant about not allowing you into the meeting. I did well to weasel Lenore in." He chuckled softly. "I even had to play my trump card and say that I couldn't take notes for myself."

Lenore tapped his hand as if to infer that he was a naughty child. "He put on such an innocent air and said he had no objection to their own stenographer, and, of course she'd transcribe the notes into Braille for him, too, since I wasn't allowed to see them."

Annie giggled. "Oh, Pa."

"Well, they were being unreasonable. I understand about national security, but it wasn't as if I'd brought Mata Hari with me."

"I don't know about that. Mum does look rather mysterious and alluring in all those silk robes you keep buying her," Annie teased.

"That's why I buy them," Alan said.

"Stop it, both of you." Lenore's tone of voice told them she meant it. "And as for Alan's performance, it was a rather sneaky ploy."

"Yes, and it worked, too, didn't it?" He smiled, remembering the silence in the boardroom as the impact of his edict sank in. "So David Levinson gave you a tour. What did you think of the place?"

"I don't know enough about shipbuilding to give an educated opinion, but everyone seemed busy. There didn't seem to be any confusion about what was being done."

"What did you think of David?" Lenore asked, settling into the circle of Alan's arm across the back seat.

"I thought he was arrogant, condescending, and rude." Annie frowned, then smiled as his face came to mind. "He's also very handsome."

"Arrogant, condescending, and rude?" Alan

asked.

"He kept questioning the fact that I, as a woman, would be interested in business, and I'm sure that he also felt I was incompetent." Annie felt her cheeks grow hot with the anger she hadn't allowed herself to display earlier. "And he called me a *little debutante.*"

Lenore laughed. "She's quite worked up, Alan."

"Red cheeks?"

"Very."

"Mum, that's not fair. You've been in business your whole life, and you started when most women stayed home and had families."

"I didn't have a family to take care of until you came. After that, I had to work to support us, and then I grew so interested in working with Alan that I didn't want to stop after we married. Mrs. Swane runs the house more efficiently than I could anyway."

"And I needed you," Alan added. Lenore leaned over and kissed his cheek.

"Why does the name Levinson sound familiar to me?" Annie asked.

A sudden silence replaced the good-humored banter.

"Mum? Pa?"

Lenore leaned forward to touch Annie's shoulder. "Your...Albert Rycroft was employed at Levinson's Emporium in Barnwell."

"Papa?" The name slipped out before Annie realized it.

"Yes, your papa," Alan said.

"David told me that he's from Texas. It would be a coincidence, wouldn't it, if there was a connection?"

"Actually, my dear Annie," Alan said after a moment, "there is a connection."

"You're serious!" Annie's fingers tightened around the steering wheel.

24

"Quite. Where are we?"

"Just a few miles from Georgetown."

"Suppose we stop for dinner, and I'll tell you what I know of him."

****

With her barely-touched dinner pushed aside, Annie turned her coffee cup between her hands. "So David Levinson is the grandson of the man who owned the store in Barnwell."

"Do you remember meeting the elder Mr. Levinson?" Alan asked.

"I don't think so. I was at the store several times, but...no, I don't think he was ever there."

"He didn't live in Barnwell," Alan said. "His son, David's father, was also in the mercantile business. He and David's mother were, I believe, killed in an automobile accident some years ago."

The small amount of dinner she'd eaten lay leaden in Annie's stomach. "You said you'd met him before."

"When we did some business with the shipyard before I purchased it."

"You never mentioned him to me." Annie hoped she didn't sound accusing.

"There didn't seem to be any way to broach the subject, Annie. You never ask questions, and whenever Lenore and I mention your father..."

"You're my father."

"Whenever the conversation turns to the past, to Albert Rycroft, you have nothing to say, or you simply leave the room."

Annie didn't reply.

Lenore put her hand over Annie's. "Does it really matter, Annie dear?"

"No." Annie's reply was too quick, her head shake too vigorous. "No, it doesn't matter. It's over."

****

Lenore and Alan lingered in their sitting room

after telling Annie goodnight. "We've made a beginning," Alan observed, "and I don't believe that it doesn't matter to her."

"Perhaps we should just let it go," Lenore said, a quiver in her voice betraying her anxiety.

"I disagree, but I will abide by your wishes, darling Lenore." He gathered her in his arms and realized that she was trembling. "She's in denial about her past, just as I denied that my blindness had changed my life. It will catch up with her as it did with me."

"Albert Rycroft knows where she is."

"And has never contacted her, that's true. But he knows about her, thanks to Roth's willingness to be the go-between."

"Would Emory Roth give you more information if you insisted?"

"I don't need more information. It's enough that he sees that our communications with Rycroft are facilitated. The man has shared Annie's life as much as possible through pictures, school reports, copies of awards and newspaper clippings. He's had everything."

"Except her."

"Obviously, he doesn't want to be part of her life. I don't understand it, but it's been to our advantage."

"She's been happy with us."

"Yes, she has."

Lenore put her face against Alan's. "It's just possible that she doesn't even think of him anymore except when something happens, like today."

Alan sighed. "If you think that for a moment, you're fooling yourself, my love. Bobbie is still with us, and she's still her Papa's shining star."

Chapter Three

Alan twirled the dial on the radio until the static faded. The frantic voice of the announcer, punctuated by the staccato sounds of others amid obvious chaos, filled the room. Lenore and Annie sat in silence, almost forgetting to breathe.

"Well, it's finally happened," Alan said, sitting back in his chair. "Pearl Harbor. It was an obvious target."

"So we're at war?" Annie asked.

"I'm sure the President will ask for a formal declaration tomorrow."

"Now what?" Annie asked.

"We've been making contingency plans for this day," Alan murmured. "And now it has come."

"I can hardly believe it." Lenore's fingers played with the doilies on the arms of her chair.

Aland held out his hand to her. "Unfortunately, the 'war to end all wars' did not accomplish that purpose. Wilson knew that. He was firm in his belief that Versailles was not a peace but rather a truce for twenty years. We've realized the truth in those words since Hitler invaded Poland in thirty-nine. Now it's our turn."

"Will we fight Germany, too?" Annie asked.

"I'm afraid so, Annie. The world is at war again."

****

Just after the first of the year, Trent Young telephoned Annie to ask if she was still interested in working for him. "You were second on the list, you know, after Jack Shaw. He feels obligated to enlist."

"Couldn't he get a deferment because Ashley

Enterprises is involved in producing war materials?"

"I've spoken with him about trying for one, but he doesn't agree. Not that I can blame him. I know I'm asking you to leave a permanent position just for the duration of the war, but you know the business, Annie. There's no time to train anyone else."

"When do you want me to start?"

"Whenever the bank will let you go."

"I'm sure they can replace a teller without too much difficulty."

"I knew we could count on you, Annie. You do understand that..."

"Of course, Uncle...Mr. Young. Jack's position will be waiting for him when he comes home."

"God willing."

"Yes, sir. God willing."

****

"I'm proud of you, Annie." Alan accepted the cup of coffee she placed in his hands. "I know you were disappointed when Trent hired Jack Shaw."

"I understood that Uncle Trent felt Jack was the best candidate, and I wouldn't have wanted it any other way. I learned from you, remember?"

Alan gave her an approving smile. "You did indeed."

"You're in a position to advance at the bank, and you like it there," Lenore said.

"The bank understands. My supervisor said he couldn't tell me I could come back after the war, but he'll give me a good reference."

"You're quite sure then?" Alan asked.

"I'm sure, Pa. And besides, I'll enjoy...well, you know, I didn't like living in that boarding house. It reminded me too much of..." She stopped, not looking at Lenore. "I'll be glad to be home again."

****

"It's the right thing to do, Gram." Annie reached for the butter cookies. "You were going to retire and go to live with your sister, but you've stayed here because of the war."

"You might've ended up president of the bank."

Annie laughed. "I don't think so. Anyway, something would've come up for me eventually at Ashley Enterprises." She reached for Mrs. Swane's hand as the woman sat down at the kitchen table. "I'm glad you're staying. It wouldn't be the same without you."

"Everybody's going into war work these days. I don't know who Miss Lenore would get to run this house."

"Oh, she'd find somebody, but they wouldn't do things your way. We're all pretty spoiled, you know."

"I didn't spoil you."

"Yes, you did, and you know it."

"You turned out all right."

"I hope so. I want Mum and Pa to be proud of me and..." Her voice trailed off.

Gladys Swane sat silent, wondering if Annie would finish her sentence. When she didn't, the housekeeper asked, "Do you ever think of your father, Annie?"

Annie's mouth twisted. "Pa is my father."

"All right, your *Papa* then."

"Why did you bring him up?"

"I don't know. I've been thinking a lot about my family lately, the ones that are gone. My husband, my parents, all my brothers and sisters except two. I'm getting old, I suppose."

"You're not..." Annie began.

"Mr. Alan mentioned the other day that you never ask any questions."

"What good would it do? What's done is done, like you always say."

"You're going to get married someday, Annie. What are you going to tell your children?"

"I don't have to tell them anything. They'll grow

up knowing that Mum and Pa are my parents and their grandparents."

"You really don't think about what happened before?"

Annie shut the cookie tin. "It's all a jumble now, Gram. That night, after I knew Grandfather Harcourt was dead, I tried to stop thinking about it."

"Did you ever wonder how he died?"

"He fell down the stairs and broke his neck."

"Is that what they told you?"

"Jerry told me."

"You know that I fired my gun at him."

"Yes, and Pa aimed at the sound and ended up shooting you."

"You said that your Papa was in the house, that he took you upstairs to the secret room."

"And left me there and never came back. I don't want to talk about it anymore, Gram."

Mrs. Swane sighed as Annie rose. "Someday you're going to have to talk about it, Annie." She shook her head as the young woman hurried out of the kitchen.

****

"I don't know what made me bring it up," Mrs. Swane said to Lenore later as they shared a pot of tea while going over the household accounts.

"She just doesn't want to think about it, that's all. Alan says...well, we don't agree about this, as you know. But thank you for trying."

"She reminds me of Mr. Alan, the way he was after the war. He built a wall around his circumstances, too, but you tore it down."

"Perhaps someone will tear down Annie's wall, too, Mrs. Swane. We'll hope for that." She frowned. "I think."

****

True to Trent Young's expectations, Annie stepped into Jack Shaw's position with minimal difficulty. As Ashley Enterprises geared up for war production, Alan asked Trent to take the responsibility for the shipyard, so Annie found herself the liaison between Ashley Enterprises, the shipyard's executive offices in Canon City, and the main facility in Portsmouth. When she was in Canon City, she often lunched with David Levinson, whom she began to consider interesting, though she still disliked his overbearing self-assurance.

In early March, a series of meetings required her to stay several nights in Canon City. At the end of the first day, David overheard her telephoning for a taxi to take her back to the hotel. "You don't have your car?"

"It went up on blocks in the garage as soon as I went to work for A-E and could ride to work with Mum and Pa. I take the train when I travel. Besides, gas will be rationed soon, just like rubber."

"Other people will pull strings to get extra gas coupons."

"Pa won't, not for himself or for me."

"I'll be glad to drive you to your hotel. I'll even take you out to dinner."

"That would be nice."

"Dinner, too?"

"Why not?"

He drove her to the hotel to check in, and from there they walked two blocks to a small café. "Good home-cooking," he assured her. "I recommend the baked chicken."

He took her coat as she slid into the booth. "Will you stay on at Ashley Enterprises after the war?"

"Not as Mr. Young's assistant."

"Why not?"

"Only four employees have enlisted or been drafted and refused deferments, and their positions are being held open with temporary workers. That's what I am."

31

"It sounds very strange to me."

"That's part of Pa's business philosophy. These men are risking their lives, and they should have something secure to come home to. He's asked Mum to keep in touch with their families and make sure they don't go without anything they need while the men are overseas."

"That's admirable, I'm sure."

"It's the right thing to do. Ashley Enterprises is more than a business. It's a family."

"So what will you do when the war ends? Go back to the bank?"

"It depends on whether or not there's a position available for me. My supervisor couldn't promise me anything."

"What about the secretarial pool at Ashley Enterprises?"

She frowned at the derision in his voice. "It's honest work."

"For a woman with a college degree?"

"For anyone. Why are you baiting me?"

"Is that what I'm doing?"

"It seems that way to me."

"I'll change the subject then. Do you have a boyfriend?"

"That's really none of your business."

"You do, then."

"I don't."

"Good. I'm interested in the position."

"You're very sure of yourself."

David laughed. "There's nothing wrong with that. You could use a dose of self-confidence yourself."

"What do you have in mind? Marrying the boss's daughter?"

"I might."

"The boss's daughter isn't interested."

"That can change."

"I don't think so. Not where you're concerned."

"Why not?"

"I plan to marry someone as much like Pa as possible, and you're not in the least like him."

"I might be more like him than you think."

"I don't think so, Mr. Levinson. He's one of a kind." She unfolded her napkin and spread it in her lap as the waitress brought their plates. "I hope the baked chicken lives up to your recommendation."

"It will. And so will I. You might start by calling me David."

Annie lifted her eyes to meet his. "I don't intend to *start* anything."

****

He drove her from the shipyard to the hotel every evening, but when she declined further dinner invitations, he didn't insist. On the last evening, he waited for her to check out of the hotel and delivered her to the railway station. "Will you be back soon?" he asked as he took her luggage out of the trunk.

"I have no idea."

"Will you miss me?"

"Definitely not."

He laughed and carried her bags inside to check them. "You're brutally honest." He handed her the claim tickets.

"I don't know how to be anything else."

"What would you do if I showed up in Rumers Crossing some weekend? At least your parents like me."

"I'd be busy, so don't bother, unless, of course, you're coming to visit my parents."

"What would you do if I kissed you?"

She put out a gloved hand. "Goodbye, Mr. Levinson. Thank you for the transportation."

Before he could speak, she stepped onto the train.

Chapter Four

"He is without question the most arrogant man I've ever met," Annie said as she ate dinner with Alan and Lenore the next evening.

"Lenore used that adjective to describe me once or twice." Alan held out his cup for a refill. Annie took it and went to the sideboard.

"I can't believe you were ever like David Levinson." Annie placed the cup exactly at two o'clock beside Alan's plate.

"Ask Lenore."

Lenore pressed her lips in a tight line of disapproval. "Alan, really."

"You did call me *arrogant*, my love."

"You deserved it...then."

"Mum!"

"He did, but he's improved considerably." Lenore put her hand over Alan's.

"You've been a good influence on me," he replied. "Perhaps Annie will soften Mr. Levinson."

"I'm not interested in softening Mr. Levinson," Annie retorted. "Will you two stop playing matchmaker?"

Mrs. Swane put her head through the swinging door. "This is my bridge night."

"I'll clean up, Gram," Annie said. "We're dawdling." She twirled her fork in the uneaten mashed potatoes. "He had the nerve to suggest he might come here one weekend."

"Why, I told him he had an open invitation," Lenore said. "He's..." She stopped.

"You told him that? Oh, Mum."

"He's a nice young man," Lenore insisted. "I like him."

"I don't."

"Where is Trent sending you next?" Alan asked.

"I'm not sure. It seems I'm home less and less these days."

"I don't like you spending nights alone in a hotel," Lenore said.

"Would you prefer she spend them *with* someone?" Alan asked, then chuckled at his own joke.

"Alan! What a thing to say."

He patted Lenore's arm. "She's a grown woman, my love."

"Well, yes, but..."

"He was teasing me, Mum. Why are you blushing?"

"I'll go and see what Mrs. Swane has for dessert." Lenore dropped her napkin beside her plate and hurried off.

"Pa, you shouldn't embarrass her."

"She was actually blushing?"

"Like a rose."

"You really don't like David Levinson?"

"No, I don't."

"Well, people change, Annie. I *was* an arrogant young man. Perhaps it wasn't entirely my fault, but it stung when Lenore commented on it. I valued her opinion and wanted her approval."

"Obviously she approved of you. You've been married quite happily for ten years. Speaking of that, are you going back to that little hotel in the Catskills for your anniversary next month?"

"We're thinking of it."

"I think you should. You both need to get away."

"I'll admit that we're already feeling the strain. Everyone at Ashley Enterprises is tired these days."

"The war can't last forever."

"I'm afraid the war is only getting started." Hearing Lenore return, he turned and smiled. "Do I smell fresh apple cake?"

"Still warm from the oven, and there's whipped cream." Lenore replaced his dinner plate with a smaller one and slipped a new fork into his hand. "Don't get the cream on your tie."

"Did you bring me a bib?"

She bent to kiss his cheek. "You don't need one, Alan dearest."

He managed to capture her wrist and draw her closer so that he could find her lips.

"You two are still billing and cooing like newlyweds," Annie said, spreading whipped cream on her cake. "And I won't settle for anything less, so keep that in mind when you're matchmaking."

"Don't *settle* for anything, my dear Annie. Expect only the best." With casual precision, Alan brought a bite of cake to his mouth. "Like me."

"Oh, now listen to him, Mum."

Lenore shook her head. "Alan, I don't know what's gotten into you tonight."

"I'm thinking ahead to our second honeymoon."

"You mean the tenth, don't you?" Annie asked, noting Lenore's pink cheeks. "And she's blushing again."

"If you two don't stop, I'm going to take my dessert upstairs," Lenore said.

Alan laughed. "We'd better cease and desist, Annie."

Lenore didn't look up, but Annie saw her mouth twitch with amusement. "Yes, you'd better."

****

Business took Annie to Massachusetts in March around the time of her parents' trip, so Rod drove Alan and Lenore to the station. "I'll plan on meeting your train on Sunday," he told Alan.

"You might call the house to see if Annie is home

before you come. And you'll take care of seeing about young Wilhite's wife...widow...while we're away?" Alan asked Rod after tucking the baggage claim checks in his pocket.

"Mary and I will go over there."

"Make sure that she isn't in need of anything."

"She'll get his insurance. I'm sure she knows that."

"Tell her that Jerome Vannoy will be glad to help her decide how to use it, but only if she'd like his counsel."

"I'll tell her. Have a good trip, Mr. Ashley...Mrs. Ashley."

****

They settled into their seats for the four-hour trip. "It will be dark by the time we arrive," Alan mused.

"There was no way to reschedule that meeting this morning."

"Things just keep piling up. Meetings, contracts, employee turnover...and young Wilhite."

"You need a rest, Alan. We both do." She sighed. "It's such a shame about Billy Wilhite."

"Unfortunately, he won't be the last. As for business, we'll have to plunge in as soon as we return. Annie's tired, too."

"She's young."

"Are you saying that I'm old?" He lifted her hand to his lips.

"Of course not."

"I am, but a week totally alone with you will rejuvenate me considerably."

She laughed softly and scooted closer to him. "I hope so."

****

"This bungalow seems like a second home after ten years," Alan said as they stepped inside. "Has anything been moved?"

Lenore glanced around. "Nothing."

"Is a fire laid?"

"Yes, and I see the champagne bucket."

"Naturally. I like you tipsy."

"Oh, Alan, I don't get tipsy."

"You get very sleepy, and then I can carry you off to bed and have my way with you."

"I should think that after ten years you don't need permission or champagne to have your way with me."

"That's true, but it sounds more daring."

Lenore changed into her new robe before their light supper was delivered. "What color is this one?" Alan asked as she joined him on the sofa.

"Lavender. It's extravagant to buy a new peignoir set every year, you know."

"But I like it."

"That's the only reason I do it." She began to serve their plates. "There's no more silk to be had in the stores these days. This is one of those new synthetic materials."

When they'd finished, she stacked everything on the rolling cart and set it outside the door. "Yes, before you say anything, I'm going for the champagne in the kitchen," Lenore said. She returned with the chilled bottle and a corkscrew.

"I could do this blindfolded," Alan joked as the cork popped and fell onto the floor.

"You've certainly had enough experience." Lenore picked up the cork and set it aside. "Only half a glass for me, Alan dearest."

"Then you'll only be half as much fun."

"You're making very bad jokes tonight."

"You love them, admit it."

She watched him fill both glasses with a skill that never failed to amaze her. "I love *you*."

"To us...to Annie...to love," he said, lifting his glass. "We've known so much happiness, my darling

Lenore. I want the same for Annie."

****

She was already drowsing beside him when he began to remove the pins from her chignon. As her hair cascaded down her back to her waist, she roused and reached for the brush on the table. "It's still like silk," Alan commented as he began the nightly ritual they both enjoyed.

"There are more than a few white hairs, and you have absolutely none."

"Does that mean it's more difficult being my wife than being your husband?"

"It means that my mother's hair was solid white by the time she was fifty, and mine will probably be the same."

"Then people will mistake you for my mother, and we can't honeymoon here anymore." He lifted her hair and kissed the back of her neck, then began to knead her shoulders. "Lenore, do you think Annie is interested in David and that's why she protests so much that she's not?"

"I don't know, but I'm glad we told her who he is before anything developed between them."

"They say truth is stranger than fiction. It's enough of a coincidence that Albert Rycroft, the very man who saved my life in France, is Annie's biological father. To add yet another twist of fate, that David Levinson is connected to Rycroft also..."

"Only indirectly. I don't suppose he ever met Annie's father."

"I'm sure she hasn't shared any personal information with him."

"I doubt it."

Alan stood up. "Why are we discussing David and Annie on our anniversary?"

"Because we're parents," Lenore said, holding out her hands.

He grasped them and lifted her to her feet. "I

love making love to you even more than I did ten years ago. You're everything to me, Lenore. Wife, best friend, partner, lover..." His mouth came down on hers as he crushed her closer his arms.

Chapter Five

It was July before Annie went back to the shipyard headquarters in Canon City. Irritation nibbled at her when she saw David waiting on the platform. "I was appointed," he said, grinning at her obvious displeasure.

"It's been a long day, and I have a meeting very early tomorrow morning."

"Hello, David. How are you, David? So nice of you to meet my train, David." He grinned at her.

Annie glared back. "None of the above. Here are my baggage claim checks, and I'm staying at the same hotel as before."

He stepped back and gave a mocking salute. "Yes, ma'am, boss lady!"

"Don't call me that," she said between gritted teeth. "I'm very tired, David, and in no mood to play verbal ping-pong with you."

"But you do it so well. Did my ears deceive me, or did you just use my first name?"

"Just leave it alone."

He took the checks. "You know my car. Go ahead and get in."

Annie found the car and laid her head back against the seat. She'd have to make sure that David wasn't her driver this trip. Surely there was someone else who could see that she got to and from the hotel, and if not, she didn't mind calling a taxi.

She reflected that she hadn't lied to him when she said she was tired. She'd spent exactly four of the past thirty nights at home, and she *was* exhausted. Her parents were exhausted, too, and she didn't like the fact that Lenore had lost weight she didn't have to spare. Hopefully, two weeks in Maine this summer would help restore all of them. The only permanent restoration, of course, would be the end of the war, and that didn't appear to be on the horizon.

She closed her eyes and thought of the members of the Ashley Enterprises away at war. Jack Shaw, a bombardier with the Eighth Air Force; Billy Wilhite, supervisor of the metal shop, dead in the Pacific within days of arriving there, leaving a young wife and a baby he'd never see grow up; Yeary and Hartsfield, also in the Pacific; Rod's oldest son, Peter, only eighteen, in basic training; and Jimmy, the son of James the doorman, bound for an unknown and undoubtedly dangerous destination.

Some of the women in the secretarial pool had left to follow their husbands to distant stations all over the United States. Those remaining had to take up the slack since replacements were hard to find. No one was looking for work these days. If nothing else, the war had improved the economy.

She startled as David slid behind the wheel. "You really *are* tired," he said with no hint of the usual cynicism in his voice.

"I've slept in my own bed four nights this month."

"How are your parents?"

"Hanging on."

"It's going to be a long haul, you know."

Annie closed her eyes again. "Maybe once we get production organized…"

"Don't count on it."

"You might humor me."

"If that means lying to you, I can't do it. I might as well tell you, Annie, I have my replacement trained, and I'm leaving at the end of the month."

Her eyes flew open again. "You've been drafted?"

"I enlisted."

"David, why?"

"Why not?"

"You could have stayed here because of your job."

"My replacement is just as good as I am. Better maybe. He's 4-F because he had polio as a child and still wears a brace on one leg."

"But you're going to..."

"To war? That's what it's all about, isn't it? Surely you're not worried about me."

"Of course, I am! I'd be worried about anybody. My friend Bea's husband is going to the Pacific as a Naval chaplain, and Jack Shaw, the man I replaced at Ashley Enterprises, is in England right now. We just lost the metal shop supervisor. His baby girl is only six months old."

"It's too bad, but I don't have anyone to worry about me."

"What about your family?"

"My parents are both dead. I haven't seen my half-brother since their funerals six year ago, and we correspond infrequently. That's it."

"I'm sorry."

Neither spoke until they were inside the hotel. "When do you leave, David?"

"At the end of next week."

"But you'll be here until then?"

He nodded and set down her bags at the desk. "Right."

"Does Pa know?"

"I suppose that's information you'll take back with you in your report. The hiring is done here, not at Ashley Enterprises."

"He'll be sorry to hear that we're losing you."

David's eyebrows arched. "Really? Well, you're tired, so I'll leave you alone."

"Thank you for meeting my train."

"I wanted to do it."

"David, have you...that is..."

"Yes?"

"I was going to say that I haven't eaten a bite since noon."

"Neither have I. Would you like to go around the corner for a hamburger?"

"I'll meet you back here in five minutes."

Annie berated herself as the elevator crawled toward the fourth floor. *Why did I suggest getting something to eat? I don't even like him, not that much anyway...but he's going to war. He might not come back.*

****

"Is this a one-for-the-boys gesture?" David asked as he held the door for her.

"Why are you always so suspicious? You're downright cynical, as a matter of fact."

"No reason. I wasn't beaten as a child or anything like that."

"Is it just me that you like to irritate?"

"That's the only way I can get any indication that you're alive."

"What do you mean?"

"I mean that you're an icicle, Annie."

"I resent that. Just because I'm professional..."

"Uh-uh, professional doesn't explain it. It's pretty obvious I'm interested in you, but I don't think it makes a difference who's interested. You're not."

"That's a pretty broad statement."

"Well, you're what? Twenty-two? No boyfriend and totally oblivious to any attention I pay to you."

"It's business, David."

"Does it have to be?"

Annie didn't like the way his words muddled her thoughts. "I think it does."

"Well, I tried, anyway. How do you want your

hamburger?"

"No onions."

David gave the waitress their order. "How did you end up living with your step-aunt? Isn't that what you said Mrs. Ashley was before she married?"

"It's a long story."

"It might be a long wait for the burger."

"Then it's none of your business."

He settled back. "Then make it my business. I'm interested.

"It's complicated, David."

"You said you were born in Texas."

"A little town called Barnwell." She watched for recognition in his expression.

"My grandfather had a store in Barnwell."

"I know. My father, that is my biological father, was the manager."

"Albert Rycroft?"

"How did you know his name?"

"I've heard about him all my life. Whatever happened to him?"

"What did you hear about him?"

"That he got framed for a robbery at the store, and his wife left him and took their daughter. I guess that was you." David sat forward, waiting.

Annie frowned and chewed her lip. "A robbery?"

"An inside job, supposedly, but my grandfather swore that Albert Rycroft wasn't responsible."

"Papa wasn't a thief." Her stomach knotted.

"I believe I just said that."

"Oh."

"It's a small world."

"Yes, it is. Did you know that Papa was the man who saved Alan Ashley's life in France?"

"No, I didn't. You're right. It *is* complicated."

The waitress brought their hamburgers. David didn't attempt further conversation, but Annie had the feeling that he was watching her. Afterwards, he saw her to the elevator in the hotel lobby, said a quick, impersonal goodnight, and left.

****

He was lounging against the wall by the elevator when she came down the next morning. "Breakfast?"

"All right."

"Is the same place around the corner all right with you?"

"Of course. I've been thinking about what you told me last night."

"About your father? Is he still alive?"

"I think so."

"You don't know?"

"I suppose Mum and Pa know."

"But you've never asked."

"When Mamma took me away from Barnwell, Papa promised to come for me. He had his chances to take me with him later, at least two of them, actually, and didn't do it."

"So you're angry with him."

"In a way."

"What happened to your mother?"

"She was married to Mum's brother for awhile. He'd already sent me to live with Mum and her mother before they divorced. She never wanted me anyway."

"Is she still alive?"

Annie shook her head.

"But you've lived an idyllic life with the Ashleys."

"That doesn't make up for it. He was my father. I loved him."

"If you say so." He opened the café door for her. "What's on the agenda today?"

"Meetings and more meetings."

"Are you free tonight?"

"I should be, but..." She shrugged. "If you're

inviting me to dinner, I accept."

****

He took her to the Canon Club, where the live orchestra was better than the food. After dinner, they stayed to dance. Annie hated herself for crying when the music ended at ten with "I'll Be Seeing You."

David offered her his handkerchief but made no comment. At the hotel, he walked her to the elevator. "I'd like to come up," he said when the door opened.

She frowned. "Why?"

"I know you're smart about the business world, but personally there's a lot you don't know about the real one."

Her face flamed. "It wouldn't look right. I know that much."

"Do you care?"

"Of course I care."

"I don't. Not really."

"If you were a gentleman, you'd be more concerned about my reputation than about what you want."

"Did I say I wanted anything?"

"Well, don't you?"

The elevator doors slid shut, but he pushed the button again and stepped inside close behind Annie. "I just said that I wanted to come up. That's all."

****

Though she'd attended a girls' school and college, Annie hadn't lacked for escorts to any function. Still, her experience with members of the opposite sex was limited. She was, she admitted when she came up for air on the sofa in her room, out of her league with a man like David Levinson.

"This is completely improper," she sputtered. "I don't even like you."

"You like what I'm doing." He sat back, smiling

at her disheveled appearance.

"I shouldn't." She got up and walked a safe distance across the room. "You might as well know that I'm not planning to give anything away until I'm married."

"That's all right. Marry me."

"You're insane."

"Why? Because I asked you to marry me?"

"I don't even like you," she repeated in precisely-measured syllables.

"Why?"

"I don't know. First impressions, maybe."

"We're a lot alike, Annie."

"We're not in the least alike."

"The Ashleys come from backgrounds more diverse than ours."

"They adore each other."

"We might learn to adore each other, too."

"I don't think so, David. You'd better leave now."

He shrugged. "I'll be in the lobby at seven-thirty to take you to breakfast and drive you to the office."

"I can get a taxi."

"I'll see you tomorrow." He stepped out into the hall and left the door standing open as if he knew she would follow him into the corridor. She watched him until he disappeared around the corner toward the elevator.

****

Annie had dinner with David every night that she was in Canon City. He didn't suggest coming up to her room again until the last night. "I told you, David, I'm not...well, I'm just not."

"Did you ever want to?"

"I never thought about it."

"I still have a week before I report. I'd like to see you again before I go."

"Why?"

"I'm attracted to you."

"And that's why you asked me to marry you? Because you're attracted to me?"

"Well, you wouldn't believe me if I said I was in love with you."

"Are you?"

"Strange as it may seem, I believe I am."

"You're insane."

"You've said that before."

"What makes you think that you're in love with me? We hardly know each other."

"You can't explain love, Annie. It just happens. It's just there. Why did the Ashleys fall in love?"

"I never asked. They just did, that's all."

"Maybe it's time your aunt..."

"She's my mother!"

"Maybe it's time your mother had a long, serious talk with you."

"I know about the birds and the bees, thank you very much."

"Uh-huh, well, maybe you need to know *why* they do what they do."

"Goodnight, David!" Annie reached past him and pushed the elevator button.

"I guess this means I can't come up."

"Absolutely not."

She was certain that his intentionally exaggerated sigh could be heard all over the lobby. Before she could step into the elevator, he grasped her arms and pulled her toward him, kissing her long and hard despite her struggle to get away.

She put both hands against his chest and pushed. "Don't!"

He let her go. "I'll see you around, Annie. You can count on it."

Chapter Six

Annie joined her parents in the drawing room after dinner, curling up on the floor with her head in Lenore's lap. "Why, Annie, you haven't done this since you were in school." Lenore stroked the younger woman's hair.

"I've missed it, too, Mum."

"You've had very little transition from girlhood to womanhood with the war coming on like it did," Alan said.

Annie reached for Lenore's hand. "Sometimes I wish I could go back. I really do."

"Why?" Alan lit his pipe and placed the match squarely in the glass ashtray on the table beside him.

"Why do I wish I could go back?"

"I believe that's what I asked."

"It was all so simple then, just being Annie Ashley."

"Aren't you still her?" Alan asked.

"Yes, but she's...it's just not the same, Pa. This is only the fifth night this month that I've been home."

"We're well aware of that, Annie. Lenore and I miss you when you're not here."

"I had dinner with David Levinson in Canon City."

Lenore's fingers continued to stroke the dark hair almost identical to her own. "How nice, dear."

"Did you know about the robbery at the store in Barnwell?"

Alan nodded. "Emory Roth made a thorough

investigation of everything connected to your background."

"David said that his grandfather never believed Papa was responsible."

"In all likelihood, your grandfather or one of his cohorts was involved and somehow made it look as though your father was to blame."

Annie started to retort that he, Alan, was her father, but decided not to. She knew what he would say. "When did it happen?"

"Shortly before your mother left with you."

"Were there any charges filed?"

"No."

"So then he left, too?"

"Roth said there was a fire on the square which destroyed several buildings, including Levinson's Emporium. When Mr. Levinson decided not to rebuild, your father left almost immediately."

"What about the house, the one we lived in?"

"It was sold for taxes several years later."

"So he really just got up and left everything behind." She didn't add, *including me.*

"It appears so."

"I wonder why, if he wasn't guilty."

"That, my dear Annie, is something we've never been able to ascertain, but it seems to tie in with whatever reason your grandfather sought you out."

"The night he was killed, Papa was here...why?"

"You said that he carried you to safety in the secret room."

"But why was he here?"

"To keep Robert Harcourt from taking you, I should think."

"How did he know what Grandfather was going to do?"

"I have no idea." Alan sat forward. "How well do you remember that night, Annie?"

"I don't think about it anymore."

"Perhaps you should."

"Grandfather was dead, and you and Mum got married and adopted me. That was all I cared about then...all I care about now."

Alan turned his face toward Lenore. Annie often thought that their eyes met and spoke to each other despite Alan's blindness. "Your father has always known where you are, Annie. We've kept in touch with him through Emory Roth. Through the years we've sent pictures, newspaper clippings, copies of school reports...anything that might help him share your life."

Annie's head came up. "Why?"

"He's your father."

"I wish you'd stop saying that! You're my father!" She scrambled to her feet.

Lenore tried to coax her back. "Annie..."

"I'm going up. Goodnight." She kissed Lenore, then Alan, and hurried away without another word.

Alan opened his arms, inviting Lenore into his lap. She responded quickly. "She doesn't want to talk about all this. Do you really feel we should push her?"

"I've explained my reasoning, Lenore."

"Would you have told her that Albert Rycroft killed her grandfather?"

"I debated whether or not this was the time. However, she might suspect that's what happened."

"I wish Emory Roth hadn't put everything in a written report. What if something happened to us, and she found it in your safe?"

"All the more reason to tell her while we have the opportunity to help her understand." Alan worked the pins from Lenore's hair and smoothed it over her shoulders.

"Do you think she's interested in David Levinson?"

"Are you trying to get her married off?"

"Oh, Alan, you know I'm not. It's just that I want to see her settled more than she is now. Even her employment isn't permanent, and she hasn't anyone except the two of us and Mrs. Swane."

"She and Bea are as close as sisters."

"But Bea isn't here anymore, and she's also married. That makes a difference."

"I suppose it does. Are you ready to go up?" Alan traced her lips with the tip of one finger.

"I'm always ready to go up these days. We never seem to get caught up at the office anymore." She slid off his lap.

"We can't give up trying." Alan took her arm as they started for the door. "I want you to see Rolf Sims soon. Mrs. Swane says you've lost weight."

"I'm all right, Alan. Mrs. Swane shouldn't tell tales."

"Make an appointment tomorrow, my darling."

"Are you going to be difficult?"

"Very."

"All right." She flicked the light switch as they left the room. "If you'll let him look you over, too."

"I don't need looking over."

"Those are my conditions."

"Perhaps I can offer you a bribe." At the foot of the stairs he took her in his arms. "I can be very persuasive."

Lenore offered her lips. "If you can stay awake long enough."

He laughed as he took her arm and started up the stairs. "Maybe this weekend."

****

Through her half-open door, Annie heard her parents laughing as they came up the stairs. "I'll just go check on Annie and be along," Lenore said.

Annie came to the door. "I'm all right, Mum."

"We haven't had a cozy bedtime chat in a long time."

Annie stepped back. "Come in."

They sat on the cushioned window seat. "We were surprised to hear that David has enlisted."

"He says his replacement is better than he is."

"Maybe just as good." Lenore took Annie's face in her hands. "Are you interested in him?"

"I spent a great deal of time with him in Canon City. He drove me from the hotel to the shipyard offices and took me to dinner. We even went dancing."

"How very nice!"

"No, it wasn't, Mum. I don't know how it happened, but he came upstairs with me and...oh, nothing happened, but he'd have liked for it to!"

"You know the facts of life, Annie."

"Yes."

"I, on the other hand, was quite ignorant, even at the age of thirty-three, when Alan and I married."

"You were engaged before."

"Yes, but it wasn't the same. My David and I were children together. We danced, took long walks in the park, sat in the porch swing on warm evenings. Everything was very chaste. So when I felt such a strong attraction for Alan, it was frightening."

"David seems to think I'm attracted to him," Annie interrupted.

"Are you?"

"I don't know."

"You've never really had any experience with that kind of relationship."

"We don't have a relationship. He's so arrogant!"

Lenore laughed. "So was Alan Ashley when I first knew him, but beneath that was a warm, wonderful person I'm grateful not to have missed."

"You're very happy, aren't you?"

"I can't begin to put it into words, Annie. Alan and I have shared ten years of pure joy and contentment."

"That's what I want, too. David said I was an icicle."

"Why?"

"Because I don't have a boyfriend at my age and because I keep him at arm's length."

"With a few exceptions."

"Mum, I swear that nothing happened. It's just that I never..."

"You never knew a grown man before. That's what Alan said about me when I was hesitant to accept his physical attentions before we married."

"But you wanted to."

"Very much, although he wouldn't have...well, you understand."

"And I'm not going to."

"I'm glad. When does David leave?"

"In a week. I think that's why he mentioned coming here."

"Would you like for me to invite him?"

"Let me think about it."

Lenore reached for Annie, cradling the young woman in her arms like a child. "I want you to be happy, Annie. Once all I could hope for was to keep you sheltered and fed and safe, but now I can expect happiness for you as well."

"I've always been happy with you, Mum, and then I was happy when Pa came into the picture."

"Happy as our daughter, yes, but I want you to find fulfillment as someone's cherished partner as I've found it with Alan."

"Someday."

"Yes, of course. Someday. Goodnight, Annie dear.

****

My best little girl, my shining star...Bobbie...Bobbie...

Papa? I can't see you, Papa!

You don't have to, Bobbie. I'm always here.
Don't go, Papa! Stay with me. Please, Papa.

Annie sat straight up, clutching the sheet around her. Moonlight streamed in through the open drapes. On the floor beside the bed, Prince snored on, his back legs moving in tandem as if he were chasing a squirrel on the broad expanse of lawn below.

"Papa, I'm not Bobbie anymore, don't you know that? You left Bobbie behind forever." Sliding out of bed, Annie huddled against the dog's warm bulk. He roused and licked her face.

An intense longing swept over her, but she didn't know what it was that she wanted. Papa? A love of her own? David? Certainly not David! She sat up and wiped her eyes. But there was something...something...she slipped back into bed and tried to sleep again.

My best little girl...marry me, Annie...my shining star...love can't be explained, it just happens...

She sat up clutching her pillow against her face. "Leave me alone," she screamed into it. "Just leave me alone! I don't want you...either of you!"

Prince lumbered to his feet, growling, and thrust his nose over the side of the bed. "It's all right, boy," she murmured. "I'm crazy tonight, that's all."

She lay back, her hand still resting on Prince's head. "We were both orphans of the storm, weren't we, Prince? We knew the minute we saw each other at that shelter that we were meant to be together."

Prince slid from beneath her hand and settled his arthritic joints back into his pillow.

"I'm not an icicle. David was mean to say that. I can love. I love you, Prince, and Mum and Pa and Gram and...but I don't love David. He's leaving, probably going to get himself killed. Why would I love anyone who leaves me like...like Papa did?"

Prince began to snore again.

"You're no help. That's the problem, isn't it? No one can help me with this. Pa was right when he said that I could change my name but not who I am."

Bobbie...my best little girl...my shining star...I'll always take care of you...

"But you didn't, Papa. You left me, and David is leaving, and I'll never trust...I'll..." Unable to finish her thought, Annie buried her face in her pillow and wept.

Chapter Seven

Lenore suggested that Annie go alone to meet David's train on Saturday morning. "I'm not sure that's a good idea, Mum. I'm not sure it was a good idea to invite him at all."

"You agreed."

"Yes, but...oh, well."

Mrs. Swane caught her on the way out. "Stop at the market and get some cream. Heavy cream like I use for whipping. Miss Lenore asked for chocolate mousse tonight."

"Doesn't that take a lot of sugar?"

Gladys Swane lifted her eyebrows. "Don't ask the cook for her secrets. The three of you give me your ration books every month, and what I do with them is my business. You haven't starved yet, have you?"

Laughing, Annie hugged the older woman. "No, Gram. I'll get the cream."

David stood on the platform, his bag at his feet. "I thought maybe you'd changed your mind," he said.

"Sorry I'm late. I had to stop at the market for Gram," she said. "We're on our own for lunch. Mum and Pa have gone out to the Young's farm, and Gram is working her culinary magic in the kitchen for dinner tonight."

"I don't mind."

"I need to take her the cream, and then we can get a sandwich downtown."

"Why do you call your housekeeper Gram?"

"She practically raised Pa, and I think of her as a grandmother."

"Didn't you have grandparents?" David swung his bag into the trunk.

"Everyone has grandparents. I don't remember mine very well." Annie swallowed the lie. While she remembered Robert Harcourt with frightening clarity, the happier memories of her father's parents had dimmed almost beyond retrieval.

After lunch, David suggested a drive. "I've never been here before. I'd be interested to see the architectural style of the older buildings."

"Most of them date from the early to mid-1800s. You'll have to ask Pa about their history. His family was one of the first to settle here. He'll give you a tour of the house, too, and tell you about the secret room."

"The secret room?"

"Pa can tell you the story better than I can."

"How is it you have a car if the Ashleys are out?"

"I drove them early this morning. Uncle Trent will bring them home. And before you make a snide comment, I call him Mr. Young in the office."

At the city park she pointed out the statue of Alan's great-grandfather. "He started the bank, that red brick building on the corner."

"It reminds me a little of Barnwell, the way the businesses are built around the courthouse that way."

"Oh? I don't remember Barnwell very well. Actually, I don't remember the town at all, only the house we lived in."

"I saw it after you did, I expect. I went back with my grandfather after the fire. I didn't tell you about that, did I?"

"Pa did."

"How did he know?"

"He had to hire an investigator when...I told you it was complicated, David. But Pa knew, and he told me."

"Granddad went back to get some papers from the courthouse so that he could file for the insurance. They weren't there, so he went to the abstract office, and found out that he'd never owned the building at all."

"I don't understand."

"The papers had been fixed. Somebody named Harcourt owned the whole block."

Annie choked. "Robert Harcourt was my grandfather."

"Annie, I'm sorry." David touched her arm. "Pull over for a minute."

Annie steered the car to the side of the road and leaned her head against the steering wheel. "He tried to get custody of me, but he died before it could go to court."

"From what I understand, he was the county's claim to organized crime."

"I didn't know that."

"Mr. Ashley doesn't know?"

"He didn't mention it, but he probably knows. I don't like to talk about it." She hesitated. "David, about the robbery at your grandfather's store. What was taken?"

"Diamonds."

"Diamonds? I thought it was just a general store."

"My grandfather was very involved with the Zionist movement, helping Jews leave eastern Europe where they were being persecuted. In 1921, he and some others put their money into diamonds, which they planned to resell to finance the passage of about two hundred Jews out of Russia, hopefully to Palestine."

"He...your grandfather really didn't think that my...that Albert Rycroft took them?"

"Albert Rycroft was Jewish, too, or didn't you know?"

"Vaguely, but he took me to Sunday School at the Methodist church."

"He was very involved with the Zionists, too. In fact, he still had extended family in Russia, and the *pogroms*, the movement against Jewish communities there, had escalated. He had a legitimate interest in seeing the money put to good use."

Annie started to ask how David knew more about her family than she did, but changed her mind. "Were the diamonds ever found?"

"Grandfather always said that they were safe and would turn up when they were most needed."

"How could he know that?"

"I don't know, but the others who'd invested with him believed what he said. Most of them are dead now, too."

"What if they really were stolen?"

"I don't know, Annie. So far they haven't surfaced."

"Do you think they will?"

He shrugged. "Are you all right?"

"I don't like to talk about him."

"Your grandfather or your father?"

"Either one. Sometimes I dream about Papa." Immediately, she regretted speaking her thoughts aloud.

"Bad dreams?"

She nodded.

"Do your parents know?"

"I'd never worry them."

"Don't they have a right to know? You're very insistent that they're your parents."

Annie started the car again. "I'll drive by Ashley Enterprises so that you can see where we work."

****

"Mrs. Swane, you've outdone yourself," Alan said.

"She's even going to join us," Annie said.

Alan pulled back Lenore's chair. "You're truly a guest of honor, David. Mrs. Swane has such a busy social schedule that she usually eats in the kitchen and is gone before we're finished."

"And leaves me to clean up," Annie said.

Mrs. Swane unfolded her napkin. "It happens that I don't have an engagement tonight."

Annie hugged her. "I'll clean up anyway. You've been cooking all day."

"It's certainly a challenge with new rationing every day, or so it seems," Lenore said. "We just give her our ration books and trust that dinner will be on the table."

Alan sat down. "We're glad you could join us, David. You'll be missed at the shipyard."

"I trained my replacement myself, and frankly, Mr. Ashley, he has a lot more talent in that area than I do."

"You'll be in basic training for awhile."

"At Camp Edwards."

"That's a long way from Rumers Crossing, but if you get leave, you must feel free to make this your home away from home."

"Since I've given up my room in Canon City, that's a welcome invitation."

"Do you know where you'll be sent after training?" Lenore asked.

"Europe, I guess. The sergeant at the induction center was interested in the fact that I speak German."

"Fluently?" Alan asked.

"My grandparents were immigrants, and it was my mother's first language, so I learned it along with English."

"That may keep you off the front lines," Alan said. "You'll be valuable as an interrogator."

David shrugged. "I haven't really thought about it, Mr. Ashley. The rumor is that Hitler is trying to rid Europe of Jews any way he can."

"I've heard that, too." Alan felt for his roll and broke a small piece from it.

"My grandfather had two sisters who didn't emigrate. No one has heard from their families since before Pearl Harbor."

"Oh, David, I'm so sorry," Lenore said.

"I didn't know them, but they're family, after all."

"This war was inevitable," Alan said. "And it's going to be costly in men and material. I hope we wind things up better than we did in 1918."

"Do we have to talk about the war tonight?" Annie rose. "I'll get more tea."

****

David lent a hand in the kitchen after dinner. When he and Annie went into the drawing room, it was empty. "I guess they've gone up," she said.

"I don't mind being alone with you."

"I don't think it's a good idea."

"Oh, come on, Annie, we had a little romp on the sofa in your hotel room. It didn't get out of hand."

"It might have."

David laughed. "And you don't even like me."

Annie crossed to Lenore's chair and sat down. It was, she considered, a safe distance from the sofa. "Is it really true that Hitler is killing the Jews in Germany?"

"And the other occupied countries."

"Why?"

"You're half-Jewish, Annie. Don't you know anything about your heritage?"

"Nothing. I told you, I was raised in the Methodist Church, and my parents and I attend the Episcopal church here. I was confirmed when I was fourteen."

"You should get in touch with that part of yourself. I don't attend synagogue regularly or keep kosher, but I appreciate my history."

"It's odd, isn't it, both of us coming from the same background?"

"I told you we had more in common than you think."

"Maybe speaking German will keep you out of action after all."

"Are you actually thinking of my welfare?"

"Don't be mean, David. Of course, that's what I was thinking."

"Sorry. On the other hand, my skill with the language might put me in the middle of the action. Who knows? I'll cross that bridge when I come to it." He let his eyes rest on her. "You're sitting there like I'm going to attack you."

She unfolded her arms from in front of her. "I didn't mean to suggest that."

"Actually, I'd like to. Attack you, that is."

She sighed. "David, please stop."

"I'll send you my address when I get to camp, if you'll write to me."

"Gram likes you. She'll send you butter cookies." He patted the place on the sofa beside him. "Come over here, Annie."

"No, David, it's not a good idea."

"You've really never been attracted to anyone before?"

"I didn't say that."

"But it's true. You haven't."

She shook her head. "I went to a girls' school, you know."

"Then at least one side of your education has been neglected. Come here."

She sat unmoving for a long moment, then rose and walked to the sofa. "Behave yourself."

"No promises."

"David…"

He put his arms around her and noticed that

she didn't resist. "I don't know why I love you, but I do, and maybe you'll change your mind about me by the time the war is over."

"What if I don't?"

"Then you don't." He traced her lips with the tip of one finger, then kissed her briefly. "You taste better than the chocolate mousse, but don't tell Mrs. Swane I said so."

Chapter Eight

Trent Young sent Annie back to Canon City two days before David reported for basic training. He met her train and drove her to the hotel. "I'm staying with a friend. She'll keep my car while I'm gone."

"She?"

"Are you jealous?"

"Not in the least."

"She's sixty-two, if you're interested."

"I'm not."

"She was a friend of my mother's."

"Oh."

"I thought you and I might go to dinner tonight."

"With your friend as a chaperone?"

"Do we need one?"

"Maybe." Annie fished around in her purse for a tube of lipstick and made liberal use of it. "You took a lot for granted the weekend you visited."

"You seemed to enjoy it." He grimaced. "Can't we just for once stop this verbal sparring and be friends?"

"If that's all you want to be." Annie snapped her purse shut with more force than necessary.

David made a sound between disgust and resignation. "I enjoyed the weekend in Rumers Crossing. The house is really something. It would be an architect's dream to restore something like that."

"It doesn't need restoring."

"No, but if it did, I'd want to do it. Mr. Ashley said the tunnel from the secret room was closed up."

"It was dangerous."

"I can believe that. Were you ever in it?"

"Not the tunnel." The memory of the room stirred a sudden chill in her bones. "How is your replacement working out?"

"Like I said, he's better than I am." David parked by the main building in the shipyard and opened the car door for her. "I'll be around somewhere all day, so I'll try to check in from time to time in case you finish early."

Annie tried to keep her mind on the meeting, but despite her best efforts, David intruded in her thoughts. Her stomach fluttered when she found him waiting for her in the main office.

"I want to check into the hotel before dinner, if you don't mind."

"Sure." He took her arm, and the flutter became a tidal wave.

"David, I..."

"What?"

"Nothing."

"You're hugging the door," he observed as they drove. "Are you thinking about jumping out?"

"No, of course not, I..."

"You can't seem to finish a sentence."

"It's just that what I want to say is difficult."

"If you want to say that you're madly in love with me and suggest that we look up a justice of the peace before dinner, I'm all for that."

"You have to have a marriage license."

"All right, we'll get one tomorrow."

"Don't be ridiculous."

He was silent for a moment. "I'm serious, Annie."

"I know you are, but...David, I like you better since I've gotten to know you. I might even be a little fond of you, but marriage is another story. You're leaving day after tomorrow."

"I'll get a furlough after basic, before I ship out. I

could come to Rumers Crossing."

"Maybe."

"A couple of nights is better than nothing."

"Not to me."

He maneuvered the car into the last space in front of the hotel. "I've never wanted anyone as much as I want you."

"But you've had them. Other girls, I mean."

"That's not important. This is now."

"So now you're ready to marry me if you can't get me any other way. Is that what this is all about?"

"You know better than that."

Annie chewed her lip. "I'll write to you. We'll see how things go."

"I guess I'll have to settle for that."

"I guess you will."

****

They went to the Canon Club again for dinner and dancing afterwards. This time, when the orchestra ended with "I'll Be Seeing You," Annie didn't even try to pretend she wasn't crying.

David put his arm around her waist and guided her off the dance floor. "I'd like to think you're crying because I'm leaving, but I know you're not."

"Of course, I'm sorry to see you go off to war."

"Just sorry?"

"I don't want to fight with you, David. I told you that I like you better than I did, but I'm not in love with you."

"Would you know if you were?"

"What do you mean?"

"I mean that you keep your feelings on ice, Annie, and I wish I knew why."

"That's not true."

"It's occurred to me that it has something to do with your real father and who you were before you became Annie Ashley."

"That's ridiculous. I've been Annie Ashley longer

than I was Bobbie Rycroft."

"Is that who you were?"

"I'm not her now."

"You're a Cinderella who's not quite sure she wants to leave her nice familiar kitchen to marry the prince."

"You're no prince!"

He chuckled. "I could be. I don't know the whole story, but from things you've said, I wonder if you don't trust me because of your father. Because he abandoned you."

"He didn't abandon...he left me with Mum and Pa because he wanted me to have the best, and I have."

"I wish you'd talk to me honestly, Annie. Sometimes that helps to sort things out."

"I told you that it's none of your business."

"Maybe not, but I suspect that if you don't get in touch with Bobbie Rycroft, you're not going to be very successful as Annie Ashley."

"I'm doing quite well as Mr. Young's assistant."

"That's business. What about your personal life?"

"That's all right, too."

"Then what about love, Annie? Don't you want that someday?"

"With the right person."

"How will you know who Mr. Right is if you don't let yourself feel something?"

"This is a ridiculous conversation."

"Is it? Oh, you're fond enough of the Ashleys and Mrs. Swane, but it stops there."

"You're just being mean because I won't do what you want."

"Sleep with me?"

"Stop it, David."

"You'll go so far, and that's it."

"I told you that I'm not interested in a one-night

stand."

"Annie, it's not all about sex. It's about feelings, and yours are so bottled up that they're ready to explode."

"So you have a degree in psychology as well as architecture?"

"Forget it."

He drove her back to the hotel where they said goodnight without touching each other.

****

Annie felt more relieved than bereft with David at Camp Edwards. She responded to his regular, oddly impersonal letters with a cultivated detachment and told herself that he'd meet someone else. Still, she wasn't surprised when he wrote to ask if he could spend his leave after basic training in Rumers Crossing.

"If you were in love with him, you wouldn't ask me what I thought," Lenore said when Annie confessed that she had misgivings about David's proposed visit.

"He's nicer than he was at first, but he makes me feel...strange."

"Physically?"

"More in my head."

"You'll have to explain that a little better."

"He makes me feel like I'm not a whole person," Annie blurted. "It's like I'm flying into a million pieces when I'm with him."

Lenore frowned. "Not a whole person?"

"Like I don't know who I am."

"Oh, Annie dear!"

"He thinks I should know more about where I came from...my Jewish heritage, he calls it. And he knows too much about Papa."

"About what happened in Barnwell."

"You and Pa know, too, don't you?"

"Emory Roth brought us a great deal of

information. We've been waiting for you to ask."

"I don't want to know."

"Why not, Annie?"

"It doesn't have anything to do with me. I'm not Bobbie anymore."

"Are you sure?"

"I don't want to be her."

"Alan feels there are things you should know. I'm not sure that I agree with him, but perhaps not knowing isn't good for you after all."

"Please, Mum, I don't want to talk about it."

Lenore sighed. "All right. What about David? If you don't want him to come, write and tell him so."

"I don't know if I want him to come or not."

"Then you must decide. You're not a little girl any longer, Annie. I can't make your decisions for you."

****

Albert Rycroft came again that night. *Bobbie...Bobbie...my best little girl...my shining star...it was a mistake, Roberta and me, but not you...not you.*

****

The next morning Annie announced that she was going to invite David to spend his leave at Rumers Crossing.

"Is this serious?" Alan asked.

"I don't know, Pa. I like him."

"You have to like someone before you can love them."

"He says that he loves me and wants to marry me."

"How do you feel about that?"

"I don't know how I feel. He keeps pushing me about the past, and I don't want to dredge it up again."

Alan slid his fingers toward his orange juice at one o'clock. "The past is always with us, Annie. I told you years ago that Bobbie and Annie were one and the same. A change in name doesn't change a person's identity."

"Pa, I'm happy as your daughter."

"That gives me a great deal of satisfaction, but the fact remains that you came to me with your personality fully formed."

"Not really. You and Mum are responsible for much of who I am, don't you think?"

"In some ways, perhaps. Still, denying where you came from won't resolve anything."

"I think Annie has to make her own decision," Lenore said. "She's a grown woman, after all."

Alan's eyebrows lifted. "All right. We have more to do than repeatedly argue the point without resolving it."

****

"Talking about the past upsets Annie," Lenore said when they reached the privacy of Alan's office. "Don't you think we should leave it at that?"

"I didn't bring up the subject at breakfast. She did."

Lenore slipped her purse beneath her desk. "I wish she had better memories, but she doesn't. We can't change that."

"And I can't seem to change the fact that you're still afraid of losing her after all these years."

"I can't help it, Alan. If he should want to contact her..."

"What would be so terrible about that? Are you so insecure about her feelings for you?"

"I don't know. Am I?"

"It seems so to me."

"There's also the matter of what he did that night."

"Killed Robert Harcourt, you mean."

"You know that he did. That frightens me...that he could commit murder."

"I killed men during the previous war."

"That was different."

"Is it, Lenore? Taking a human life is a terrible thing, but I'm not convinced that Albert Rycroft didn't have cause for everything he did. And we can't forget that he left Annie here with us, not once but twice, because he believed it was best for her."

"You're sure that's what he thought?"

"I'm absolutely convinced of it."

"I've never known you to be wrong about someone's character." She uncovered the Braille writer. "I'll have some notes ready for you in half an hour."

Chapter Nine

January 5, 1943
Dear David,
You can come here on leave if you like. I don't suppose you have anywhere else to go. I have to tell you that I've made the decision to put everything in my past behind me, so it's not up for discussion. If you're in love with Annie, there might be a future for us. If you just want to resurrect a child you never knew, we don't have anything to talk about. Maybe this will settle things between us once and for all.

If you decide to come under those conditions, let me know when to meet your train.
Annie

David arrived with candy and flowers for Annie, Lenore, and Mrs. Swane, and a box of pipe tobacco for Alan. "I got it at the PX. It's supposed to be good stuff."

Alan turned the box in his hands and inhaled. "I was partial to a similar Dutch brand before the war, but I can't get it now. I'll look forward to trying this. Thank you, David."

"It's all a bribe, you understand," David said, winking at Mrs. Swane. "I'm really tired of mess hall food."

"I happen to know there's roast beef and lemon meringue pie for dinner," Alan said. "I've been smelling it all afternoon."

"No aperitif?" David asked, wiggling his eyebrows at Annie.

She flushed. "Certainly not. I'd suggest you take your things upstairs and get washed. You know which room is yours. Gram doesn't like to be kept waiting when she announces dinner."

****

Alan and Lenore went up early, leaving Annie and David alone in the drawing room. David added another log to the fire. "This is nice."

"Don't get too comfortable," Annie said.

"I thought we were going to talk."

"I told you there's nothing to talk about." Annie sat down in Lenore's chair.

"I know what you said, Annie, but I still feel that the problem between us lies in not reconciling yourself to what happened to you before you became the Ashleys' daughter."

"There is no *us,* David, and you have no idea of everything that happened to me," she flared.

"Then tell me."

"I told you I wanted to leave it in the past."

"That's just it, Annie, it's not. It's hovering around you like a big black cloud."

She sighed. "If I tell you, will you leave it alone?"

"What can I do except listen?"

"My grandfather used to hit me for no reason. My mother let it happen. He was always making threats. When I was five years old, he told me he was going to take me out to the cemetery and put me in one of the graves that was covered with a rock slab, and I'd never get out. I was terrified! And later he tried to…" She broke off abruptly, but she knew from the way David jerked upright on the sofa that he knew what she was going to say.

"Are you sure?"

"Of course, I'm sure! I knew you wouldn't understand!"

"I'm trying, but you said you were only five. How would you know if he tried to molest you?"

Annie sprang up from the sofa. "You think I made it up? You think I didn't know that when he

75

put his hands under my clothes..."

David's fingers closed around her wrist and brought her back down beside him. She struggled briefly, then gave up.

"Look, Annie, the whole idea makes me sick for you. Finish the story."

"I told Papa about some of it, and I heard him tell Mamma that he'd kill Grandfather if it ever happened again. I knew that if he did, he'd go to jail, maybe forever."

"So you never told again."

"No, but...I think Papa killed him anyway."

"Why do you think that?"

"When my grandfather found out that I was here, he tried to get custody of me. Pa's attorney said that with my testimony and what the detective had uncovered, the judge would rule against him. He must have known that, too, because one night just before Mum and Pa married, Grandfather broke into this house. He might have gotten me, but Papa appeared out of nowhere. He took me to the secret room and left me there. I never saw him again."

"What happened to your grandfather?"

"Later, after Pa found me, the security guard that Pa hired said Grandfather fell down the stairs in the dark and broke his neck."

"Did you believe him?"

"Yes, but just recently Mrs. Swane said something that made me wonder." She got to her feet and began to pace, her hands clenched in front of her as if she were trying to ward off some invisible threat.

"Barnwell County would probably have pinned a medal on Rycroft for getting rid of Robert Harcourt."

Regretting her admissions, Annie started for the door. "I told you that I didn't want to talk about any of this."

"I think you need to talk to someone. Someone

who's not as involved as the Ashleys. You don't like to upset them." He held out his hand. "Come sit down, Annie. I swear I'm not going to do anything but hold your hand."

"I don't trust you."

"That's the problem, isn't it? Trusting."

After a few minutes, she sat down by him.

"Good for you. That's a step in the right direction. Tell me about the orphanage."

"It burned down."

"I didn't know that."

"Papa was there, too. That was the first time he left me. He took Rebekah, my cousin, but I guess, if I hadn't been outside with him, I'd have died like the others when the furnace exploded. The whole building went up like it was made of paper." She shuddered as the inferno roared through her mind again.

"I'm sorry. Why did he take your cousin?"

"She was...slow. Her stepmother didn't want her and convinced her father to put her in the Home. I guess Papa knew that and wanted to give her a better life."

"But he knew you'd have a better life with the Ashleys."

"I guess so."

"What about the others, the ones who didn't get out?

"The children and staff are buried in Potter's Field in Greenfield. Pa organized a memorial service and put up a marker with all the names."

He squeezed her hand. "It must have been terrible for you."

"Now can you understand why I just want to forget?"

"If you haven't forgotten by now, you're not going to. I'm more convinced than ever that you need to just deal with it and move on."

"All of it happened to Bobbie Rycroft. I'm Annie Ashley now."

"I'm in love with Annie Ashley."

"David..."

He brought out a jeweler's box from his pocket. "Marry me, Annie." He opened the box to reveal a wide gold band. "I've got twenty-five of my thirty days left. It would be a start, and after the war..."

"It wouldn't work."

"Why not?"

She shook her head wordlessly.

"So if I promise to love you and stay with you forever, you can't accept that because of what Albert Rycroft did for your own good?"

"No, David, it's not like that."

"That's exactly it. How is it you could trust the Ashleys?"

"Because they've always been here, and you're leaving," she blurted. "Maybe you won't come back."

"Only if I die, and that's always a possibility."

She covered her face with her hands. "I don't want to think about it."

He put the box back into his pocket. "All right."

"I don't know what I feel for you, David."

"Have you let yourself feel anything?"

"Maybe not."

When he pulled her into his arms, she didn't resist. "I know you're attracted to me physically, but that's not enough. I want you to think about spending the rest of your life with me, having my children, growing old with me."

She studied his face. "My college roommate would have said you look like a movie star. She'd have snapped you up in sixty seconds."

"I'm tall, dark, and handsome?"

"All of that."

"I'm a Jew, Annie, and so are you. We share a cultural history."

"Only half, and I don't know anything about it."

"You could learn."

"Maybe."

He brushed her lips lightly. "Just think about it. Think about what you really feel and why. I won't mention it again until you do."

****

The next night after dinner, Alan invited David into his study. "Do you have your orders yet, David?"

"I report on the twentieth of February."

"Not quite a month."

"I've asked Annie to marry me before I go."

"Is that rushing things a little?"

"I guess it is, Mr. Ashley, but this is war, and wars have a way of wiping out everything but today."

"That's quite true. Has Annie shared anything about her history with you?"

"Last night she told me a little, enough for me to understand why she's afraid to trust me."

"I've considered that I may have done her a grave disservice by letting her become Annie Ashley twelve years ago. The name change was practical, but she thought that would change who she was, and of course, it didn't." Alan swiveled his desk chair around and joined David in front of the fire. "She adored her father. Her whole reason for living, according to Lenore, was waiting for him to come for her."

"And when he didn't...or rather, he did and left her behind again...she tried to leave Bobbie behind, too."

"You're very perceptive, David."

"It wasn't that hard to figure out."

"I adore my wife. She completes me. She's my first thought when I wake in the morning and the last before I sleep at night. We've shared a physical passion that has transcended anything I ever

79

imagined." He turned his face toward the other man. "I tell you these things because I want them for Annie, too. She is the daughter of my heart if not of my body."

"I understand."

"Lenore was emotionally fragile when I married her. She'd experienced losing her home, near-starvation, feelings of failure because Annie was taken to an orphanage, and finally the fear of losing her permanently. She couldn't trust me either, not at first."

"Obviously she does now. I've watched her look at you, Mr. Ashley, and wished that Annie would look at me the same way."

"If she doesn't, David, then perhaps you'd better rethink your plans."

"I'll think about what you've said, Mr. Ashley. I'll consider everything very seriously."

****

The Ashleys went up early again, and David told Annie about his conversation with Alan. "If I've moved too quickly, I'm sorry. I'm twenty-eight years old, Annie, and I thought I knew what I was doing."

"You did come on a little strong."

"I've backed off now. It's all up to you."

"You don't get much experience in a girls' school."

"None of your friends dated?"

"Most of them did. I used to listen to them talk about their boyfriends and wish I could join in, but...there was just never anyone special. And I've always had the idea that I'd meet someone like Pa someday."

"No two people are exactly alike."

Annie studied David's face for a moment. "You're like him in one way."

"Oh?"

"You know who you are."

"I guess I do. Do you know who *you* are, Annie? Really know?"

"Pa doesn't seem to think so. He says that just changing my name didn't change who I was...who I am."

"So who was Bobbie Rycroft? Tell me about her."

Annie leaned her face against David's arm.

"She was always lonely and afraid until she went to live in Brookston with Mum and Grandmamma. She tried to be cheerful and optimistic for Mum's sake when things got bad, and when she lived in Greenfield, she believed what the director, Miss Ervin, said—that she had to make the best of things and look ahead."

"Did you look ahead?"

"Oh, yes. Living there wasn't so bad. We were never really hungry, just cold sometimes when the furnace was cranky. We all cared about each other...really cared." Her expression changed. "Then there was the fire and being afraid that Grandfather would take me. That was the worst."

"But as Annie Ashley, you expected to live happily ever after."

"And I have, David. I've had so much love and every opportunity and material possession. I'm safe now."

"So Annie Ashley is safe, but Annie Levinson might not be."

"I guess that's about it."

"Life is a risk, Annie. Albert Rycroft took several risks for you and for your cousin Rebekah."

"I realize that."

"Have you ever opened up like this to anyone?"

"No, not really." She let him fold her hands inside his. "It's how I survived, I suppose. You were right when you said I didn't want to upset Mum by talking about it."

"You're like her—strong on the outside and

fragile on the inside."

"I suppose I am. Pa takes care of both of us."

"Ultimately you have to take care of yourself, Annie."

"I realized that when I finished college, but...I've tried to put it off."

"Working with your parents, living at home."

Annie nodded. "Nothing's changed."

"Everything's changed. That's the problem."

She closed her eyes and let her body relax against his. *Papa used to hold me like this, in the swing on the front porch. He was so strong. Nothing could hurt me with his arms around me. David's strong, too, but...he's leaving, just like Papa left, and maybe he's never coming back...*

"David."

"Hmmm?"

"If...if I love you...will you promise never to leave me?"

"You know I can't do that, Annie."

"What can you promise?"

"To love you for whatever time we have. To come back to you if I can."

"That's not enough."

"It's all we have."

She buried her face against his shirt again. "Is it enough?"

"It is for me." He put his lips against her hair.

She snuggled closer, whether to a real man or a memory, she wasn't sure. "Hold me, David. Just...just for tonight, hold me."

Chapter Ten

Thomas Greer, the rector of St. John's, where the Ashleys attended, conducted the wedding ceremony in front of the fireplace in the drawing room. Annie, wearing a white suit reminiscent of Lenore's wedding outfit, came down the stairs on Alan's arm. David wore his dress uniform and a broad grin.

Bea, who managed to get time off and space on a train, served as second matron of honor beside Lenore. Mrs. Swane baked and decorated the wedding cake and served brunch to the guests. Later, Rod drove Annie and David to the station as he'd driven Alan and Lenore for their trip to the same hotel in the Catskills.

They arrived after dark and found champagne waiting in their bungalow. "Pa must have sent it," Annie said with a laugh. "He says that Mum drank it, for the first time ever, on their wedding night and got quite tipsy."

"Does he tell that story in front of her?" David carried their bags into the bedroom.

"Not often," Annie said as she followed him.

"Will I have a story to tell?" He reached for her, but she stepped away.

"We'll see. I'll change while you open the champagne."

"Change as in..."

"You'll see."

****

David stirred up the fire and returned to sit

beside Annie. "You're beautiful, but you can't be very warm in that." He toyed with the lace at the throat of the filmy pink peignoir.

"The champagne warmed me up."

"Are you tipsy yet?"

"Just sleepy."

He took her glass away. "We can't have that. Not now."

He worked the covered buttons through the satin loops on the robe and pushed it off her shoulders. "Nice." He pushed aside the straps to her gown, too. "Very nice."

"I thought you'd like it."

"I didn't mean what you have on."

"I didn't really think you did." She folded her arms around his neck.

He felt her trembling. "Nervous?"

"Shouldn't I be?"

He tilted her head and put his lips against her neck. "Just relax, Annie. I'll make things good for you."

Her voice was muffled against his shoulder. "I'm not really an icicle, am I?"

"I shouldn't have said that. I'm sorry."

"It's just that I…"

"I know." He stood up, then lifted her in his arms. "It'll be good, Annie, I promise."

****

Alan lifted the covers for Lenore to slip in beside him. "Annie was a beautiful bride," she said for the dozenth time that evening.

"Almost as beautiful as you were."

Lenore smiled against his cheek in the way she'd learned to do to help him be aware of her facial expressions. "I still wonder if perhaps they didn't rush things a bit."

"It's happening all over the country, darling

Lenore. I'm afraid that, in wartime, people live for the moment."

"I had one or two friends who married quickly at the beginning of the last war, but I never considered it. My parents wouldn't have allowed it, anyway."

"Did you ever regret it?"

"No, I didn't. I thought later that maybe it meant that David Broome and I simply weren't supposed to marry at all." She draped one arm across him. "I hardly remember him, Alan. In a way, it's very sad that someone can be forgotten so easily."

"I can still see the faces of the boys in my company, but I can't remember their names. We slogged through miles of mud together, ate and fought together, but they're gone. I can't remember anything but their youth and, sometimes, their fear."

"War changes men, doesn't it?"

"Forever."

"So David will be changed when he returns."

"In some ways, most certainly."

"How will that affect their marriage?"

"I couldn't begin to know. They'll have ten days, not long enough to even taste what marriage is really like."

"I remember our wedding night as if it were yesterday." Lenore kissed each of his eyes. "I remember thinking that you saw me, really saw me completely in a way that you wouldn't have if you'd just glanced at me."

"That's true."

"And I still discover new things about you even after a dozen years."

Alan put his lips against her hair. "For example?"

"Oh, things you know about that surprise me. Just the other day, I was listening to you discuss ball bearings with George Hunt in the metal shop.

You had the details at your fingertips."

He laughed. "Quite literally!"

"Don't tease me, Alan. I'm serious." She tapped his chin for emphasis.

"If I don't know what I'm talking about, I can't expect my employees or clients to have any faith in my judgment or decisions."

"I remember you said before we married that it was exhausting to always appear confident."

"It's more so now, considering all the technical issues I have to deal with. Having you makes all the difference. You're more than efficient in the office and restful at home."

"I want to be."

"You're everything I ever dreamed of and more."

"Do you think…Alan, do you think that David really understands Annie's needs?"

"I think he understands as well as he can. Whether or not he can provide for them is another question altogether." He stroked her cheek. "For years, I was obsessed with wanting the return of my sight. Instead, you became my vision. Sometimes our needs are met in ways that we don't anticipate."

"I thought I needed a guarantee against the things I feared, when what I really needed was to learn to trust. To trust you."

Alan turned toward her. "Is the mother of the bride very tired?"

"Not too tired for what I expect the father of the bride has in mind."

He smiled into the darkness and put his lips against her throat.

****

David woke in the night to the sound of Annie moaning as if she were in pain. "Papa! Papa! Please don't go. Come back, Papa."

He shook her awake. "Wake up, Annie, you're dreaming."

She beat him away with her fists. "No! You can't make me stay. You can't. You promised to take me with you."

He cradled her in his arms. "Annie, sweetheart, wake up. You're all right. I'm here."

"Why, Papa? You said I was your best little girl, your shining star. What happened?"

David took her face in his hands. "Open your eyes, Annie. Your papa's not here."

"I hate you, Papa! I hate you for leaving me!"

He shook her with more force. "Annie."

Her eyes flew open. "David, what..."

"It's all right, sweetheart."

She burst into tears. "I'm sorry. I'm so sorry."

"You're all right." He rocked her in his arms like a child. "You were dreaming, that's all." When she was finally quiet, he wiped her face with a corner of the sheet. "Can you tell me about it?"

She shook her head.

"It might help."

"No, it's all over. I don't know why I keep dreaming the same thing."

"About your father leaving you behind? It really is over, Annie, but we're not. We're just beginning."

She turned her face away from him. "But you're leaving me, too."

"Not forever."

"Maybe you won't come back."

"I'll come back, Annie, I promise." He pulled her closer to him. "I love you."

She made an odd sound that he couldn't interpret. He pushed the hair out of her face and began to kiss her. "Was it good for you, Annie? Did I make you happy?"

"Very happy."

His lips moved to her bare shoulder. Without warning, she clasped his neck so tightly that he had to reach up and loosen her arms. "Easy, sweetheart."

"Love me, David."

"I do love you."

"Promise you'll love me forever."

"I'll love you forever."

"Make love to me again."

He smiled. "Exactly what I had in mind."

Chapter Eleven

"Slide over here behind the wheel, Annie. Don't get out."

"Why not?"

"I don't want my last memory of you to be standing alone on an empty railroad platform at eleven o'clock at night."

"It was your idea to take the later train."

"So I could spend the last possible minute with you." He smoothed her hair. "Just stay here, sweetheart."

"If that's what you want."

"I do." He touched her face. "I love you, Annie."

"I love you, too."

"When I come home, we'll decide what we want to do and where we'll live, and we'll give the Ashleys some grandkids."

"How many?"

"A couple or four or five."

"Two would be fine."

"I think so, too." He pulled her closer. "I'll miss you. Especially on cold nights."

"Oh, yes, especially then." She buried her face in his shoulder. "David, I wish you weren't going. I know, I know, it's just the way things are."

"For us and a million others."

"I'm afraid."

"I'm no hero, Annie."

"Don't be. I want you to come back."

"Hopefully in one piece."

"With the most important pieces anyway." She struggled with her tears. "Just come back, David."

Their last, long kiss ended only when the train whistle blew. David opened the car door and stepped onto the pavement. He didn't look back as he strode toward the train.

****

Annie put her feet over the side of the bed and slid them along Prince's shaggy back. He was fourteen now, and the vet said that she was going to have to make a decision about him soon. His stiff joints made climbing the stairs painfully difficult for him. Mrs. Swane pureed his food since his teeth were bad. Sometimes Annie had to feed him with a spoon like a baby.

The dog took a long shuddering breath and let it out as if complaining about being disturbed. "I wish I could lie around all day," she said to him. "I can't seem to get enough sleep these days." A sudden wave of nausea swept her, and she plunged toward the bathroom.

****

"Did you not sleep well?" Lenore asked when Annie appeared at breakfast a little late. "You look rather pale."

"I'm all right." Annie helped herself to toast and coffee from the sideboard. "I have three meetings today, but at least they're in town."

"We all have to pace ourselves," Alan said. "There's still a long way to go before this war is won."

"I just want it to be over."

"We all do," Alan said.

****

In the middle of the first meeting, Annie had to excuse herself, barely making it to the ladies room before she lost her breakfast. *Too much pork roast last night. And apple pie.* She retched again. *I ate too much, that's all.* She bathed her face in cool water and returned, still queasy, to the meeting.

It happened again after lunch. This time she collapsed in the hall and woke up on the sofa in Alan's office.

"You fainted," Lenore said, patting her face with a damp cloth. "Dr. Sims is on his way."

"For a faint?" Annie struggled to sit up. "He has more important things to do."

"He was just leaving his office for a late lunch," Alan said. "He can get a bite downstairs after he sees you."

Bile rose in her throat as her empty stomach heaved. *I'll never eat again.*

****

Dr. Sims sent everyone out and pulled a chair close to the sofa. "Did you skip lunch?" he asked as he checked her pulse.

"No, but I lost it. And breakfast this morning. I think it was the pork roast we had last night."

He took her blood pressure and had her sit up so he could listen to her heart and lungs. "Did it just start?"

Annie frowned. "I've been a little queasy the past few days, but..." Spoken aloud, her thought took on a terrifying reality. "Oh, no."

Rolf Sims chuckled as he put his stethoscope back into his bag. "Come by the office tomorrow and let me examine you."

"I'd rather not."

"Bring Lenore if it will make you feel better."

"I can't be...I mean, David and I haven't been married that long!"

The doctor laughed. "The word you want is *pregnant,* and you don't actually have to be married at all."

Annie's face flamed.

He patted her. "I'll see you tomorrow."

Alan and Lenore were waiting for him in the outer office. "I told her to stop by the office tomorrow so I could check her again. She's all right. Don't worry."

"I'll bring her before we start work," Lenore said. "You're sure it's nothing serious?"

He hid his smile behind his hand. "I'm sure it isn't, Lenore. Just bring her in."

****

"I'd say around the first of December," Dr. Sims said as Annie wept on Lenore's shoulder. "Come, Annie, it's not the end of the world."

"But we didn't plan…"

"Most people don't."

"I think it's wonderful," Lenore said. "David will be so pleased, and I'll have to restrain Alan from buying out the stores."

"Just take it easy for awhile," the doctor continued. "I'll give you a prescription for some vitamins and something for the nausea. It won't last forever."

Despite Lenore's attempts to cheer her, Annie couldn't stop crying as they drove back to the office. "I know you didn't plan to have a baby so soon, but things will work out."

"Mr. Young depends on me to travel for him."

"You can do that for awhile longer, I'd think."

"I deal with men, Mum. When I start to show, it will be embarrassing."

Lenore bit her lip, remembering how she'd surveyed herself daily in the mirror, hoping to see some change in her flat profile. She shook her head to dispel the memories. "Grown men certainly know the facts of life," she said. "Now dry your eyes, Annie, and don't be gloomy for Alan."

"Bea said once he could hear a butterfly belch, and sometimes when he turns his eyes on me, I swear he's reading my mind."

"He may well be. He's very astute."

"He'll spoil him rotten, you know."

"Him?"

"I think David would like a boy first."

Lenore smiled. "Most men would, but we'll just hope for a healthy baby."

****

Dearest David,

You know those two children we're going to have when you get home? Well, one of them will meet your train. I'm sick every morning and through the day, and I think I hate you.

All my love,
Annie

****

My darling Annie,

I was careful. What happened? Sending you a thousand kisses,

David

****

David, you idiot, what do you think happened? Sending 999 kisses back.

Annie

****

Dearest, darling Annie,

I am completely out of my mind with excitement, and I hope you are, too. Okay, so we didn't plan it—uh, him—and I really hate that I won't be there with you, but that's the way things happen sometimes. At least I don't have to worry about you since I know the Ashleys will treat you like priceless china. I wouldn't mind a few pictures of your "progress" if you can arrange it.

I can't tell you what I'm doing, so this is another boring letter for the censors. Stick in some socks and a summer sausage with the next box of butter cookies. While you're dining in style for two, I'm stuck with army chow.

I wonder just exactly when David, Jr. got started? Whenever it was, I enjoyed every minute of

*it. You did, too. Don't deny it. (Hope the censors won't
cut that out!)*

    All my love forever,
    David

****

Dearest David,

    *I'm feeling better, no thanks to you, but I have to
pin my skirts now. I'm going to Canon City again
tomorrow. It may be my last trip. Mr. Young has
been very understanding. He says that whenever I'm
ready to stop traveling, to let him know. He thinks
that the executives at the shipyard can make a trip or
two here for a change, and I can sit behind the
boardroom table, camouflaged, you see.*

    *Dr. Sims says that everything is as it should be
and that he can hear a heartbeat. I haven't felt the
baby move yet, but he says it should happen any day
now.*

    I love you and miss you.
    Annie.

****

Seeing a light under Annie's door, Lenore
tapped lightly.

"Come in, Mum. I'm still up."

"I just came to see if you're ready for your trip
tomorrow."

"Just about." Annie held a scarf against a suit
she was folding. "Does this go?"

"Quite well."

"It's long and hides the fact that my jacket isn't
buttoned. I can pin the waistband of my skirt closed
but not the jacket."

"I'm sure it will look fine."

Annie folded the suit with tissue paper in the
creases and laid it in her bag. "It will just have to,
that's all."

"I wish you didn't have to stay overnight."

"Only two nights this time. At least it's not all

week. Two days without a letter from David."

"They'll be here when you get back."

"I know, but..." She snapped the bag shut and slid it onto the floor.

Lenore took Annie's hand and led her to the window seat. "Letters are your only connection."

"Ten days. That's all we had, Mum. Sometimes it doesn't seem real."

Lenore laid her palm on the slight swell beneath Annie's robe. "This makes it real."

"Maybe it will be more real when I feel him move. Dr. Sims says any day now."

"I'm looking forward to it."

Annie thought she heard the barest hint of regret in Lenore's voice. "Mum, did you ever...I mean, you and Pa might have had children of your own."

"It wasn't meant to be, Annie. Besides, we had you."

"But I wasn't yours, not that way. I never really thought about it until now." She put her hand on top of Lenore's. "This baby is part of me in a way that you never experienced."

"You *are* part of us, Annie, in a very special way."

"I know, but a baby..."

Lenore leaned to kiss Annie's cheek. "Alan and I are joyfully anticipating being grandparents. Now, you need to go to bed."

Annie clung to Lenore for a moment. "I didn't mean that you aren't my mother. You are."

"I never thought of myself as anything else. Goodnight, dear."

****

Alan emerged from the bathroom buttoning his pajamas. "Is Annie ready for tomorrow?"

"Yes. I wish she didn't have to go."

"Trent told her that whenever she was ready to

stop traveling, he'd arrange to have the meetings here in Rumers Crossing. It just seemed more efficient for one person to travel as opposed to several."

Lenore sat at her dressing table and waited for him to take down her hair and brush it. "She asked me if I wished that we'd had children because she wasn't really ours that way."

"What did you tell her?"

"That it just wasn't meant to be and that we were content with her and eagerly awaiting our first grandchild."

Alan drew the brush through the hair that she kept unfashionably long because he liked it. "Is it still a great regret for you, darling Lenore?"

"Only that we had the promise, and it wasn't fulfilled. If it had never happened…"

"It was beyond belief that it did. I told you that after I was so ill in prep school, the doctor made it clear to me that I'd never father a child."

"Doctors don't know everything. And maybe it was my fault."

"There is no fault, Lenore. Dr. Sims explained that. Sometimes a pregnancy mercifully terminates itself when something isn't right."

She leaned forward and covered her face with her hands. "Am I terrible to envy Annie this experience?"

"Of course not." He put down the brush and wrapped his arms around her shoulders. "She'll be here for awhile, at least until David gets home, so we'll be able to enjoy every moment with her."

"I'm glad of that."

"So am I. I've been thinking about becoming a grandfather. Young David Jr. will learn to read from the *bumpty book* before he reads print, just as Bea did."

"I was thinking that we'll have to attach bells to

his shoes when he begins walking, so that you'll always know where he is."

"And teach him not to get under my feet. Prince seemed to know that instinctively."

"Alan, a decision must be made sooner rather than later about Prince. Annie knows it, but she can't bring herself to say goodbye."

"Perhaps Prince will know when it's time and just sleep away. That would be easier for all concerned."

"I hope so. Poor old fellow still insists on sleeping by her bed, and the stairs are really too much for him. Mrs. Swane made him a nice bed in the kitchen, but he won't use it."

"He even slept by her bed when she was away at Vassar, remember, and refused all invitations into our room."

"Well, I hope it happens sometime when Annie is away."

"Perhaps it will, if she doesn't choose to see him off voluntarily."

"No decision is going to be made tonight, and I expect you're as tired as I am."

"The days just aren't long enough lately."

"They won't be until the war is over." He took her arm and walked toward the bed. "Sims mentioned that he'd like to see you the next time he sees Annie."

"I had a check-up just recently."

"Six months ago."

"That long? All right, I'll go in."

"Young David will need a healthy grandmother, you know."

Lenore slid across the bed and snuggled against him. "It will be nice to have a baby in the house, won't it?"

Chapter Twelve

Annie paid the cab driver, then glanced at her watch. Only four-thirty. Thankfully, the meeting had gone smoothly and ended ahead of schedule. Lunch, eaten on the run between sessions, hadn't been satisfying, and she was aware of an empty sensation in her stomach.

Then she felt something else, something tentative, that soon became more defined. A vision of the butterflies that danced among the daffodils ringing the terrace in early spring came to mind. *Butterfly wings.* The baby was moving like a butterfly fluttering its delicate wings. She'd read that in the book Bea sent a few weeks ago. She put her fingertips against her belly, and this time the soft drumming grew stronger against them.

It was real. David's son was real. *Oh, David, why aren't you here to experience all this with me? Why did you have to leave me, too?*

Realizing that she was standing in the middle of the sidewalk, Annie moved on toward the door. "Afternoon, Miss Ashley," the doorman said, touching the brim of his hat.

She wanted to correct him, but she'd made the decision to continue using the name with which everyone was familiar, at least for now. She greeted him with a smile. "I'm married, you know," she said on impulse.

"No, I didn't. Congratulations, ma'am!"

"Thank you." She leaned closer. "And we're going to have a baby."

"Not really!"

She nodded. "In December."

"So we won't be seeing you around here for awhile, I guess."

"This is probably my last trip."

"Your husband's in service?"

"He's overseas. Europe."

"He'll have a lot of reasons to look forward to coming home, won't he?"

"Oh, yes, he will. He really will." A smile spread across her face as she continued through the lobby. *David's coming home to a real family. He's coming home to me...and to his son.*

Sitting at the desk in her room, she felt the baby move again as she took a sheet of hotel stationery out of the drawer and picked up her pen.

Dearest David,

Your son is a butterfly making his presence known with his tiny little hands and feet. It just happened when I got out of the taxi at the hotel a few minutes ago.

I'm going out to celebrate at that little café around the corner, the one where we went the first time you asked me out, when I didn't even like you.

I like you now. In fact, I love you so much that I can't even tell you, and I miss you. Take good care of yourself, dearest David, and I'll take good care of your son.

With all the love of my heart,
Annie

****

She lingered over her salad as she scanned the evening paper, wondering if David was part of the offensives detailed in print. He might be anywhere.

It was already dark when she left the café for the short walk back to the hotel. Noticing that the streetlight was out on the corner, she slowed her steps on the sidewalk she could barely see. Then, remembering the alley between the hotel and the building next to it, she picked up her pace again.

She'd had an aversion to the shadowy spaces between tall buildings ever since her experience in the alley behind the Greenfield Home. Sometimes in her dreams she saw her father striding away from her there. She could even hear her own cries echoing among the jumble of trash barrels and discarded boxes in that sinister, suffocating space.

Relief flooded her as she caught sight of the hotel. Then, just one step out of the light streaming from the lobby, hands closed around her arms above her elbows, dragging her into the darkness. "Make a sound and it'll be your last."

"Please don't hurt me! I have some money in my purse..."

"Not a sound, or I swear you're dead...Bobbie."

The voice's owner shoved her ahead of him along the rough pavement of the alley, his arm around her throat making it difficult to breathe. The rough material of his sleeve scratched her cheek. *Bobbie...he called me Bobbie.*

She heard the hum of a car engine close behind them, but there were no lights. "Inside," the man said, jerking her upright as the car glided alongside. She cried out in pain as he grasped a handful of hair and shoved her toward the rear door.

"Avenall!" Another voice, one she'd heard before, pierced her panicked brain. "Let her go, Avenall! This is between us."

"Yeah, it's between us all right, and you know what I want."

"She doesn't have them."

"She'll do until you decide to be reasonable."

"Let her go." Annie caught a note of desperation in the voice. "Just let her go, and I'll..."

"Yeah, you'll make good, because you know what'll happen if you don't."

The familiar voice let out a chilling oath. "I'll kill

you, Avenall! By God, I'll tear you apart! Let her go!"

"I'm not stupid enough to let you get close enough for that. Harcourt was a fool, but I've got a gun, Rycroft. Any closer, and she's dead. You know where to find me." He shoved Annie again. This time she stumbled and fell, the corner of the car door slicing into her abdomen like a knife. She moaned as waves of pain and nausea washed over her.

She heard the sound of scuffling, and then the car's engine rumbled to life again. She scrambled to her feet and moved back until a brick wall halted her. It was then that the car's lights came on, blinding her as it inched toward her. "No, no...please..." She put her hands against her stomach, shielding the frantic fluttering that had begun again. "Please, no..."

"Don't, you fool! We ain't got nothing without her!"

"Run, Bobbie! Run!"

Later, when the police asked about the gunshots, she could only tell them that she'd heard the sound of the car making contact with the wall...and her body.

****

"It's all right, Annie, Alan and I are here with you."

Annie forced herself out of the gray, cloying mist. "Mum?"

"You just had a little accident, Annie dear, but you're going to be all right." Lenore pressed Annie's limp hand to her cheek and smoothed her tangled hair.

Alan's voice pushed back the mist even farther. "We're right here, Annie. Don't be afraid."

Somehow she found the strength to grasp his hands. The feel of the raised scars on the backs of them was comforting beneath her fingers. "Pa...they came back for me."

"It's all over, Annie. Don't be afraid."

The scent of pipe tobacco filled her nostrils as he bent over her, pressing his lips against her forehead.

For a moment she was back in the dark alley, being lifted in strong arms.

"Papa," she murmured. "Papa."

****

"You speak with him," Lenore told Alan. "I can't leave her."

Alan felt for the doctor's arm and stepped into the corridor outside Annie's hospital room. "She *is* going to be all right?"

"She's badly bruised, but there don't seem to be any internal injuries. She lost the baby, of course. I'm sorry."

"Was it a boy or a girl?"

"We don't really..."

"Which?"

"A boy. Almost five months gestation, I'd say." He paused. "We'll dispose of..."

"No!" Alan recoiled from the anguish in his own voice. "I'm sorry, Doctor. No, we'll want the baby buried."

"It wasn't..."

"He was my grandchild. I'll make arrangements with a mortuary to transport him."

"As you like."

"Thank you for your services. I'll go back to my wife and daughter now." He put his hand on the door. "We'll tell her what happened when she's stronger. Please caution the nurses not to mention it."

****

They told her the next afternoon. She didn't cry as they'd expected, but the agony in her eyes, before she turned her face to the wall, transferred itself to Lenore, and she cried instead.

"Would you like for me to get word to David

through the Red Cross if I can?" Alan asked.

Annie shook her head.

Alan's fingertips brushed her forehead. "I thought you might want to know that the baby was a boy. He'll be buried in the Ashley plot in Rumers Crossing."

"No." She closed her eyes. "Put him in Greenfield with the others."

"But that's for..." Lenore began.

"I know what it's for. I should be there, too. Papa did this. He left me for this."

It was on the tip of Alan's tongue to say that it looked very much like Albert Rycroft could now be credited with saving his daughter's life three times. "It's your decision, Annie. Do you want to name him?"

"For his father. David Samuel Levinson. When can I go home?"

"Tomorrow," Lenore said. "The doctor said you'll need to rest for two weeks."

Annie shrugged and closed her eyes again.

****

She didn't cry until the morning three days after she came home, when she woke to find Prince cold and still in his bed beside hers. Curling up on the floor beside his lifeless body, she buried her face in his shaggy fur and sobbed until her body ached.

****

Alan showed Emory Roth into his study. "It was good of you to come all this way tonight."

"I was glad to do it. How is Annie?"

"Grieving, finally. Prince died sometime during the night."

"I'm sorry. He was getting on in years, wasn't he?"

"Almost fifteen."

They sat in front of the empty fireplace. "I've been able to determine that Albert Rycroft used his

103

passport to come here about two weeks ago," the investigator said.

"Do you know why?"

"Apparently he's been working with the underground in various places to rescue Jews who haven't been picked up yet by the SS, but that takes money. He was here to solicit funds, I think."

"Or to get the diamonds?"

"Maybe."

"Annie told the police that her father called the man Avenall."

"I've always thought that Floyd Avenall was the man driving the car the night Harcourt broke in here. I've kept an eye on him. Oh, I know you didn't ask me to, but I had the feeling that all this wasn't finished, and when you told me what your son-in-law said about the diamonds, I knew Annie was still a pawn."

"If they were meant to aid Jewish immigration, and Rycroft had them, then they're gone."

"I don't think he ever had them, but I think he knows where they are."

Hearing the door open, both men rose as Lenore came in with the teacart. "I thought you might like some coffee."

"Thank you, my dear. Can you stay and hear what Emory has to say?"

"For awhile. I just checked on Annie. She's asleep." Lenore sat beside her husband and began to pour the coffee. "Thank you for coming, Mr. Roth."

Alan offered a brief recap of the detective's new information. "Is there anything else, Emory?"

"Not at the moment. The police in Canon City aren't pursuing Avenall's death too actively. They found out about his background. He was Texas's problem, and now he's dead."

"Do they know about Albert Rycroft?"

"If they do, they're not putting it out."

"Annie told them there was another man and that she didn't know who it was. I suppose I should have urged her to be truthful with them, but she didn't actually see him and only thought she recognized his voice." Alan held out his cup for a refill.

Lenore bit her lip. "She heard the other man, Avenall, call his name. She knew who it was."

"It was Albert Rycroft, Mrs. Ashley," Emory Roth said.

"He killed Floyd Avenall, didn't he, just like Robert Harcourt?"

Roth didn't hesitate. "We know that, but no one is asking us, just as they didn't push too hard about Harcourt's death."

"And we're not offering the information." Lenore slipped her hand into Alan's. "I was naïve to think it was over twelve years ago."

"I haven't been able to determine anyone else who knows about the diamonds or might be looking for them," the detective said. "I think the man with Avenall was something of a minor lackey. So perhaps it's really over now."

"Is that your honest opinion?" Alan asked.

"As honest as I can be at this point."

"Will you pass on the information to Rycroft as if he weren't involved?"

"About the baby? Yes, I think so, unless you object."

"He should know," Alan said. "We agreed that he should share her life as much as possible."

Lenore sat up straighter. "I didn't really agree, Alan. I only accepted your judgment in the matter."

"It was my best judgment," he said. "I still believe I was right."

"Does Annie know that Avenall is dead and that her father killed him?" Roth asked.

"She doesn't want to know. She's angry," Lenore

said. "She blames him for what happened. For leaving her here all these years to be in this situation."

"Well, she has to blame someone, I suppose," Roth said. "But it's too bad that it must be the same man who seems to always be around just when she needs him."

****

Alan came back after seeing Emory Roth out. "What are you thinking, darling Lenore?" He sat down and took her in his arms.

"My thoughts are muddled, Alan, much like they were when I was about to take Annie and go across the border into Canada."

"Do you wish you could go back and make another decision?"

"You know I don't."

"It was a foolish question." He found her lips. "I can't imagine these dozen years without you."

"We've had so much happiness. I wanted the same happiness for Annie."

"She'll have it. The war will be over, and David will come home. The doctor didn't seem to feel that the loss of this baby meant there couldn't be others."

Lenore put her face against his neck. "I've relived my own loss these past few days and thought of telling Annie, so she'd know that I understand."

"Perhaps it's the right time to tell her."

"She told me that she felt the baby move for the first time just hours before the attack. I'm rather glad that didn't happen for me."

Alan stroked her shoulders in silence.

"It would have been more of a loss, I think. The baby was real to me, but feeling it move…"

"You grieved nonetheless."

"Too much, I think. I've come to realize that the most important thing is that I have you. We have each other."

"Just as Annie will have David when the war is over." Alan stood up and held out his hand. "It's late." He waited for Lenore to switch off the lamps.

"Annie says that she hates her father, that he's to blame for every bad thing that ever happened to her."

"Did you remind her that he's also responsible for every good thing that's happened to her in the past dozen or so years?"

"I tried. She didn't want to listen."

"We may have to force her to listen to the facts so that she can put things into perspective."

"I don't think it's that simple, Alan."

"Perhaps not, but eventually she's going to have to accept the reality that she can't change what's happened, and go on from there."

Chapter Thirteen

"She's out there again." Lenore stood at the study window overlooking the back lawn that sloped to the river. Her heart turned over at the sight of Annie kneeling in the grass beside the spot where the gardener had buried Prince.

Alan followed the sound of Lenore's voice. Moving behind her, he circled her waist with his arms. "Yet she won't allow us to take her to Greenfield where her baby is buried."

"She says she couldn't bear it right now."

"She can't avoid it forever."

"I think she'd like to try." Lenore turned in Alan's arms and laid her face against his chest. "I've made up my mind to tell her about our baby. Perhaps that will help."

"What about the rest? About Albert Rycroft and the fact that he killed for her yet again?"

"I think she knows that, but she's so angry with him...and to tell you the truth, so am I. It seems that somehow he placed her in this situation when he took those diamonds. He didn't think about how it might involve her."

"If he took them."

"Why else would her grandfather want her? Why else would Floyd Avenall try to abduct her? She's been a pawn, Alan, and you know it!"

"I expect she has been, but there was no changing the situation, was there? I had the house guarded day and night for six months, and Jerry stayed on for another two years, until his brother finished college."

"I don't mean to criticize you, Alan. You did everything you could and more. And you weren't the one who endangered her to begin with. Her own father did."

"Roth seems to feel that it's over now."

"I wish I felt sure of that."

"Well, perhaps we should just let it go now, as you wanted to do before. She's a grown woman. We can't force her to feel differently."

"That's just it, Alan, she's not a grown woman. Inside she's still that frightened six-year-old who was handed off the train to me in the dead of the night and who sat by the front door for hours on end, waiting for her Papa to come for her."

"Do you want me to talk to her?"

"Not now. I don't think she'd listen anyway."

****

Dearest David,

Dr. Sims says I can go back to work next week. That will be good for me, I think. I just sit here alone all day and think of you and of our baby. I don't even have Prince to talk to anymore.

Annie chewed her pen as she considered her next words. She hadn't told David the whole truth about the miscarriage. Mum and Pa said that he had a right to know, and maybe he did, but he'd worry more if he knew what really happened. Besides, she wanted to forget, and he would tell her that forgetting wasn't the answer.

I saw Dr. Sims today for my last check-up. He says there's absolutely no reason why we can't have more children, and we will. Two or three or four, whatever you want.

I miss you so, David. Take good care of yourself, and hurry home.

All my love,

Annie

She folded the paper and put it inside an

envelope, then went into the bathroom and changed into her robe.

Lenore was waiting on the window seat when she came out.

"I just came in to say goodnight."

"Mum, I'm all right. You worry too much about me."

"I saw you on the back lawn again today."

"There's nothing wrong with that."

"You should let me drive you to Greenfield, Annie."

"I don't want to go. Not yet. When I'm ready, I'll drive myself."

"I wish you'd come with us to choose a marker."

"Pa designed the one for the children from the Home. He can take care of this one."

"It's a little more personal to him this time. It's for his grandchild."

Annie shook her head. "I wish I hadn't felt him move. He wasn't exactly real to me before that."

"He was real from the beginning." Lenore stood up and walked a few steps, then returned. "Annie, I want to tell you something. Perhaps I should have told you before, but you were in school and..."

She sat down again. "In the spring of your junior year at Vassar, I discovered, much to my surprise and delight, that I was going to have a baby."

"Mum!"

"I couldn't believe it. After eight years, I'd almost given up hope. Alan and I were thrilled, though he was concerned for my health. We both felt, however, that you were almost grown up now and wouldn't feel displaced."

"I wouldn't have felt that way before."

Lenore took Annie's hands. "We'd concentrated so hard on you, trying to make you feel secure and to give back the childhood years you'd lost. We always felt it was best for you to receive all our attention."

"Mum, I wouldn't have felt left out. You deserved a child of your own."

"No, let me finish, Annie dear. We were confident that we could concentrate on another child now without neglecting you. Dr. Sims was surprised. I was past forty, and he said things would be more difficult, but I wasn't worried at all. I was too excited to be worried."

Lenore gazed out the window, remembering. "We agreed to wait to tell you until you came home in the summer. By then the baby would be very obvious, and we could all anticipate together."

"What happened?"

"I was almost three months along the night I woke and realized that something was very wrong. Alan called Dr. Sims. He came immediately and stayed the rest of the night until it was over."

"Oh, Mum, I'm sorry!" Annie put her arms around Lenore. "I'm so very sorry!"

"Dr. Sims said that, being so early, it was probably for the best. I didn't see things that way, of course."

"Was Pa terribly upset?"

"He was more worried about me, but Dr. Sims assured him that I was in perfect health. I only missed a week at the office. Alan just told people that I had a bad cold and didn't want to expose anyone else."

"Why didn't you tell me?"

"It seemed unnecessary. Alan and I did our grieving and put it behind us."

"Did Gram know?"

"Oh, yes, from the beginning, and Sam and Ellen, too."

"I wish you'd told me."

"This seemed to be the right time. You need to know that I understand your feelings of loss."

"It was more *how* it happened with me. That

man in the alley, the car...and Papa."

"He saved your life, Annie."

"He killed the man, didn't he? He shot Floyd Avenall."

"The police in Canon City are calling it a homicide by an unknown person."

"No one saw him carrying me to the hotel?"

"No one saw or heard anything, it seems."

"It was the diamonds, the ones David told me about."

"Emory Roth feels that's possible."

"But how did Papa know..."

"No one knows that, Annie, not even Mr. Roth."

"He just seems to come and go like the wind." She turned her head to look into the darkness beyond her window. "Each time I step into the future, something jerks me back into the past."

"All of us have a past, Annie. We just have to move on."

"I don't want to live in the past, Mum. I really don't."

"And you shouldn't, but you have to accept it before you can put it behind you."

"Did you put your baby behind you?"

"Perhaps not completely. I suppose I was reliving that time through you."

"So you've had a double loss."

"We still have each other, Annie, and when David comes home, you'll have another baby. Dr. Sims said there was no reason why there couldn't be another one."

Annie nodded. "Yes, I know." She savored Lenore's soft arms around her. "Thank you for telling me about your baby, Mum. I wish things had been different."

"There's so much I wish for you, Annie dear. It breaks my heart that I can't protect you from the bad things in life, but I can't. I never could."

"You took good care of me, Mum."

Lenore sighed. "I tried. That's all any of us can do, I suppose."

****

Dear Annie,

Just what the hell were you thinking? I didn't live in a vacuum in Canon City, you know. I have friends and acquaintances who read the newspaper. How do you think I felt when I got letters from friends sympathizing with me for the attack on you that led to the loss of our baby, and I didn't even know about it?

It wasn't that you lied to me outright. It was what you didn't tell me. I suppose you'll say it was because you didn't want me to worry, but that's unfair of you to deny me the opportunity to share all of this with you.

I'm disappointed in Alan Ashley, too. We had enough man-to-man talks that I thought he'd be responsible enough to make sure I knew the truth.

When I get home, we're going to have to straighten out a lot of things, Annie. Our marriage isn't worth much if we don't really share our lives. There's still a part of you I don't know, even though I thought I did. I don't know Bobbie, and I'm not sure you know her yourself. We've got to find her, find your Papa's shining star, or we'll lose each other.

Love,
David

****

Dear David,

I did what I thought was right, and so did Pa, so you'll just have to be disappointed in both of us. As for the other, Bobbie doesn't exist anymore, and if you think she does, you're way off base. Maybe we rushed into this marriage too quickly. If we did, at least there isn't a child to consider.

Annie

****

NOVEMBER 5, 1943

MRS. ANNIE LEVINSON 1 ASHLEY ROAD RUMERS CROSSING NY

THE SECRETARY OF WAR DESIRES ME TO EXPRESS HIS REGRET THAT YOUR HUSBAND, 2ND LT. DAVID S. LEVINSON, HAS BEEN REPORTED MISSING IN ACTION SINCE 17 SEPTEMBER 1943 IN ITALY. IF FURTHER DETAIL OR INFORMATION IS RECEIVED, YOU WILL BE PROMPTLY NOTIFIED.

OFFICE OF THE ADJUTANT GENERAL

****

Alan stirred up the study fire and returned to sit beside Lenore. "There's always hope."

"I'm not sure Annie can hope anymore."

"Why?"

"She's lost so much, Alan."

"Unfortunately, she's lost herself, as well. I've had occasion to wonder if I made a mistake in not trying to track Albert Rycroft down and convince him to make contact with Annie and explain all the circumstances."

"He could have taken her that night in Greenfield after you told him where she was. I know you were glad that he didn't, but..."

"Lenore, you know how much I love Annie. She's my daughter in every way."

"She adores you, Alan."

"She's replaced her own father with me because I was available."

"That's not fair to her, is it? She loves you for yourself."

"Yes, but I'm also a replacement for what she lost. It was a natural thing for her to do."

"We've been a good family, Alan."

He nodded. "Yes, we have, and I don't regret a moment of these past twelve years. But I can't help feeling that I failed to give her something...the strength, the courage...something...to help her understand and accept what happened to her."

"What could you have done? What could anyone have done?"

"Outside of dragging Albert Rycroft back here to tell her why he left her behind, there's probably nothing."

"When David comes home..."

"I pray that will happen, Lenore, but if it doesn't...if David doesn't come home, she'll feel abandoned again."

"It's done, Alan. And you just said that there was always hope."

He sighed. "I had to speak the words, at least." He pulled her closer to him. "I hope David didn't get Annie's last letter. The anger in her words..."

"She hopes so, too. She regretted it immediately, but it was too late."

"Now she'll live with guilt as well as loss."

"David was hard on her."

"I advised her to tell him everything. I even considered writing to him myself."

"We discussed all that, Alan. It was up to Annie to tell him the truth."

"Yes, it was. I believe that, yet..."

Lenore reached to remove his glasses. "I've never known you to question yourself like this."

"I don't think I ever have."

"Then you shouldn't begin now." She polished his glasses and laid them aside.

"You don't like for me to wear those," he observed.

"I like to see all of your very handsome face."

He took her face in his hands and traced every feature. "I can't detect any changes in you at all."

"You're gallant to say so."

"I should be rewarded for my gallantry."

She kissed his eyelids. "There."

"Is that all?"

"For now. Annie says she's going to ask Trent to let her travel again. Is that a good idea?"

"Dr. Sims says she's been all right for months, at least physically."

"I'm talking about what happened in Canon City. How do we know that someone else isn't waiting to take her?"

"We don't, though Emory doesn't know of anyone else connected with Harcourt who might become involved."

"You suggested some security."

"I've had second thoughts about that."

"Why?"

"I think she'd feel more threatened and that she'd resent someone following her around."

"But what if..."

"Lenore, you've lived too much a prisoner of *what if's*, don't you think?"

"This isn't about me."

"I think it is. Annie is part of you."

"And of you."

"Yes, but we can't shelter her forever."

"I haven't sheltered her at all, it seems."

"You could have done nothing to protect her from what happened when she was a child, any more than you could keep these latest tragedies from befalling her."

"It seems as if I should have been able to do more."

"You made the decision not to run away, and as a result she's had a secure home and all the advantages you wanted for her."

"You're right, of course."

"We've both had to move past the unfortunate circumstances in our lives, and Annie will have to do it, too. I just wish I'd equipped her better."

"You're stronger than I am, Alan."

"I don't get any satisfaction from it. My heart breaks for her just as yours does." He rose and stirred the fire again. "What about some tea now?"

"I'll get it."

"And the..."

She laughed. "And the butter cookies."

Chapter Fourteen

Annie moved around her room with slow, aimless steps, avoiding the empty bed and Prince's empty place beside it. *I miss Prince more than I miss David. I knew him longer and better. Prince isn't ever coming back, but David...maybe he'll be back...maybe I'll get another telegram telling me that he's a prisoner of war somewhere...or maybe that he's dead.*

Her slippers made no sound on the thick rug as she padded to the window and opened the drapes to stare at the starless sky. *If he got that letter...if those are the last words he had from me...oh, David, I'm sorry! I want you to be all right, really I do! I want you to...*

Was she going to say she wanted him to come back? She wasn't sure. He said she had to find herself, to find Bobbie, but she didn't want to. *Bad things happened to Bobbie. I didn't want to be her anymore.* But bad things, it seemed, happened to Annie, too.

She glanced at the bed, remembering the last night she'd slept beside David. They'd made love less passionately with but more tenderness than ever before. Aware that he was leaving in a few hours, he seemed to be trying to memorize every detail of her body.

It was so long ago now. She could barely see his face unless she looked at his picture, and when she tried to remember his touch, it eluded her.

She did remember the night she agreed to marry him. She said that she loved him, but now she wondered if she'd just convinced herself that marrying him was the thing to do. She couldn't even remember what she'd been thinking before she said yes.

Annie turned away from the window and sat on the edge of her bed. From the beginning, she'd been aware of how deeply Alan and Lenore loved each other. They showed it in a hundred ways. A touch, a word, even a glance, although some would say that was an impossibility.

What had David done except make love to her? What had she done except let him? A marriage wasn't made in ten days, but she thought they'd made a beginning. Now she wasn't sure. Now she might never know.

She turned on the lamp beside the bed and tried to see more than just David's face in the bronzed frame. What was behind that slightly cocky smile? Was anything readable in his deep-set eyes? Who was this man she'd promised to love *until death us do part?*

She reached to touch his face, then withdrew her hand as if the image burned her. If he didn't come back, this picture would be her only reminder of what they'd shared for such a brief time. If he did return, had they shared enough to build a life on? Would they be two strangers sharing a home and a bed? Did she want that for the rest of her life?

The baby she'd carried for too short a time might have been a bond between them, but that, like everything else, was gone, too. Everything. The Home, Miss Ervin, her best friend Lucy, all the others. The house in Barnwell with the swing on the front porch where she sat and waited for Papa to come home in the evening and where, in pleasant weather, he read aloud to her. All the happy times had vanished.

Even Papa was gone, despite the fact that he

kept turning up. Somehow she couldn't reconcile her gentle, smiling Papa with the man who had killed twice for her. Had she ever really known him any better than she knew David? Did she want to know him now?

Outside, clouds scudded across the sky, obscuring the moon and casting an odd shadow on the china doll propped against a cushion on the window seat. Only Alberta remained, all that was left of Bobbie. As she rose from the bed, her sleeve brushed the picture frame, knocking it to the floor. Annie heard the shattering glass, but she didn't stop until she held Alberta in her arms.

"You're all I have left," she murmured, pressing the painted curls to her cheek. "Bobbie's gone, and Annie only exists on a piece of paper. Oh, Alberta, where do we go from here?"

****

"I need to work," Annie insisted when Lenore suggested that she take some time off. "Staying home isn't going to change the fact that David's missing."

Trent Young kept her busier than ever, adding two more subsidiaries to her list of regular contacts. More often than not, during the first few months of 1944, she was away from home four out of five weeknights. On weekends she slept late and then repacked her suitcase for the next trip.

"She's working too hard," Lenore said to Alan as they waited for her train the evening of the second of June.

"Has she seen Sims recently?"

"I reminded her that it was time for her check-up last month, but I don't think she went."

"It's company policy. We're working short-handed enough. That's why I instituted the visits to Sims every six months for every employee. Annie is no exception. I'll speak with her."

"She says work helps."

"Helps what? To ignore her circumstances?"

"Alan, be gentle with her."

"When have I ever been anything else?"

"You've always been strict."

"But not demanding."

"No, I think any demands to achieve, she's placed on herself."

"I've failed to equip her for life, Lenore. She had a difficult beginning that it seems nothing could overcome."

"You said that I overprotected her."

Alan held out his hand and felt Lenore's slip into it. "We never stop being parents, do we?"

She sighed. "She was a sweet child, but I wonder now if she was ever really happy. Maybe I just wanted to think she was."

"She's no longer a child, and she has to take charge of her life."

"Hasn't she done that?"

"Professionally, perhaps."

"Alan, it's been six months with no word about David. Do you really think there's still hope?"

"We have to hope."

"I don't think Annie does anymore."

"I..." The sound of the train cut him off, and he reached for the door. "She's here."

****

Alan called Annie into his office on Monday. "This is your week in town," he said. "Make an appointment to see Dr. Sims."

"I don't have time, and I don't need to see him anyway." Annie tried to rein in her irritation, but she knew that Alan recognized it.

"It's company policy, Annie. No exceptions."

She scowled, guilty of being glad he couldn't see her expression. She startled at his next words. "Wipe the martyrdom from your face, Annie."

"How do you always know?" Some of her ill-humor dissipated.

"I make it my business to know. Now go and telephone Sims for an appointment."

Annie rolled her eyes at Lenore who was coming into the office. "How do you live with him?"

"Quite cozily, actually," Lenore said, patting Annie's arm. "Why?"

"He's impossible."

"Well, I love him anyway."

Alan cleared his throat. "Did you bring those figures from Jerome?"

"I have them, Alan."

"We'll go over them and leave a little early for our Monday evening at Giovanni's."

"Your weekly date?" Annie asked. "Both of you are impossible."

"Romance keeps a marriage fresh, my dear Annie," Alan said. "And the fettuccini at Giovanni's isn't to be dismissed."

"Honestly."

"But you are. Dismissed, that is."

Annie rolled her eyes at Lenore again and left.

"I told her to make an appointment with Sims," Alan said when he heard the door close. "And I expect you to let me know when she sees him. Now, let's have a look at those figures."

****

On the sixth of June, Mrs. Swane, who always switched on the radio in the kitchen before starting the coffee, heard the news first. "It's begun," she announced to Alan, Lenore, and Annie as she set the small radio on the sideboard and plugged it in. "Maybe it's the beginning of the end."

Arriving late at the office, they found others straggling in, too. "It seems the radio stopped time for all of us this morning," Alan observed. "Lenore, send a memo to Jerome not to dock anyone who was late clocking in this morning."

James, the doorman, was listening to a small radio he'd brought from home. "I hope you don't mind if I have it in the lobby, Mr. Ashley."

"As a matter of fact, we need to round up any radios in the building and place them strategically. Work can't stop anymore than the war can, but we need to learn as much as possible about what's going on."

"I can take care of that, sir."

"Thank you, James. Have you heard from your son this week?"

"Had a letter waiting when I got home yesterday, Mr. Ashley. He's finished his missions."

"That means he can come home, doesn't it? I'm glad for you and Mrs. Guthrie."

"Be a load off our minds, I can tell you. I don't guess there's any word about..."

"Not yet, but maybe this will make the difference. We must keep up hope." Alan extended his hand to the man. "My heartiest good wishes for your family, James. Tell Jimmy to stop by and say hello when he gets home."

****

Lenore turned on the radio in Alan's office and left the door open so that Mrs. Fenton could hear it, too. After lunch, Annie stopped by to say that she was going to keep her appointment with Dr. Sims.

The doctor gave her some vitamins and told her to gain ten pounds. "Lenore needs at least ten, maybe fifteen. Isn't Mrs. Swane feeding you?"

"Quite well, actually."

"Just asking."

"We're tired, that's all. Work has taken our appetites."

"Well, get them back. I told Lenore to drink milkshakes twice a day, and I'll tell you the same thing. That doesn't mean replace meals with them."

He hesitated. "Any news of David?"

She shook her head.

"I'm sorry, Annie, but now that we've got a toe-hold in Europe, more information will be coming out."

"You were in the last war, weren't you?"

"I'd just finished my internship. You might say I substituted the war for a residency."

"So you weren't at the front where the fighting was going on."

"On the contrary, more often than not I operated by lantern light with shells exploding too close for comfort."

"David is fluent in German. I'd hoped his language skills might keep him away from the fighting, but it didn't happen."

"For awhile, I had visions of working in a nice clean hospital, but that didn't happen either." He came around the desk and put a hand on her shoulder. "Don't give up hope, Annie. I saw a few miracles in the last war. I think there'll be some in this one, too."

****

Annie and her parents sat up late that night to hear President Roosevelt address the nation, ending with:

"Almighty God,

Our sons, pride of our nation, this day have set upon a might endeavor, a struggle to preserve our republic, our religion and our civilization and to set free a suffering humanity. They will be sorely tried by night and by day without rest until the victory is won. Some will never return. Embrace these, Father, and receive them, Thy heroic servants, into Thy Kingdom."

"Amen," Alan murmured, reaching for Lenore's hand, then Annie's. Lenore turned off the radio, and they sat in silence for a long moment before going upstairs.

In the corridor, Alan embraced Annie. "Goodnight, my dear Annie. It's always darkest before the dawn." She held back her tears until she reached her own room. In the closet, under a pile of sweaters, she found the glassless frame containing David's picture and put her lips against his face. Then she returned it to its hiding place and got ready for bed.

****

The cost of this temporary victory was high. It seemed that everyone Annie met in her travels knew someone who had lost someone on the beaches of Normandy. Since she had stopped wearing her wedding ring long ago, no one questioned her about who she had *over there*.

She tried not to think about David, and usually she succeeded. When he did come to mind, she sent up a quick prayer for his safety, but she didn't let herself fantasize what a positive answer to her petition might mean.

****

As the demands for more materials increased, everyone worked harder and longer than ever. Annie thought that if she never saw the inside of another train or hotel room, she wouldn't mind.

She barely made it home from Albany in time for Christmas Eve. "You decorated the tree without me, and Gram has already gone to her sister's," she complained as they ate their traditional clam chowder in front of the fire and listened to a rebroadcast of the New York Philharmonic's Christmas concert.

"She caught the last possible bus," Alan said.

"Did you give her my present?"

"I tucked it into her suitcase myself," Lenore said. "And she left yours under the tree."

Annie glanced at the huge tree with only six gifts beneath it. "My friends always thought it was strange that we gave and received only one gift apiece."

"That was settled your first Christmas," Alan said. "I had a number of things in mind for you, but Lenore said I would spoil you."

"You probably would have. I developed a rather avaricious little soul after I came here and saw such riches."

"I never knew you to be mercenary," Lenore protested.

"When Pa began to give me pocket money, you said it was too much, but I insisted that I needed every penny," Annie reminded her.

"For books," Alan said.

"My library outgrew the bookcases you had built in my room."

"A good investment."

"I never gave away a single one. I always imagined reading them to my children someday."

"And so you shall," Alan said. "Someday soon, I hope."

"Pa, I..."

When she didn't go on, Alan said, "Finish your thought, Annie."

"No, it's too gloomy for Christmas Eve."

"You're thinking of David."

"Yes."

"You never mention his name anymore," Alan went on. "Is there a reason why?"

"We had ten days, Pa, and I didn't know him very long before that. Sometimes I can't remember the things I should remember."

"You never spent a Christmas together," Lenore mused.

"We never had a chance to share any of the things that are special to me. Our Christmas traditions, for instance. Clam chowder and music on Christmas Eve, dinner with Aunt Ellen and Uncle Sam on Christmas Day. Even the employee luncheon you and Mum host before we close on the twenty-third."

"You can make up for lost time," Lenore said. "After the war."

"I don't believe that David is coming home."

"Do you want him to?" Alan's question sliced through her growing self-pity like a knife.

"Of course, I do, Pa! How can you ask that?" She began to stack their empty bowls, then paused and shook her head. "All right, I don't want him to be dead, but as for coming home, I guess I don't know."

"Then you'd better make some decisions about what you'll do if he does," Alan said without any sign of surprise. "He deserves that much."

Chapter Fifteen

In May, Annie was returning from Canon City on the train when word began to spread through the passengers that the war in Europe was over. Alan and Lenore, waiting for her at the station, confirmed it. "But there's still Japan," Alan cautioned. "And, barring something catastrophic, they'll fight to the last man, woman, and child."

****

Annie thought that nothing could be as bad as the news coming from liberated Europe. Like most Americans, she'd heard the term *concentration camp,* but she knew now that no one had even begun to comprehend their horror. Now, newsreel pictures of bodies stacked like cordwood, walking skeletons in striped rags, and gaping ovens which hadn't quite consumed the last remnants of bone haunted her dreams.

She comforted herself that if David were alive, he would have been in a POW camp. Supposedly, those were humanely regulated by the International Red Cross. Alan had used his connections in Washington to obtain information on any unreported prisoners in German or Italian hands, but without success.

As the celebrations of May's V-E Day turned into redoubled efforts to finish off Japan, Annie made the conscious decision to give David up for dead. Her resolve lasted a month, until his letter reached her, even before the official telegram.

Dearest Annie,

I'm alive and well, having spent the last eighteen

128

months as a "guest" of the Gestapo in a camp called Dachau. For some reason, I guess because I speak German, and perhaps because I'm a Jew, I was considered a spy and sent to a concentration camp instead of a regular POW camp. If anyone asks you if Hell exists, tell them it does. I've been there.

Even though we were liberated at the end of April, the brass are still sorting through names, and I think the red tape may delay any sort of official notification of my status. I'm full of bugs and down to 120 pounds, pretty skinny for someone over six feet, but I'm getting good care in a place I won't mention in case the censors are still at work.

I don't know if you've thought of me as missing or dead all this time. Hopefully, you'll be as glad to get this letter as I am to write it. When I know more about being shipped home, I'll let you know, too. Mail sent to the same address as before should reach me. I wouldn't mind some of Mrs. Swane's butter cookies.

I can't forget what I said to you in the last letter I wrote, and I'm sorry I judged you for what you deemed to be a decision in my best interest. I've never stopped loving you, Annie, and all I want is to come home and hold you in my arms forever.

All my love,
David

****

This time Alan could get more information, though he was unable to cut through the red tape to speed up David's return. Being in better shape than some, he would have to wait his turn for transport to the States.

Annie vacillated between relief and dread. Her memories of their ten-day marriage were vague. David would be a virtual stranger in her bed. To assuage the guilt of her mixed emotions, she retrieved his picture from the closet and had new glass cut for the frame. Almost as an afterthought, she put on her wedding ring again.

Dear David,

Whatever I say will seem trite, I'm sure. Almost two years with no word and then, out of the blue, your letter appears in the mail. I don't even know where to begin. Quite honestly, I just tried not to think about it, to pretend it was all a nightmare that would end someday. I'm sure that doesn't surprise you. Then, a week after Germany surrendered, I decided that you weren't coming home. I guess I've been in shock since your letter arrived. But come home, David, and we'll pick up where we left off. I'm sure we've both changed, but we'll get to know each other again, hopefully better than before.

With love,
Annie

****

While she waited, the catastrophic event of which Alan had spoken finally occurred. The first of two atomic bombs consumed much of the populace of Hiroshima, vaporizing some and leaving others agonizingly burned. For Annie, the pictures of the mushroom cloud boiling over the Japanese city brought back memories of the flame and smoke rising from what had been the Greenfield Children's Home.

Images of the concentration camp survivors and victims haunted her dreams. The ten pounds she'd acquired with twice-daily milkshakes dropped off. Alan insisted that she see Dr. Sims, who took one look at her and said, "Talk to me, Annie. I'm a doctor, not your judge. Nothing you say will go any farther than this office."

She told him about the nightmares, even the ones about Albert Rycroft. He offered her some pills to quiet her nerves and help her sleep. When she refused, he nodded in approval. "I felt obligated to offer them, but they're not the answer, Annie." He held her eyes. "Have you shared any of this with Alan and Lenore?"

"They've had enough on their shoulders without me adding to their worries."

"The war's over now."

"Pa says it's over as far as the fighting is concerned. He says it will be a fight in itself to return to any semblance of normalcy."

"He may well be right. Have you given any thought to what you and David will do?"

"It still seems unreal that he's alive."

The doctor shifted in his chair and leaned across the desk. "Sometimes when a man has lived under David's circumstances...I'm speaking of starvation, disease, and abuse...there are problems."

"Are you saying that he might be unbalanced?"

"Nothing like that. I'm speaking of his physical health. I know you want children, but David may have a problem fathering a child, maybe temporarily, maybe permanently."

Her blank look told the doctor that she had missed his meaning. "I simply mean, Annie, that what the imprisonment has done to his body may delay, or even prevent, his ability to procreate. It might even mean that a normal relationship isn't possible right away."

"Oh." She looked away.

"I'm sure David is getting the best medical care available, but I'd be glad to see him if he wants to come in."

"I'll tell him." She got up to go. "Do you think the nightmares will ever go away?"

"I'm a surgeon-turned-family sawbones, not a psychiatrist, but I can refer you to someone."

She looked at him as if he'd grown an extra head.

He smiled and put his arm around her shoulders as he walked her to the door. "Annie, Alan is one of my closest friends. I've taken care of Lenore and watched you grow up. I want the best for you, whatever that is."

"I don't know myself, Dr. Sims. I wish I did."

"I got that idea from what you told me. Just be kind to yourself, Annie. Give yourself time to readjust to having David with you. Give him time, too. No man who's been to war is ever quite the same."

She left the office feeling worse than when she'd come.

****

She received two more letters from David before the Army notified her that they were shipping him home at the end of September. His words weren't impersonal, but she sensed a restraint that she supposed came from her own less-than-ardent attempts at communication.

As Ashley Enterprises began to shift into peacetime pursuits, Annie wondered when her position as Trent Young's administrative assistant would end and what she would do after that. A week before David's scheduled arrival, Trent called her into his office.

"As you know, Jack Shaw made it through and is coming back."

"I'm glad for him. And for me. Now you can be Uncle Trent again."

"You've done a good job for me, Annie. A good job for Ashley Enterprises. As I said, Jack made it through, but not entirely unscathed."

"He was injured?"

"Unfortunately, yes, almost at the end of the fighting. He's going to be in a wheelchair for the rest of his life."

"Oh, no! Oh, that's terrible! He's so young, and...wasn't he engaged before he went overseas?"

"Yes, well," he cleared his throat. "She decided,

under the circumstances, that she didn't want to marry him after all. I spoke with him long-distance last night, and he offered to step aside because of his disability. I told him we wouldn't consider it."

"At least he has something waiting for him, even if his fiancée isn't."

"I reminded him that Alan's personal disability hasn't hindered him in business. On the other hand, Jack would have difficulty traveling, so it occurred to me that you might become his assistant for that purpose. I'm only a few years from retirement, and Jack is capable of stepping into my position when I decide to leave."

"He'd certainly have the best training."

"I haven't discussed any of this with Alan yet. I know it all depends on what David's plans are."

Guilt consumed Annie as she realized she hadn't considered what David would want to do and that it probably wouldn't involve remaining in Rumers Crossing.

"He'll be home next week."

"That's why I waited to mention it. Take some well-earned time off, Annie. You've got vacation time coming if you want to use it and get paid, or just take off on your own. I don't think you're in danger of starving or living under a bridge." He winked at her.

The man across the desk was Uncle Trent now, not her immediate boss. "I'll have everything caught up by Monday. When will Jack be here?"

"Jean and I invited him to visit us at the farm and get reacquainted with Ashley Enterprises before he takes over from you. He'll be here on Friday."

"I'll have a final summary report on your desk then. He can read it this weekend. If he has any questions..."

"We won't call you," Trent said, laughing. "You'll be on your second honeymoon."

Annie managed a weak smile. "I...that's right. I guess I will."

****

Money being no object, Annie was able to find accommodations in New York City at one of the better hotels. She took a cab to the pier where David's ship would dock, arriving early to position herself behind a pillar where she would be able to see him before he saw her.

As she waited for the passengers to disembark, she alternately perspired and shivered. The day before she left home she'd spent a long time looking at David's picture, wondering if she'd even know him. Alan had echoed Dr. Sims' caution that David was sure to be changed. "The doctors haven't erased almost two years in a few weeks," Alan said.

Annie saw her husband first after all, slightly stooped and with an obvious limp. His uniform hung loosely from his bony shoulders without appearing to touch any other part of his emaciated body. When he paused at the end of the gangplank to look for her, she tried to move from behind the pillar, but her legs refused to go forward.

She took him in again, this time in more detail. His eyes, sunken in a face that was no more than skin stretched over skull, scanned the dock again. She saw him set down his duffle bag as if it had suddenly become too heavy to hold. Only with a supreme effort did she step out from her hiding place and call his name.

****

At the hotel, he stayed in the shower for a long time. After awhile, Annie opened the bathroom door a little and said, "David, would you like for me to order room service instead of going out to dinner?"

"I want a nice thick steak, medium rare. Real beef, not..."

"I'll try for one," she interrupted. "Good cuts of

134

meat are still scarce."

"A place like this will have a good one. Order some onion rings and a baked potato, and see what they have for dessert."

"Are you that hungry?"

"Annie, I've been hungry for two years." His voice accused her.

Stung, she mumbled, "I'm sorry."

"Never mind."

"I packed a bag for you. Mrs. Swane sent all your things to the laundry and the dry cleaners. Would you like your robe or something else?"

"My robe may be the only thing that doesn't fall off me."

"All right. I'm putting it on the vanity."

She dropped some slippers on the floor of the bathroom, too, before she went to telephone room service. "Forty-five minutes until they bring dinner," she called through the door. "Aren't you running out of hot water?"

"Not yet."

She heard the shower go off. In a few minutes he came out tying the belt of the robe that almost went around him twice. "I hung everything in the closet," Annie said, dropping her eyes. "You may have to buy some things to tide you over until you gain some weight."

"I got all my back pay before I came home."

"The allotment checks went into a special account at the bank, so you have a nice nest egg. In fact, I withdrew some cash and bought you a new wallet." She pushed the leather billfold toward him across the lamp table.

"What's your status with Ashley Enterprises?"

"Jack Shaw's coming back, but in a wheelchair. It's permanent, so Uncle Trent offered me the opportunity to stay as Jack's assistant and do the traveling for him."

"What did you tell him?"

"He didn't want an answer right away. He knew we'd have to talk it over."

"Do you want to stay?"

"I suppose I do, but the decision about where we live is yours." She'd rehearsed the words for days, hoping that his decision would be the one she wanted.

He picked up the wallet, opened and closed it, and set it down again. "I don't know yet."

"You don't have to make a quick decision. I'll spend a few weeks helping Jack get settled in."

"I guess I look pretty bad." His eyes held hers, preventing any pat answer.

"Yes, you do, but I expected it. I saw the pictures."

"Of the camps?"

She nodded. "The newsreels were full of them."

"Pictures don't even begin to tell the story." He rubbed his eyes. "You know what they're saying, Annie? That six million Jews died in those camps. Six million!"

"I hadn't heard that number."

"Hitler said he'd make a *Judenfrei welt*, and he damn near did it!" David's shoulders twitched.

"I don't understand German, David."

"Sorry. A Jew-free world. That was what saved me, you know, being able to speak German."

"I thought that's what got you into trouble to begin with."

"It was. The German lieutenant who picked me up was determined I was a spy. He got a handsome reward for turning me in, I guess."

"Picked you up in Italy?"

"I forgot that you don't know the story. The telegram should have told you that I went missing in Holland."

"No, it said Italy."

"I was there before I parachuted into Holland to provide some backup for the underground. Unfortunately, I landed in a tree, and before I could cut myself loose, Jerries were swarming all over me." He sat down in a chair and picked up the newspaper he'd bought in the lobby.

"Surely that's not all the story."

"No. They hauled me around for awhile before shipping me back to Germany. I was in a few other places before I wound up in Dachau. Being able to speak and understand German kept me one step ahead of the guards."

He stopped and looked away from her, then back. "I wasn't sure you'd wait for me."

She felt her face flame. "I'm your wife, David."

"We didn't have much of a marriage. Ten days, and from what I remember, we spent most of that time in bed. We can't spend the rest of our lives there."

"I always wondered if that's why you married me," she said before she thought. "Because you couldn't get me any other way."

"Is that what you thought?"

"Well, you said..."

"I know what I said, but you had a choice, didn't you?"

"I guess so. Yes."

"Well, assuming that I married you because I wanted you, why did *you* marry *me*?"

Her mind raced frantically for some kind of answer that would be honest but not heartless. David would know if she was telling the truth.

Taking a deep breath and expelling it slowly to buy time, she said, "I don't know, David."

"I didn't think you did. Do you want a divorce?"

"You haven't been home but a few hours. I don't think this is the time to discuss anything so...so final."

"When do you think it will be time?"

"What do you want, David?"

"You, Annie. Just you. I was in love with you. I still am."

"We hardly knew each other."

"I remember telling you once that love can't be explained. It just happens."

"I think we're both overwhelmed right now."

"I'm not. I spent two years just trying to stay alive, and I made it. The fact doesn't overwhelm me, just gives me a great satisfaction that I beat those monsters. I'm not going to waste a minute of the rest of my life, not after what I've been through."

"What do you want to do? Be an architect?" Annie changed the subject neatly.

"Maybe. I need to get my skills back."

"At the shipyard?"

"No, my place is filled. They didn't promise me anything like Trent Young promised Jack Shaw."

"Pa and the board of directors decided that was a good policy for Ashley Enterprises."

"I agree with them, but they're in the minority. Life over here moved on while the rest of us were fighting the war."

"We were fighting, too, you know."

"I didn't mean to minimize the home front efforts."

"I know it wasn't the same."

He was silent for a moment. "You really waited for me."

"Did you think I wouldn't?"

"To tell you the truth, Annie, after awhile I didn't think about much of anything except how to get some extra food and stay off the worst work details and out of the way of the guards. At first I thought about you a lot, but after awhile I couldn't handle not knowing if I'd ever see you again."

"I understand."

"Do you?"

"Truthfully, I didn't think about you that much either, David, just because there was so little to think about."

"We didn't have much time, did we?"

"No."

"Maybe we should have waited. I'm sorry about the baby."

"I'm sorry I didn't tell you the truth."

"I shouldn't have written what I did."

Annie caught her breath. *He didn't get that awful letter!* "I wrote back, and then I regretted what I said. I'm glad you didn't get the letter. For awhile I felt so guilty that those words might be the last memory you had of me."

"Letters aren't a very good substitute for conversation. But we're talking now."

A knock on the door cut off Annie's reply. "That must be dinner."

"Good. I'm starved. Literally."

*****

David finished the very large rib-eye and all of the onion rings, a baked potato, a side salad, and his own slice of custard pie plus half of Annie's. "Man, that was good!" He sat back in the chair and folded his hands over his almost-absent midsection.

Annie pushed the cart into the corridor. "I suppose that will hold you until breakfast tomorrow."

"Maybe. Do they have twenty-four-hour room service?"

"I doubt it."

He moved to the sofa. "Come sit with me, Annie. I'm not going to throw you into bed."

She joined him. He curled his fingers in her hair. "You changed your hairstyle."

"I usually wear it up like Mum."

"I like it down the way it is now." He took a

strand and held it under his nose. "It even smells familiar."

"I'm a creature of habit, I guess. I'm still using the same shampoo that Mum buys for us. She used to shop for everything I needed and send me a box every couple of months when I was at Vassar."

"You didn't have much autonomy, did you?"

Annie shrugged. "I think it made her feel better after all those years that we didn't have anything, but she and Pa never interfered with any of my decisions."

"When you wanted to make them. Like marrying me in such a hurry."

"They didn't oppose that, no. They did question if I'd really thought it through."

"Had you?"

"No."

"I didn't think so, but I wasn't going to rock the boat. When you said yes, I didn't argue with you." He put an almost weightless arm around her shoulder. "I was pretty spoiled as a kid, Annie. I always got what I wanted. I don't think you did."

"Pa would've spoiled me."

"With material possessions? He always seemed strict with you in most ways."

"He was strict to offset Mum's being over-protective. But he would've given me the moon if I'd asked for it. He insisted that I should have Prince even when Mum and Gram said he was too big."

"I'm sorry about the old fellow."

"He's buried under a tree in back of the house. Pa asked the gardener to take care of it." She willed herself to relax against David before she said, "Pa told the doctor at the hospital that he didn't want the baby...disposed of."

David's arm tightened around her. "What do you mean?"

"It...he *was* a baby, David. I'd just felt him move

a few hours before...before it happened. I carried him almost five months."

"Spit it out, Annie."

"He's buried in Greenfield with everyone from the Home."

"In a Potter's Field? Why?"

"It was my idea. I suppose I've always felt I should be there, too."

With surprising strength, David crushed her against him. "And you would be, too, if it wasn't for your father! All right, for Albert Rycroft! What is it with you, Annie? Do you feel guilty to be alive? I do, in a way, when I think about the others who aren't, but I'm not sorry I made it."

"I don't know what I feel, David." Even as she spoke, unexpected desire stirred in her, though she felt a certain fearful reluctance when David's lips came down hard on hers.

He drew back. "We don't have to do anything tonight if you don't want to."

"But you do."

"To tell you the truth, I'm tired. I've got a full belly, and I could use a good night's sleep in a bed that doesn't go up and down and shake like a wet dog the way that ship did."

Relief mingled with disappointment. "Go on, then. I'll just sit up and read for awhile.'

"I didn't say I wouldn't like to fall asleep next to you." The sleeve of his robe fell away, exposing a tattooed number on his forearm.

Annie recoiled. "What..."

"It's permanent," he said, covering it hurriedly. "We all got them."

She shook her head in disbelief.

"I know it's not pretty, but I'm not ashamed of it."

"You...shouldn't be...ashamed."

"Look, Annie, I made it back. A lot of guys

didn't. But like I said, I'm not going to feel guilty because I survived."

"Why would you?"

He shrugged. "I'm going to bed." There was a question in his eyes.

She got up. "I'm coming, too."

Chapter Sixteen

On the second night, when they finally made love, Annie felt removed from the whole proceeding. Though David fell asleep almost immediately, she lay awake listening to him breathe hoarsely through his mouth—a result, he had explained briefly, of a broken nose inflicted by one of his captors.

She tried to remember what she'd felt before, but the memory was gone. Turning on her side, she traced the outline of his jaw with the tip of her finger, lightly so as not to wake him, and wondered if he really did love her as he'd said—or if he simply felt obligated to make an attempt at preserving their marriage.

Why did I marry him? Did I love him then? Did I even know what being in love was all about? What about now? We just made love for the first time in over two years, and he had to know that I didn't feel anything.

His mouth twitched, and he turned his face away from her. She lay back and closed her eyes. She'd heard the old adage *Marry in haste, repent at leisure,* and now she understood what it meant. Could they find anything to salvage from their too-short marriage? Did David really want to make the effort? Did she?

The next morning, David suggested going home. "I know this was supposed to be a sort of second honeymoon, but it seems a waste of money to stay in this expensive hotel for a week. You probably need to go back to work and get Jack Shaw squared away."

"Uncle Trent said I could take as much time as I

needed."

David covered his face with shaving cream. "I don't think you've got that much time."

"What does that mean?"

"It means that a week in New York City isn't going to ease us back into what we never had."

She leaned against the door of the bathroom and watched him use an old-fashioned straight razor to scrape away the overnight stubble. "A marriage."

"Right. I railroaded you into it, Annie, I admit it. We should have waited."

"I suppose so."

"I'm willing to try to work things out if you are."

"I think we should. Try, that is."

"You don't sound hopeful."

"I'm confused, David. I've hoped before and been disappointed."

"Is it a one-time effort in life? And I'm not your father, by the way."

She shook her head. "We both need some time."

David wiped his face and turned to take her in his arms. Annie could see and feel every one of his ribs. "Maybe we wouldn't have gotten married if it hadn't been for the war. I guess I thought if we didn't do it then, we might never get the chance."

"There are a lot of wartime marriages in trouble, from what I hear."

"I had two or three buddies who got *Dear John* letters. At least you never wrote me one of those."

"I wouldn't have done that, David."

"Well, we're married, and we made a baby. That's something between us."

"I've never been to visit his grave." She buried her face in his bony shoulder. His hands came up to caress her hair.

"I'd like to go. Maybe you'll go with me. It might be a step in the right direction."

****

Once they were back in Rumers Crossing, Annie thought David acted more like the way she remembered him. She could tell, from his easy smile and frequent laughter, that the welcome he received from Alan, Lenore, and Mrs. Swane pleased him.

When Annie went back to work, he appeared content to spend his time reading and doing what he called *reconnaissance* in the kitchen. Mrs. Swane complained, though not too seriously, that she had to come up with more places to hide the butter cookies.

Their occasional lovemaking, like their conversation, remained impersonal. Annie responded to David's tenderness and consideration, but she'd learned to live without his touch and thought she still could.

David and Alan spent a lot of time closeted in Alan's study. "What are they talking about?" Annie asked Lenore with some irritation.

"I think David's looking for some direction, don't you?"

"He could go back to school and take some refresher courses in architecture, if that's what he wants to do."

Lenore changed the subject. "Trent says that things are going well for Jack Shaw, with your help."

"He's grasped the whole picture without a problem. I understand why he was the best choice four years ago."

"Annie, with David back, we don't have much private time to talk, but I'm still here."

"I know, Mum. There's nothing to say. We're just taking one day at a time."

"I sense that you're struggling. So does Alan."

Annie nodded.

"Alan and I are so close, almost like the same person. It's the best feeling in the world, Annie dear. I hope you and David can develop that same relationship."

"You and Pa are so much alike. David and I aren't."

"I sense that, too."

"He's a good person."

"So are you."

"He says his parents spoiled him, that he had everything he wanted."

"You did, too. It's just that you didn't want very much."

"I had milk to drink and my beautiful pink room and Prince...money to buy books whenever we went into Lowell. That was enough."

"Don't forget the regular Bea-boxes."

"Oh, yes, those, too. I was exquisitely dressed without costing Pa a penny."

"He would have outfitted you from the best shops."

Annie fixed Lenore with knowing eyes. "When I absolutely had to have something, you took me to the bargain basement."

"I happen to know that you still check out what's there before you go anywhere else."

"You see? You marked me for life." Annie watched Lenore look away to consider her next words.

"Annie, David will more than likely find work far enough away from here that you'll have to move into your own home. Will you be all right financially? I shouldn't pry, but..."

"I have a tidy bank account, and there's the account where I put all the allotment checks since I didn't need them. We'll have a nice cushion, and I'll be able to find a job wherever we go."

"I thought perhaps you might choose not to work."

"If you mean I might have a baby, no, not right away, not until we're sure of things."

"That you're going to stay together?"

"Yes. I'm not going to lie to you."

"Alan and I have discussed the possibility that your marriage might not be on firm ground."

"More like quicksand."

"Oh, Annie, is it that bad?"

Annie shrugged, but before she could answer, Alan and David joined them in the drawing room, demanding tea and butter cookies.

****

After a month, David said he wanted to drive to Greenfield. Annie had almost hoped that he'd forgotten, but she agreed to go with him. The small stone bearing a lamb on top and the inscription *David Samuel Levinson, Jr. 1943* sat tucked in the shadow of the larger one erected over the common grave of the Greenfield residents. "Pa chose the stone," Annie said. "He designed the larger one for the people at Greenfield. Between Mum and me, we came up with all the names for it."

"You and your cousin were the only survivors, weren't you?"

"There was one more—Dick Regan, the oldest boy. He used to sneak out to work at night, so he wasn't there when the furnace exploded. Actually, he's the one who took care of me until he finally called Pa and told him where I was."

"You never mentioned that."

"Someone was after me that night, too. One of my grandfather's thugs, I suppose. Dick found me running for my life and hid me in an old garage. I...I lied to him...told him Papa was coming back. I don't think he believed me, but he went along with it until the other man came back. Then he knew he had to get me out of there."

"Did he know why?"

"He was the oldest, so Miss Ervin probably told him about the guards Pa arranged for after my grandfather tried to back out of the custody suit for fifty thousand dollars."

"Fifty...seems like there are a few gaps in the story you told me."

"It didn't seem important, David. I wanted to forget."

"But you didn't."

"I might if you didn't keep pushing me to remember." She stepped away from him, but his hand closed around her arm and pulled her back.

"What happened to Dick?"

"Pa tried to find him, but he couldn't. It was over...don't you understand?"

"Not really. You said that your grandfather broke into the house and tried to take you."

Annie's knees buckled, but David caught her before she hit the ground. "Annie, I'm sorry. I'm not trying to upset you."

"Can't you just let it go?"

"For now...but one of these days, we've both got to find Bobbie."

"She's gone! Why can't you understand that?"

"No, she's not. I married her. Oh, she goes by the name of Annie now, but Bobbie's in my bed, and that's why..." He broke off and pulled her closer. "Look, we didn't come out here to talk about this." He squatted beside the baby's grave. "Thanks for choosing the name."

"I knew you'd want him named for you."

"I thought about him that way before...well, before." He ran his fingers over the lettering cut into the granite. "Annie, when the car pinned you to the wall..."

"I wasn't injured, not really, only bruised. The doctor said then that I could have more children, and Dr. Sims confirmed it."

"I don't see how you could have kept from being seriously injured."

"I don't know either, except that the car didn't

hit me that hard. Dr. Sims said that perhaps the baby was already in trouble for some reason and that the trauma just brought on the miscarriage sooner rather than later."

"You said you felt him move."

"Just before it happened."

"Were you sorry that you miscarried?"

Annie gasped. "How can you ask that, David? Of course, I was sorry!"

"We didn't plan it, not so soon, anyway."

"I'll admit I was upset at first, but I got used to the idea."

"Do you want another baby?"

Annie shook her head. "Not right now."

David walked over to the larger monument. "It was nice of Mr. Ashley to do this."

"He told the county officials he'd take care of everything, but they'd already put them here in the Potter's Field. What was left of them." She choked a little. "So he told them he was going to have this monument done. They couldn't say much about it without appearing heartless."

"I have to ask again why you put our baby here."

"I'm not sure. At the time, it seemed fitting. I might have been here, too."

"I told you about survivor's guilt, Annie, and it doesn't do anyone any good."

She shrugged. "I can't help what I feel."

David put his arm around her. "I understand that much. Okay, no more questions. Maybe this was the right spot for him after all. Maybe he's more connected here than with the Ashley ancestors."

"Mum and Pa didn't understand. It helps that you do."

Back in the car, he said, "I saw a diner on the way out to the cemetery. Are you hungry?"

"No, but we'll miss dinner at home. Maybe we should stop."

149

"Probably." He turned the key in the ignition. "Thanks for coming with me, Annie."

"Why wouldn't I have come?"

"I know you didn't want to. You could've given me directions to come by myself."

"He was ours, David. It was the right thing to come together."

He reached across the seat to take her hand. "Thanks, anyway."

****

Trent Young sent Annie to Canon City for three days of meetings. David drove her car, now in service again, to meet her train. "How was the trip?"

"Everything went well, and everyone at the shipyard sends their greetings."

"That's nice. How's my replacement doing?"

"I didn't see him, but I hear he's continuing the outstanding job he did during the war."

"Good. That's good."

"Something's on your mind."

"I've made some decisions I'd like to tell you about."

"I'm listening."

"Not this minute. In private, after dinner."

"Do Mum and Pa know?"

"I'll tell them later."

"Does it involve a move away from Rumers Crossing?"

"Yes, a big one."

"I see."

"There's nothing for me here, Annie."

"I understand that. I just thought with all the new homes going up, you might find something as a draftsman. It would be a start."

"I looked into it, but the company doing the construction is fly-by-night. I don't mean they're not putting up quality homes, but they move around wherever the work is. They're not established."

"Well, of course, you'll want something settled."

"We'll talk about it after dinner."

****

Annie stared at her husband in utter disbelief. "I can't even begin to understand what you're talking about."

"I'm talking about going back to Germany to look for the remnants of my grandfather's family, anyone who survived the camps."

"Why?"

"I can't give you a good reason other than it's something I feel I have to do. You did what you felt you had to do with our baby, and I told you I understood."

"It's not the same thing. How can you even compare...and how are you going to live, David? You've got to eat, you know."

"I told you about the trust that my grandparents left. It's more than enough to keep me going for a few years."

"A few years! You're going to wander around Germany for a few *years*?"

"If that's what it takes. A lot of Jews are going to Palestine, if they can get in. The British won't be there forever, and there'll be an independent Jewish state someday."

"What does that have to do with you?"

"It would be a place to start fresh, Annie, to make a difference by helping build a new country."

"You have a country. You were born here."

"I'm a Jew, Annie. So are you."

"Not really."

"You are. You just don't know it."

"I don't want to know it. David, this whole plan is...unworkable." She stopped just short of saying that it was insane.

"Why?"

"Where would you start? Isn't it like looking for

a needle in a haystack?"

"There are refugee camps and lists of the dead, as well as of those who survived."

"And suppose you find some of your family? What then?"

"Then I'll encourage them to emigrate with me."

"You intend to give up your citizenship here?"

"It's possible I won't have to."

"All right, you want to do this. Where do I fit into these plans?"

"I hope you'll come with me. It will be something we'll do together, give us a common purpose in life."

"You're not serious."

"Dead serious."

"I don't know what to say."

"You'll think of something." David lifted his eyebrows. "You always do."

She headed for the bathroom. "I'm going to take a shower."

"And wash it all away?"

"That's not fair, David!"

"No, it's not, but life isn't fair. Never was and never will be. But you know that, Annie. You know better than anyone that life can dump a load of garbage on a person. You can either stay there under it and die, or you can claw your way out to better things."

"I don't see tramping around like a gypsy as better than what I have here."

"What do you have here?"

"I..." Uncertainty infused her mind and bored its way down into the pit of her stomach. "I have..." Fleeing his steady gaze, she put the bathroom door between them, then turned and pounded it with her fists.

****

For a few days, Annie thought the subject was closed between them, but on the fourth night, as

David emerged from the bathroom in his pajamas, he said, "I picked up some passport applications for us today."

Annie sank down on the side of the bed. "You really mean to do this, don't you?"

"Did you think I didn't?"

"You hadn't said anymore about it."

"And you thought it would just go away. That's like you, Annie. What you don't want to deal with, you hope will go quietly and conveniently away."

"That's not true, David! None of the circumstances of my life have gone away, no matter how much I wished for it. Circumstances even killed our baby!"

He sat down beside her. "I'm sorry, Annie. I shouldn't have said that."

"Why not? You believe it."

"I also believe you have an inner strength that you might find if you wanted to. You're a survivor, Annie, just like I am. Maybe it was born in you, or maybe it was Lenore Ashley's example, or maybe Alan Ashley put it there. Wherever it came from, you can use it for your own benefit."

"Or yours."

"Well, we're a package, aren't we?"

"I don't know anymore." Annie moved to her dressing table and began to cream her face.

"I thought we'd been getting along rather well."

"I can *get along* with anyone. A married couple should do more than that."

"I agree, but you don't share yourself with me. You don't share your feelings."

Annie wiped her hands on a tissue and tossed it away. "It's always been difficult for me."

"I don't believe that, Annie. You seem to share them readily enough with your parents."

"That's different."

"How?"

"I don't know. It just is."

He pushed back the straps of her gown and kissed one shoulder. "I love you, Annie. I really do."

"I know, and I don't want to make you unhappy, but what you're asking me to do is so huge!"

"I'm asking you to share my life."

"A life of wandering around looking for people you don't even know and then going off to live in a place that doesn't even exist."

"Israel will exist someday. I want to be part of it. It's my heritage."

"But it's not mine, David, don't you understand?"

"It could be." He laid her back on the bed and stroked her hair. "We can be happy, Annie, I'm sure of it." He reached up and switched off the lamp.

Even as she gave herself up to the needs of his body, she knew that she couldn't sacrifice herself to the needs of his heart.

Chapter Seventeen

Annie agreed that David should be the one to make Alan and Lenore aware of his plans. They reacted predictably: Lenore shocked into silence, Alan formulating his words with obvious care.

"It's a noble endeavor, David."

"Even if it's a *Don Quixote* attempt, I have to try."

"The only part of the plan I question is settling permanently in Palestine. You could easily involve yourself in another war when and if the British leave."

"I've thought of that." David took a long, slow sip from his glass. "If it comes to that, I'd send Annie home. I wouldn't put her in danger."

"You've been separated for two years," Lenore said. "How can you even consider the possibility again?"

"It's just something I feel strongly about, Mrs. Ashley."

Lenore shook her head. "I'll admit that I don't understand, David."

Alan turned his face toward Annie's place at the table. "What are your thoughts, Annie?"

"I don't know."

"You must feel free to make the best decision for yourself without regard to Lenore and me."

"I just don't know, Pa," she repeated.

"Well, I'm sure you and David will discuss it thoroughly before making a decision. It is, of course, quite a large one."

****

Later, while David was in the shower, Annie went down the hall and knocked on the door of her parents' sitting room. "We thought you might pay us a visit," Lenore said as she slipped an arm around Annie's waist and led her to the sofa where Alan was waiting. "You're not happy about this, are you?"

"It's crazy!"

"David is quite serious about it, Annie," Alan said. "I think he'll follow his heart no matter what you do."

"I think so, too." Annie curled her feet under her and rocked back and forth. "But I can't go with him. I can't do it."

"Then the marriage is over?" Alan asked.

Annie's head snapped back. "I…not necessarily."

"I think it is, Annie," Alan continued. "If you were committed strongly to David, you wouldn't hesitate to follow him anywhere, especially after the enforced separation of the war years."

"How can you say that, Pa?"

"Because it's true. A marriage is many things, not the least of which is physical attraction. Passion, if you will. But without commitment to that person to whom you've pledged your life, the marriage is nothing."

"Would you have expected Mum to follow you to the ends of the earth?" The anger in Annie's voice surprised no one but her.

"Yes, I would have," came the unhesitating answer, "and she would have done it. I did, in fact, expect her to give up the idea of fleeing to Canada with you and to trust me with your safety."

"I struggled with that, Annie," Lenore said. "You were old enough to see how it was tearing me apart."

Alan held out his hand to Lenore. "Some marriages are forged in the fire of unpleasant circumstance, and ours certainly was."

"Because of me," Annie muttered.

"Because of many things, including you. We didn't just commit to each other, Annie. We were of one mind about being your parents. We started out years ahead of most couples. When I asked Lenore to be my wife, I also pledged myself as a father."

"So you're saying that I'm not committed to David. That I don't love him."

"I'm saying that if you are committed, and if you do love him, you'll be certain of your path." Alan leaned forward, holding out his hands and waiting for her to grasp them. "Annie, Lenore and I love you more than you can imagine. You've made us proud, and not just because you've achieved academically and professionally."

"David said I was a survivor, like him."

"I agree." Alan tightened his grip on her hands.

"He said I was strong."

"You are. At least, I intended that you should be, though I've had occasion to wonder lately if I failed."

"It's my failure, not yours."

Lenore smoothed Annie's hair back from her face. "In the end, Annie, it came down to whether or not I truly loved Alan enough to trust my life to him...and yours as well. Faced with losing him, I found my answer. It seems to me, Annie dear, that you must ask yourself only one question. Are you truly in love with David?"

Annie jumped up and ran from the room without replying.

****

The next evening, David and Alan stayed in the study for two hours. When they emerged, neither man shared what had passed between them. Lenore didn't ask, and Annie prayed that David wouldn't tell her.

For the next few weeks, Annie and David shared her room and the bed as polite strangers. He began sorting through his belongs, packing some for storage, as he tried to fit a lifetime into one suitcase.

His passport arrived in the middle of November, followed by the visa that Alan had used his influence in Washington to procure. The next day he took the train to Canon City to book passage for Germany.

Annie moved through those days and nights in a surreal mist. David was going. She was letting him go, even wanted him to go, yet a growing sense of abandonment fueled silent anger in her soul.

Love. Commitment. Devotion. Her parents had those things, but somehow they had eluded her own grasp. Or had she even reached for them at all? Twice, under cover of darkness, she escaped to Prince's final resting place. Stretching out across the grass-covered mound, she let her mind drift back to the days when she'd frolicked there, carefree, with the lumbering black beast.

I want to go back. Why did you have to leave me, Prince? Why, Papa? Why didn't you take me with you? I wouldn't have cared if you'd taken Rebekah, too, but I was your best little girl, your shining star...and you promised to come back for me...oh, Papa, why did you leave me behind?

*****

On his last night, David suggested they go to Giovanni's for dinner. "Do you have everything you need?" she asked as they waited for the waiter to bring their meal. "I don't imagine you'll be able to buy much over there."

"If I get desperate for something, I'll let you know."

"Just write and ask."

"I don't know how long I'll be there. The visa is only for six months, but I can probably get it renewed. I'll come back before I go to Palestine."

"How will you get in? Pa says that the British aren't issuing visas for Jews these days."

"I'll get in."

"Maybe you'll have second thoughts after you spend some time in Germany."

"Maybe," he said, though his tone of voice denied the possibility. "Will you write to me?"

"As soon as you let me know an address."

"Alan suggested I might work with the army as an interrogator. They're prosecuting everyone they can find who was responsible for the camps."

"Why do you want to go back to a place where you suffered so much?"

"I explained it to you."

"And I tried to understand, really I did." She frowned as she looked him over. "You've put on some weight, but you're still too thin. What if you get sick over there?"

"I'll find a doctor. Besides, Dr. Sims says I'm in good shape, considering everything. Of course, regular supplies of butter cookies wouldn't hurt." He winked at her.

She smiled. "I'll talk to Gram."

"She's staying on?"

"For the time being. Pa says he'll have the front half of the third floor remodeled into an apartment for her and even put in a kitchen so she can be totally independent from the household."

"But she feels responsible for her sister."

"It's just Gram and her now, and one brother who lives in Ohio."

"That connection is important. They're family, after all."

Annie's eyes flashed. "We're family, too!"

"It's not the same, Annie."

"I don't notice you trying to connect with your half-brother."

"You know I've written to him, but the letters keep coming back. I've thought of hiring that investigator Mr. Ashley uses, Emory Roth, to look for him."

"I thought you knew where he was."

"I did know, before the war. I guess he was drafted or enlisted."

What about his family?"

"It was just his father and stepmother. They didn't have any children together. That's one of the reasons they talked Daniel into coming to live with them when he was twelve."

"And your mother agreed?"

"He wanted to go. He didn't get along very well with my father. Dad was into sports and outdoor stuff, and Daniel wasn't interested. He was a great student but not a very good athlete. I liked all those things and played every sport available, so I was the fair-haired child."

"Families get tangled up, don't they?"

"Sometimes. Annie, I'm not trying to quarrel with you, but I'm curious. If our baby had lived, would you be going with me now?"

"Would you truly want to take a child into Germany right now? Pa says it's a ruin."

"That's a fair question, and the answer is, I don't know. Maybe not. Maybe I'd be going ahead to find a place for the two of you, somewhere I could come back to on a regular basis as I traveled. Does that make sense?"

"I guess so."

"But it didn't happen, so I'm going, and you're staying." He reached across the table for her hand. "I wish you weren't, but I'm not going to fight with you about it."

****

"I want to make love to you tonight," he said as they undressed for bed. "It's the last time, at least for awhile."

Annie had anticipated his request, although she hadn't been able to come up with an equally polite answer. Her shrug changed to a nod.

"You don't mind?"

"You're my husband, David."

"In a manner of speaking. No, I didn't mean that. I'm sorry." He crossed the room and took her in his arms. "I do love you, Annie. I know you're not sure how you feel about me, and maybe I should've made certain you knew before we got married."

"I married you."

"But you don't really know why. It doesn't matter now." He unbuttoned her blouse with a casual detachment. "I'll give you a divorce if you decide that's what you want, somewhere down the line."

"Don't talk like that, David." She put her arms around his neck and realized that she wanted him to hurry.

****

They woke early and made love again before going down to breakfast. Mrs. Swane set out a feast on the buffet. "Don't be losing any of those pounds that I've worked so hard to put on you," she admonished David.

"I'll do my best, Mrs. Swane."

"You'll let us know how your search is going," Alan said. "And if you need anything, don't hesitate to get in touch with me."

"You've been very helpful, Mr. Ashley."

"I don't often take advantage of my insider status in Washington, but it seemed warranted in this matter."

"I appreciate that."

"Eat," Mrs. Swane urged him. "Who knows when you'll get another decent meal."

"Well, certainly none like this, Mrs. Swane. I'm sure of that."

****

Annie drove David to the station. "I'll cable you from New York and again when I get to Germany,"

161

he said, putting his lips against the hair at her temple. "Thanks for last night...and this morning."

"I hope you find what you're looking for, David."

"I hope you find yourself, Annie. That you find Bobbie again, her Papa's shining star."

"I'm not looking for her."

"You should be."

"I know you think so, but..."

"At least find her long enough to grieve for what she lost."

"I didn't lose anything, not really."

"You lost your father and the security that a child needs in knowing that her parent will keep his promises. I'm not sure you've ever trusted anyone again."

"Of course, I have. I trust Pa and Mum."

"But not me."

She didn't answer.

"Well, it's all right. I'll admit that I was angry with you about that for awhile, but it's something you're going to have to work out for yourself. I think Bobbie and I might have more in common than Annie and I do."

"Why would you think that? Besides, she's gone."

"Not really." He tipped her chin back so that he could see deep into her eyes. "I think Bobbie would be on that train with me."

"I don't think so."

He kissed her lightly as the train whistle blew. "Don't get out, Annie. I'll be in touch."

She watched him sprint for the train, his limp still apparent but not hindering his haste. At the last minute, she wrenched open the door of the car and ran along the platform until she spotted him in the window of the train.

"Come back, David!" she called. "Please come back soon!"

Chapter Eighteen

As Annie struggled with her guilt for letting David go to Germany alone, she began to dream about Albert Rycroft again and to wonder if she would have gone with him fourteen years earlier. In the end, he'd made the choice for her, and now she'd made the choice not to go with David.

Work kept her occupied, though not as much as during the war. She traveled in Jack Shaw's stead, but, because he took care of the detailed reports for Trent Young, there was less paperwork requiring her time and attention.

She was in Jack's office the day Alan stopped by on one of the regular visits he made to each of his employees. "Trent says you've picked up where you left off without any difficulty."

"I think so, Mr. Ashley."

"I've mentioned this before, but I hope you didn't leave the rehabilitation program sooner than optimal. Your position here was secure."

"They'd done everything they could. I'll be in this chair the rest of my life, but I can take care of myself."

"I found that particularly satisfying in my situation, though I was dependent on my housekeeper to lay out my clothes so that I didn't come to work looking like a circus clown." He laughed, encouraging Jack to do the same.

"I'd say that you had more to deal with than I do, learning Braille and all that."

"I was fortunate that it came easily to me." Alan hesitated for a moment. "I understand that we share another circumstance. You were engaged to be married before you left, were you not?"

"Yes, but she changed her mind when she found out what happened to me."

"So did my former fiancée, but I was fortunate in that respect, too. I met Lenore."

"I hope I'll get that lucky."

"I'd say a handsome young man like you stands a good chance."

"How do you know?" Jack blurted. "I mean, how do you know how I look?"

Alan laughed. "I have my sources." He put out his hand. "Jack, we all have to live with our particular circumstances, but how we do that is up to us. We can live victoriously or in defeat."

"Yes, sir."

"We're all gratified that you chose to return to Ashley Enterprises. A business is only as good as its employees, and you bring a particular strength to us."

When he'd gone, Jack turned to Annie. "He's pretty amazing."

"Yes, he is."

"And he's right about how we live with our circumstances."

Annie grimaced. "That was for my benefit as much as yours."

"He didn't know you were here."

"Oh, yes, he did. I learned the hard way that Alan Ashley sees without seeing. And he can hear a butterfly belch."

"A *what* do *what*?"

Annie laughed. "It's a family joke. By the way, Jerome Vannoy's new secretary asked me this morning if you were spoken for."

"Miss Matson?"

"That's the one."

"She's a knockout. You mean nobody's trying to

make time with her?"

"I didn't say that, but she seems to be interested in you, so I wouldn't waste any time."

"Well, maybe..."

"Do you know Giovanni's?"

"That little Italian place about a block from here?"

"It's where my parents did their courting. Some of it, anyway."

"Are you playing matchmaker, Mrs. Levinson?"

"Probably."

"I'll think about it."

"If I were you, I wouldn't think too hard or too long."

****

There was a letter from David on the table in the foyer when Annie came in from work. She put it in her pocket on the way upstairs, wondering if reading it would only worsen her guilt.

December 10, 1945

Dear Annie,

I cabled you from the ship, so you know I arrived safely. I'm in Munich, where I'm renting a room in a house that managed to survive the war. My landlady is a widow whose sons were both killed defending Berlin in the final days of the war, but she's glad for the money even if it's from an American. The fact that I speak German has helped me weasel my way into her good graces.

Tomorrow I'll start trying to see people in the offices dealing with refugees and resettlement. It will be harder to find the people who got out of the camps rather than the ones who are still there, buried in mass graves.

I left your Christmas present with the Ashleys, so you'll have something from me even if I'm not there.

Love,

David

Annie crumpled the letter in her hand. She hadn't thought about Christmas, nor had she thought about sending anything with her husband...even her love.

****

December 24, 1945
Dear David,

I'm glad you have a good place to stay. Hopefully your landlady is a good cook and will continue to fatten you up.

We opened our gifts after church tonight. Thank you for the lovely silk scarf. I wear so much navy that the softer blue will brighten it up. I'm ashamed that I didn't think ahead, but Gram made you two batches of butter cookies which are on the way.

Jack Shaw is interested in Jerome Vannoy's new secretary, and she's interested in him. I'm doing my best to further the romance.

Bea and Patrick are home for a few days. Bea just found out that she's pregnant, so they're both floating.

I stay busy here and know you are busy there also. I wish you the best in your search.

Love,
Annie

****

David wrote regularly, though each letter grew more impersonal. Elated to locate more relatives than he'd hoped for, and finding all of them eager to shake German soil from their feet, he now faced the challenge of getting them past the British patrols and into Palestine.

With each letter, however, Annie felt she knew David better as a person, not just as an attractive man who had somehow become her husband. She had married him impulsively and with little reason, she knew now, except physical attraction and a passing need for comfort and reassurance. His going away to war so quickly had left her with no responsibilities to him except to answer his letters and send him cookies.

So when she'd found herself pregnant with his child, reality set in. For awhile David had been a convenient stranger, providing her with the status of a married woman and serving the awakening needs of her woman's body. Now she had to acknowledge the reality of being his wife...and a mother.

How could I have felt that way? Was I always so selfish, so shallow?

She tried to remember the eleven-year-old girl who had fled the burning orphanage and found her way into a luxurious home where she wanted for nothing. Was she changed because of that? Was that what David meant when he insisted that she had to find Bobbie again? Was Bobbie better because Annie was spoiled and self-centered, a person incapable of giving, able only to take?

****

"Gram, do you remember when I came?" Annie sat at the kitchen table on a Saturday afternoon, helping Mrs. Swane shell peas.

"Like it was yesterday. You were hungry, dirty, and scared to death. I fed you, cleaned you up, and told you that you were a princess now."

"A princess."

"It got to be a joke."

"Did it? Gram, am I spoiled?"

"Why do you ask?"

"I let David go off to Germany without me because I wanted to stay here in my nice safe pink room and go to my nice safe job every morning."

"Is that the only reason?"

Annie shook her head.

"I didn't think so. You're not in love with him, are you?"

"I thought I was. Maybe I don't know what being

in love really is."

"If you were in love with him, you'd know. Look at Mr. Alan and Miss Lenore."

"They adore each other."

"They do."

"I always thought I'd grow up and find someone just like Pa to marry."

"There's only one of him, but other men have their special qualities, too. David Levinson has his fair share."

"I'm finding that out from his letters."

"Isn't it a little late to be getting to know him?"

"I suppose. Gram, have I changed much since you've known me?"

"You've grown up."

"Besides that."

"You were such a chatterbox. Followed me all over the house asking questions. Hung around the kitchen every morning until your tutor hauled you out for lessons. Miss Lenore said you did that with her mother. You'd seen too much of life, though. The hard times you and Miss Lenore had. The orphanage. The fire."

"And Grandfather Harcourt trying to get me."

"What about your father? Are you sorry he didn't take you?"

"Sometimes I wonder what my life would have been like with him. I wonder about Rebekah. She's two years older than I am."

"So you're glad you grew up here?"

"I've had everything."

"Yes, but you've appreciated your opportunities and taken good advantage of them."

"I've tried. When I was in the Home, we all had to work together to get by. Even the youngest child understood that. After I came here, I didn't have to do anything."

"You had chores. Miss Lenore insisted on that."

"But I loved helping you, and I knew that even if I didn't do a thing, I'd have enough to eat and a warm bed."

"You're still helping me." Mrs. Swane nodded at the growing pile of pea pods beside Annie's bowl.

"David says he was spoiled, that he never had to do anything except go to school and be a star."

"Like you. A shining star."

"Why do you say that?"

"Isn't that what your father called you?" She held up her hand to ward off Annie's retort. "I know, I know, Mr. Alan is your father."

Annie's face grew hot. "Papa called me his shining star."

"Are you? Or are you Annie Ashley? Annie Levinson."

"That's just it, Gram, I don't know, and David says if I don't find out…"

"Do you want to stay married to David?"

"I don't know that, either."

Mrs. Swane rose from the table, scooping up the bowl of peas to rinse in the sink. "Don't you think you'd better find out? And if that means finding Bobbie Rycroft again, then start looking."

****

Annie wrote to David about her conversation with Mrs. Swane and waited for his reply. It was six weeks before she heard from him, and he didn't even mention her soul-searching confession.

Sorry I haven't been in touch, Annie. I've been pretty busy, but I think I've found everyone who's going to be found. I even ran into a distant cousin who was in Dachau with me, but neither of us remembers seeing the other, which isn't unusual.

I've been in touch with a group who specializes in getting Jews into Palestine. It's going to take money, though. I haven't had to touch much of my trust fund, so I can use that if I have to. Unfortunately, there's a long waiting list of people who want to leave Germany and other places in Europe, so I don't know when our names will come up.

I thought I'd come back to the States until then. Before I left, I talked to a man in Canon City who said he probably could use me as a draftsman, so if it works out, I'll earn a little extra that way. I'll get an apartment, and whenever your job brings you to the city, you'll have a place to bunk instead of going to a hotel.

I'll let you know when I'm arriving. If you want to meet me in New York, I'd like that. If not, I'll understand.

Love,
David

****

Annie read the letter aloud to Alan and Lenore. "I suppose I should go to New York and meet him."

"Have you thought more about accompanying him to Palestine when he goes?" Alan asked.

"I don't want to do that."

"Your father...Albert Rycroft is there. Emory Roth believes that he's engaged in some sort of undercover work for the Zionists."

"Zionists? David mentioned that word."

"They favor a free Jewish state."

"Why has Papa been back to the States, then?"

"To raise money, I expect."

"So he turns up just at the right time to save me—and the diamonds!" Annie's lip curled in disgust.

"Perhaps not."

"Why doesn't he just give them to whoever was supposed to get them to begin with and be done with it? Then I'd be left alone."

"Maybe he doesn't have them."

"But twice now someone has thought that if they get hold of me, they'll get hold of the diamonds."

"I don't know what the reasoning is. Emory Roth is only speculating, though I think he knows more than he's telling me."

"Why is he withholding information? You're paying him, aren't you?"

"I've kept him on retainer, but he's not obligated to turn over any information that doesn't directly relate to the reason for that retainer. We've kept in touch with your...with Albert Rycroft through him, and that was the purpose from the beginning."

"It's like some Saturday morning serial." Distaste dripped from every word.

"Sometimes they come closer to real life than you'd imagine. Now about your trip to New York. Do you think it will happen in the next month?"

****

David's next letter told her that he'd be sailing on the first of June.

I'm glad that you want to meet me. Maybe you can get tickets for a show, and we can call it a vacation. I need one. I heard from Mr. Brower about the drafting job, and he said that I could go to work the first of July. He understands that it will be temporary.

I have so much to tell you, Annie. What I'm hearing about Israel—and we will be called Israel someday soon!—is exciting. A whole new generation of Jews will grow up knowing who they are and that they belong somewhere. I know I belong there, too, and I want you with me. Maybe we can talk about it when I get back.

****

Again, Annie was almost afraid to look for David at the pier, concerned that he might have lost weight he didn't have to lose or picked up some disease in the refugee camps. The man who strode confidently down the gangplank with hardly a hint of the old limp was still a little too thin, but his face was tanned and full.

He swept her into his arms. "Annie! It's great to see you here! Thanks for coming!"

He smelled of cigarette smoke. "You're not smoking now, are you?" she blurted.

"What kind of greeting is that? No, people were smoking in the lounge. I'll change my shirt at the hotel. You did get a hotel room, didn't you?"

"At the Plaza. And I got tickets for *Brigadoon*."

"Terrific! How long can you stay?"

"You're going home with me, aren't you? I booked a compartment for the two of us."

"If I can get my business here taken care of, sure I am."

"Business?"

"I have some people to see." Annie thought he sounded vague, but she wasn't sure she wanted to know details anyway.

"I see. Well, I asked for a week's vacation, and with the weekend tacked onto that, it should be enough, shouldn't it?"

"I hope so."

****

"Hot water was a luxury," he called to her from the shower after dinner that night. "Actually, most of the time, it was nonexistent."

She'd listened to him talk about his trip, almost without drawing a breath, for six hours. Anxiety nibbled at her consciousness and sharpened her reply. "I wouldn't know."

There was silence except for the sound of the water.

"I'm unpacking for you. You really need some new clothes."

"Yeah, I know. I'll pick up some things while we're here."

"Everyone is anxious to see you. Gram's already baking."

The water stopped. "Thanks for all the packages you sent. One always seemed to arrive at the right time. The stores are still half-empty over there, the ones that are still standing, anyway."

"Do we have to talk about that again?"

He came out of the bathroom toweling his hair. "No, we don't. What would you like to talk about?"

She shrugged. "You might ask how business is going."

"How is business going?"

"Very well. We're almost back to normal as far as peacetime production goes."

"That's good."

"Jack Shaw and Miriam Matson are seeing a lot of each other."

"I hope it works out for them."

"Jack's fiancée dumped him when he came home in a wheelchair. Like Pa's did when she found out he was permanently blind."

"I didn't know that. About Mr. Ashley, I mean."

"Well, Gram says she didn't deserve him, and Mum did."

"I'd agree that they deserve each other." He glanced at the two beds in the room. "Did you ask for these?"

Annie turned her back. "No, David, it's the way the room came."

"Just asking. I'm not going to make any demands on you, Annie."

She picked up her gown and went into the bathroom without replying.

****

David rolled over and propped himself on one elbow. "I enjoyed that," he said.

"Did you?"

"What can I say, Annie? I'm a married man. I got used to..."

"Not in ten days, you didn't, or even in the time

173

you were home right after the war."

"Why do you always choose our most intimate moments to pick a fight?"

"Is that what I do?"

"It seems that way. I told you up front that I wasn't going to claim my marital rights. You came out of the bathroom and climbed straight into my bed."

She touched his face. "I'm sorry."

"Sorry that you climbed into my bed?"

"Sorry that I'm not being nicer."

He chuckled. "I'd say you were pretty nice a few minutes ago." He wound her hair around his hand. "You haven't changed."

"Did you want me to?"

"Not really."

"I enjoyed your letters, David."

"I didn't think you were interested. I got carried away sometimes, I guess."

"I just meant that I felt like I got to know you a lot better." She snuggled against him without meaning to. "We really didn't know each other that well when we married."

"I guess we didn't."

"I like your mind."

"That's an odd thing to say considering our present circumstances." He kissed the bare shoulder resting under his chin.

"You know what I mean. You never really talked about your feelings before, what you're passionate about."

"What do you think that is?"

"Your heritage, I guess. Being a Jew."

"I told you that I wasn't orthodox. I didn't even come close to it. My parents weren't either, although Mom always lit the candles on *Shabbat*, and my father and I went to the synagogue on high holy days."

"I remember that my grandfather, Papa's father, wore a skullcap and had a long white beard. I used to sit in his lap and play with it."

"But your father never followed his religion?"

"Not in Barnwell. Maybe he does now."

"I can understand why you don't feel like Judaism is any part of you."

"It's totally foreign to me, David. I knew one or two girls in college who were Jews, but it never seemed very important to them."

"Maybe seeing Jews tortured and killed just for being Jews did something to me, Annie. Maybe it made me appreciate what I had, the freedom to be a Jew or not."

"But now you want to be one, even if it means living in a country that you don't know anything about."

"Oh, I know about it, believe me. I've talked to people and done a lot of reading, and I know I'm meant to be part of it."

"But I don't know that, David. Sometimes I think I wish I did, but I belong here in America, in Rumers Crossing. Ashley Enterprises is what I'm part of."

"You don't have to apologize for that."

"I'm not apologizing, exactly, but I'm torn. I'm your wife, and..."

"Look, Annie, you can have a divorce any time you want it."

"I told you that I didn't."

"What kind of a marriage is being separated for months, even years at a time? Once I get into Palestine, I'm not going to be leaving for awhile. I want a family, Annie, children to grow up knowing who they are."

"Like you did."

"I'm not so sure that I did, and I know that you don't."

"I've been Annie Ashley longer than I was Bobbie Rycroft."

"And you've been Annie Levinson for almost five years, out of which we've been together fewer than twelve months."

"That was because of the war."

"Not entirely."

"Maybe I could visit you..."

"Annie, anybody going to Palestine now has to commit to living there and being part of it. Helping it grow. Fighting for it. Dying for it, if need be. You can't be a part-time Jew, or a part-time wife, or a part-time anything else for that matter."

"Is that what I am? A part-time person?"

David leaned over and kissed her forehead. "You'll have to figure that out on your own, Annie. Goodnight." He turned over. "I love you."

Chapter Nineteen

For the next few days, Annie made an effort to concentrate entirely on David. During the day, she accompanied him to various offices and waited alone without complaint while he took care of any pending business. She asked, not entirely out of duty, if his meetings had been successful, without prying into what they were about, and listened if he told her more than yes or no.

They took the subway to the Lower East Side to see the historic Eldridge Street Synagogue. "Most of the first members were immigrants from eastern Europe," he told her. "Like Albert Rycroft."

He pointed out the architectural highlights of the building, something that Annie admitted she wouldn't have noticed on her own. "It's not in good repair, though. A lot of the people who attended here have moved out of the area."

"It's too bad to let such a magnificent structure go to ruin," Annie observed.

"I'd give a lot to be part of the restoration."

"How do you know it will be restored?"

"It's got too much history to be ignored. Someday someone will come along with money to fix it up."

****

They visited a few other synagogues with more active congregations. David explained about the religious symbols and objects inside. "Just from a historic point of view, they're fascinating."

"It's not quite archaeology, but it's very interesting," Annie agreed.

"There are lots of ruins still waiting to be discovered in Palestine. I'd love to be part of that, too."

"Maybe you will be someday."

He glanced at her, then reached for her hand and squeezed it. "Maybe so."

****

They ate at a different restaurant every night, saw *Brigadoon,* and replenished David's wardrobe with clothes appropriate for the temporary job he was taking in Canon City. On their last full day, when Annie spotted a bookstore specializing in rare and out-of-print books, David insisted that she skip his appointment to stay and browse. "You've got to be bored just sitting in an office waiting room. I don't expect you to follow me around like a puppy." He winked and patted her head.

"Are you sure?"

"Absolutely. Enjoy yourself."

Three hours later, he found her addressing a shipping label for her purchases. "I bought too much," she said.

"You don't have to apologize to *me*. It's your money. But where are you going to put them all? Your bookcases are bulging."

"Glass doesn't bulge."

"You can hardly shut the doors on them."

"I'll find a place."

"Well, my things will be out next week."

Annie stopped writing. "I'd forgotten about that."

"I have to find an apartment and get set up before I go to work."

"You couldn't commute?"

"It's too far, Annie, you know that. I'd spend all my time on the train."

She handed the label and a check to the clerk, then took David's arm. "Are you finished for today?"

"I'm at your disposal."

"Let's walk down Broadway again."

"Maybe we can get tickets for another show," he offered. "I hear *Finian's Rainbow* is good. Would you like to see it?"

"Not really, unless you would."

"No. We'll just walk and see what happens."

On the spur of the moment, they took the subway to Chinatown and had dinner at a small restaurant that offered outside tables where they could watch the passersby milling around.

"In a way, I wish this wasn't our last night," Annie said. "I've had a nice time, David. It's the first real vacation I've had in a couple of years, other than going to Maine with Mum and Pa for two weeks in the summer. We didn't even do that the last couple of years. We were too busy."

"You need to forget about business and relax occasionally, don't you think?"

"Pa insists that everyone take a vacation. He made the employees do it during the war even when we didn't."

"Probably good for morale, if nothing else."

"That's what he said."

"He's an astute businessman. You mentioned that he expects you to take over from him eventually."

"We've never really talked about it, but it stands to reason that I will. Uncle Trent is retiring in a couple of years, but Jerome Vannoy is younger. He might step in for awhile."

"Do you want to run Ashley Enterprises?"

"Not until I'm ready."

"I guess that makes sense. What else do you want to do, Annie, on a personal level?"

She fingered a fortune cookie from the basket. "When I was a little girl back in Barnwell, Papa bought me a dollhouse and a family of miniature dolls. When Mamma took me, it got left behind with most of my toys, and after that I never played house again. I never had a baby doll to rock or take care of, only Alberta, and she was more like my friend. At the Home, I was so bad at helping with the younger children that Miss Ervin let me stay in the kitchen or the laundry."

"What you're saying is, you never thought about growing up and getting married and having children."

"I don't think I ever did."

"What about Mrs. Ashley? I know she had you, but I wonder if she didn't want a baby of her own."

"After I miscarried, she told me that she'd gotten pregnant while I was in college and lost it very early."

"That's too bad."

"It would be nice if Pa had a son to follow in his footsteps with the business."

"You wouldn't feel left out?"

"No. Pa actually encouraged me to study history in college, since I loved it so much, but I knew that wouldn't be a living. If Mum hadn't had her business training, we'd have starved before I ended up in Greenfield. We almost did anyway."

"You don't have to worry about making a living."

Realizing that he wasn't criticizing her, only stating a fact, she bit back the sharp retort that formed on her tongue

"That's true, but I like business, too."

"Your attitude is admirable."

"Not really. It's common sense."

"What a lot of young women in your position don't have."

"You know that for a fact, do you?" She smiled across the table.

"I didn't live in a monastery before I met you. I had my share of dates. Maybe that's why I reacted to you the way I did the first day we met. Remember?"

She nodded. "You made me really angry."

"After I thought about it, I regretted baiting you."

"David, if you stayed here, in America I mean, we could live wherever you wanted to. And I'd have another baby right away."

He regarded her so steadily for so long that she dropped her eyes. "Is that your trump card?"

"I'm not playing a game with you. I just made the offer."

"It's a generous one, Annie, but no, thank you."

"So you're just going to leave me behind again?"

He leaned toward her. "Annie, I'm not leaving you behind. You're staying of your own accord."

****

"Lenore says that David looks well," Alan said to Annie as she waited for him to sign some papers the next day.

"Better than I expected."

"Mrs. Swane will fatten him up even more."

"He's going with me to Canon City tomorrow. To look for an apartment."

"Yes, so he mentioned last night after you and Lenore went up."

"I wish he'd commute and stay in Rumers Crossing."

"He says he'd spend all his time on the train."

"I suppose that's true."

"You could live in Canon City with him."

"That wouldn't be very practical, would it? Besides, he's only going to be there until his plans to go to Palestine are firm."

"That might take awhile."

"If I left Ashley Enterprises and took another job in Canon City, I'd be stranded when David left."

"You don't have to work, Annie."

"That's a strange thing for you to say."

"A few months without a paycheck isn't going to bankrupt you. What do you have to spend it on?"

"Not much, I suppose."

"You pay your car expenses and buy your own clothes. Lenore says you still shop the bargain basement just like she does."

"Poor Pa. You tried to spoil us."

"It's been very frustrating at times. Well, it's your choice to go or stay, of course."

"And I've made my choice, Pa. I'm not going to Palestine with David."

****

"The apartment is near my work, so I won't need a car," David told Alan and Lenore at dinner a few nights later.

"Will you be comfortable there, David?" Lenore asked.

"I just need a place to eat and sleep."

"It's really very nice," Annie said. "I can stay there when I'm in the city on business. He'll come home on weekends."

There was an uncomfortable pause.

"Yes, the apartment's big enough so that she won't be in my way," David joked. "I'll let her come in out of the cold if she's nice about it."

****

Annie was staying overnight in October when Emory Roth telephoned David to say that he wanted to stop by later in the evening with news of Daniel, David's half-brother.

"I'll make some coffee," Annie said. "And there are still some butter cookies."

"I don't know that I want to share those," David retorted.

"Don't whine. You'll get more next time."

"Yeah, you bring lots of goodies when you come." He grabbed her and nuzzled the back of her neck.

"David, stop it! You know I'm ticklish there!"

"All the better."

She squirmed. "David, stop, Mr. Roth will be here..."

"Not yet." He scooped her up and headed for the bedroom, tossing her on the bed like a rag doll. "Plenty of time."

"David, I said..." He cut her off with a long, hard kiss. "David..." But her arms were around his neck pulling him closer.

****

Emory Roth accepted a cup of coffee from Annie and helped himself to a butter cookie from the plate she set in front of him. "I located your brother in a suburb of Chicago," he said to David.

"Did you contact him?"

The investigator shook his head and took an envelope from his inside coat pocket. "His address and telephone number are here."

"What did you find out about him?"

"He served in the Navy during the war, and afterwards he took a job with a different law firm in Chicago. Oh, and he also married during the war. No children."

"What about his father and stepmother?"

"Both dead just in the past year."

"Well, I appreciate it, Mr. Roth. If you'll tell me what all this cost, I'll write you a check now."

"There's an invoice in the envelope. I made a few phone calls, that's all. Not even two hours of work. I'd have gotten to it sooner, but I had another case that seemed to take every waking hour."

David slit the top of the envelope with his pocket knife. "Annie, would you get my checkbook out of the top drawer of the bureau?"

She brought it to him with a pen. "How did Pa know about you, Mr. Roth?"

"I'd done some work for his attorney when his cousins were trying to take over the business in nineteen twenty-one." He laughed. "They were a sleazy pair. Dan Sutherland made mincemeat out of them on the stand."

"So later Pa hired you to find out about my grandfather."

"That's right."

"Pa said that you know where my...where Albert Rycroft is."

"They've kept in touch with him through me for years."

"Why? I never completely understood that."

"He's the reason they have you, Annie. He kept Robert Harcourt from taking you that night, and you know he was in that alley a few years ago."

"He turns up quite conveniently."

"It seems so."

"He's in Palestine, isn't he?"

"Yes, but he doesn't go by Rycroft there."

"What about my cousin, Rebekah?"

"She's there, too."

"Did he remarry?"

"No.

"How did he take care of Rebekah?"

"I'm sure he managed. I don't have any details about her beyond the fact that she's still with him. I don't ask too many questions, for reasons I'm not at liberty to discuss."

"She was, well, slow."

"So Mrs. Ashley told me. She said she was very talented artistically, however."

"Yes, she was. Very talented."

Emory Roth set down his empty cup. "So, David, you're going to Palestine, I understand. Things are heating up over there."

"That's what I hear."

"When will you go?"

"That's still in the works."

"But you're definitely going."

"Right. It occurred to me that my brother might be interested, but I doubt that he'll leave a good career."

"You never know."

"I'll write to him. We need to keep in touch, at least."

"I'm glad I could find him for you." The older man stood up. "I've got another client to see, so I'll be going."

"A client this late?" Annie glanced at the clock.

Emory Roth chuckled. "In my business, sometimes later is better." He put out his hand. "Good luck, David."

"Thank you, Mr. Roth. I'll need all I can get."

Annie carried the cups back to the kitchen and put them in the sink. "Pa says he's the best."

"That's why I hired him, but his rates aren't cheap. I'm glad it didn't take more than two hours." David put his hands on Annie's shoulders. "You might find some answers for yourself in Palestine."

"I'm not sure I want them."

"Why not?"

She shook her head. "I'm just not sure."

He kissed the top of her head. "How long are you staying this time?"

"Until Friday. Are you coming home with me again this weekend?"

"Can you wait until Saturday morning to leave?"

"I guess so."

"I'm glad you're here."

She slid around in his arms and laid her face against his shirt. "I am, too."

****

"This will be the first Christmas we've spent together," Annie said as she and David paused to listen to some carolers on a downtown corner.

"I'm looking forward to it."

"Is there anything special that you want Santa

to bring you?" She tucked her arm through his and smiled up at him.

"Can't think of anything. Just you."

"You already have me."

"Do I?"

Frowning, she took her arm away. "David, don't start."

"I'm sorry. It was a slip of the tongue." He draped his arm across her shoulders. "Do you want to go into Bonner's before we go back to the apartment?"

"I want to pick up something for Miriam and Jack."

"Right. They're getting married over the holidays, aren't they?"

"They'll be moving into Jack's apartment since it's already set up for him. Miriam's been on her own for a few years, so they have all the household things they need."

"How about something personal?"

"I thought of a peignoir set for Miriam, but I'd feel strange giving Jack something like that."

"I doubt he'd want a peignoir set." David laughed at his own joke, eliciting a head shake from Annie.

"Be serious, David. I meant giving him something personal, like a robe or pajamas."

"Uh...just curious, but can he...I mean, he's in a wheelchair, so..."

"Shhh, not in here."

"Nobody's listening."

"I have no idea. I guess so."

"What happened to him?"

"He told Mr. Young that a grenade exploded a few feet away from him."

"It's a wonder he wasn't killed."

"That's what he said."

"Do you think it's a good match? Is Miriam the

right woman for him under the circumstances?"

"Mum says so. She's talked to her more than I have. She says she's exactly what Jack needs, someone who'll stick with him through thick and thin and appreciate him for who he is." Annie's voice died away as she realized she was describing a quality in Miriam that she herself didn't possess.

"Lucky for Jack, then." David pushed the button for the elevator. "Which floor do we want?"

Chapter Twenty

Early in 1947, David arrived for the weekend with the news that he'd talked to his brother. "Daniel heard that I'd gone missing, but he never got the word that I was liberated."

"So he's thought all this time that you were dead?" Annie asked.

"Someone he wrote to for information told him that I was still listed as MIA. He wants me to visit him."

"He wants to renew family ties, so to speak?"

"His letter indicated that."

"I hope he does, if that's what you want."

"It's what I want, Annie. He's all I've got left of my family."

Annie thought of the baby buried in Greenfield. *I should have been able to give him that much. Something that's part of him. But it's too late now.*

****

At the end of January, on their fifth anniversary, Annie had a meeting scheduled in Canon City. David took her out to dinner and presented her with a diamond to wear above her wedding band. "You didn't have an engagement ring."

"We were never really engaged. We just got married."

He slipped it on her finger and kissed her hand. "Happy anniversary, Annie."

"Thank you, David. It's lovely."

"It's a good diamond. You can always hock it to pay the rent if you have to." He kissed her hand again. "I'm leaving in April."

The breath went out of her, and she sagged in the chair. "Oh, David!"

"I just found out today."

Wincing, she withdrew her hand. "Happy anniversary."

"Annie, you knew I was going."

"I guess I was hoping you'd change your mind."

"I was hoping you'd change yours." He stirred his coffee.

"You knew I wouldn't." She covered her face with her hands. "Oh, David, things have been so good between us."

"I know. I'm sorry, Annie. Not that I'm going, but that I've failed to make you love me enough to go with me."

"That's not the point."

"Isn't it? Do you love me, Annie? I mean, beyond the bedroom."

She looked away.

"That's kind of what I thought."

She shook her head. "You don't understand."

"I'm trying." The orchestra, back from its break, was tuning up again. "Let's dance, Annie."

Annie tried not to think about anything but the feel of David's arms as they moved around the dance floor. How she could almost hear his heart beating beneath his shirt. How safe she'd begun to feel when she was with him. How she would miss him when he was gone.

They danced four times before David suggested leaving. "Would you like to ride for awhile before we go back to the apartment?" he asked as opened the car door for her.

"Let's just go back," she said. "I'm tired, and I have a nine o'clock meeting in the morning."

David slid behind the wheel and turned the key. "You really like your work, don't you?"

"I enjoy it, yes."

"I know you're good at what you do. Mr. Ashley said so, and he wasn't speaking as a father."

"Mr. Young says I have an analytical mind and know how to fit things together."

"Have you analyzed our situation?"

"It's rather like a puzzle, isn't it?" Annie mused.

"Something like. You want to know how I see it?"

"If you want to tell me."

"We're two people who get along well together, like being together, respect each other's ideas, and enjoy the extra perks that we couldn't properly have outside of marriage."

"I'd agree."

"But we operate on different wave lengths. It's like building a house with a garage connected to the main structure by a breezeway, but the breezeway doesn't have anything to do with their stability. Both buildings are part of the whole, but they're separate, and anytime somebody wanted to tear down the breezeway, each of the other structures would continue to exist independent of the other."

"What's wrong with that?"

"Nothing in an architectural sense, but for two living, breathing people, it stinks. Look at the Ashleys. One without the other wouldn't be the same."

"One wouldn't stop living without the other."

"It would be different."

Annie thought of the relationship between her parents. It was true that they complemented each other, that their relationship brought depth to their individual personalities. She couldn't imagine one of them going on alone, at least not in the same way.

"I guess it would," she said finally.

"But I'll leave in April and make a new life for myself in Palestine, and you'll go on here exactly as before. We'll write polite letters and wish each other well. When and if I come back, we'll sleep together. I'll miss that part more than you will."

"That's not true, David. I enjoy being with you."

"I know you do, but you can get along without me."

"Didn't you just infer that you can get along without me?"

"I guess I did, so that makes me as guilty as you are."

"Why does there have to be guilt? We've just got a different kind of marriage, that's all."

"And you're satisfied with that?"

"I have to be, don't I? You're not going to change your mind."

"No, and neither are you."

He parked the car under the shed behind the apartment building and rested his arms on the wheel. "You've given up the idea of having children, I suppose."

"They wouldn't have much family life, would they? Not with their father an ocean away. They'd never see you."

"Annie, Hitler exterminated six million of our people. There's got to be another generation if Israel is going to survive."

"There isn't an Israel yet."

"I've told you, there's going to be."

"I'm not going to have children for a country."

"I'm not asking you to."

"Then why bring it up?"

He blew out his breath. "I don't know. I'm sorry." He got out and held the door while she slid across the seat toward him. They went upstairs in silence.

****

Annie dreamed about Albert Rycroft that night and woke calling for *Papa*. David cradled her in his

191

arms. "It's all right, Annie. I've got you. You're okay."

"I couldn't even see his face," she wept, digging her fingers into his shoulders. "I can't even remember what he looks like. Why won't he leave me alone?"

"He did the best for you that he could when he gave you to the Ashleys."

"But he keeps coming back, and I don't know why."

"Maybe he's looking for Bobbie."

"She's gone. I keep telling you that she's gone."

"Maybe not. Maybe she's just hiding. Maybe she and Annie need to work things out."

Annie's clenched fists pounded his chest without much impact. "He left me, and now you're going to leave me, too."

David stroked her hair and kissed her tear-streaked face. "Go back to sleep, Annie. I'll be here."

"But not forever," she murmured as she sank back onto the pillow. "Not forever."

****

The next time she stayed at the apartment, Annie had to navigate around two large footlockers and half a dozen boxes. "The boxes will go back with you," David said.

"You're only taking the two footlockers?"

"Some people arrive in Palestine with only the clothes on their backs."

"Do you know where you'll live?"

"One of my distant relatives from Germany knows someone who has a little business with living quarters over it. He says I can stay with him until I get established."

"What are you going to do? To make a living, I mean?"

"I'm not destitute yet. I managed to find funding for those in my family who wanted to leave

Germany. There are Zionist organizations out there who want to get as many Jews into Palestine as possible. The point is, I still have a great deal of my trust fund left."

"Do you need to hock my ring?"

He grinned. "I'll let you know."

"When are you going to visit your brother?"

"I've given notice at my job. The apartment manager lets me have this place on a month-to-month lease, so I can leave in two weeks."

"Two weeks!" She leaned against the kitchen door. "Two weeks."

"Would you like to come with me to Chicago?"

"I don't think so. There would be too many questions about why I'm not going with you to Palestine."

"I could just say we'd agreed that you should stay here until I got settled."

"That would be a lie."

"Suit yourself."

"Pa says there may be fighting between the Arabs and the Jews."

David shrugged. "That's nothing new."

"You could find yourself in the middle of another war."

"I probably will."

"How can you be so matter-of-fact about it?"

"Because it *is* a fact. Israel is going to have to fight for its life."

"Aren't you pushing your luck? You almost died in Germany."

"I'll tell you, Annie, I thought every day in Dachau would be my last, but then I made up my mind to stay alive. Dying there would've been useless. I decided that if I was going to die, it would be for a purpose."

He closed one of the full boxes and sat down on it. "*La shahna haba'ah birushalayim.* That means

193

Next year in Jerusalem. It's a blessing, but it became a mantra, a symbol of hope for those Jews who still had any hope. The Promised Land was out there, and they were going."

"That's not German."

"No, it's Hebrew. I've been studying it with a rabbi here in town."

"I didn't know there was a synagogue here."

"There's not. He's working for the shipyard while he looks for a congregation."

"I see." She went into the kitchen and began to unpack the food she'd picked up at the deli.

"Hebrew is easier to read than to speak or write," David said.

"I'm sure it is."

"But I can write a little. Would you like to see?"

"After supper, maybe."

"Okay. Sure."

"Are you ready to eat? I just picked up cold cuts."

"Any time now."

"What are you going to do with your dishes?"

"I thought I'd give all my household stuff to charity. It was secondhand to begin with, when I bought it for my bachelor digs."

"You don't have much time to dispose of everything."

"I thought maybe you'd take care of closing up the apartment if I don't get it done."

"I can do that."

He came up behind her and slipped his arms around her waist. She stiffened.

"Do you want ham or salami, David?"

****

When David came to Rumers Crossing the next weekend to say goodbye to the Ashleys and Mrs. Swane, he carried his boxes, sent earlier with Annie, from the garage to the attic. "I'll put out some poison to make sure the mice don't get into your things," Annie said as they shoved the last box into one of the deep closets.

"I'd hate to lose the picture albums and the few things I have that belonged to my parents."

"What happened to all their things?"

"I sold most of them, gave some to Daniel when he came for Mother's funeral, and some to their close friends. I couldn't cart it around."

"You didn't think of having a home for it someday?"

"I guess I didn't. I was twenty years old, Annie. They were dead. It seemed more important to get on with my life and leave theirs behind."

"Do you think it was easier for you that way? Knowing there wasn't any place to go back to?"

"I thought so at the time."

"I wonder if it would be easier for me if I knew that Papa was dead."

"Good thing for you that he isn't. Mr. Ashley was pretty clear about him saving your neck at least three times." He turned off the light and held her arm as they started down the stairs.

"It would be a coincidence if you ran into him over there."

"It might happen."

"Pa said they gave Mr. Roth the newspaper clipping about our wedding to send to him."

"It might happen, Annie. I'd let you know. Why don't you just get in touch with him yourself?"

"What would I say?"

"You might start with *thank you for saving my life three times.*"

"I'm not supposed to know that."

"Why not?"

"Even the police don't know who killed my grandfather at the foot of the stairs that night, and I... I didn't tell them he was there in the alley that night."

"You withheld information?"

"What was I going to do, David? Incriminate my own father when he kept those men from killing me?"

"I see your point."

"Pa says nobody looked too hard. My grandfather was bad news. You said yourself that a lot of people wanted him out of the way. But it was still murder, just like shooting that man in the alley."

"To save you."

"Uncle Sam says a prosecutor might take that into consideration, or he might not. Let's don't talk about it anymore, David."

"I never heard a word. Listen, I've been thinking about leaving from Chicago instead of coming back here. Would you like to meet me in New York City and see me off?"

"I'm not sure. Can I think about it?"

"Take your time."

"It's just that it will be hard to see you go, David. Maybe saying goodbye once is enough."

"I understand. But if you want to meet me, I'll leave Chicago a few days early so we'll have some time."

"Just let me think about it."

Mrs. Swane's dinner bell echoed up the stairs. "We'd better wash up and get down there in a hurry. I'm sure she's made something special for me again."

"You're pretty sure of yourself, aren't you?"

"I'm her fair-haired boy." David grinned and dropped Annie's arm. "Last one to the table is a dirty dog!"

****

When Annie took David to catch his train to Chicago, she told him she'd meet him in New York. "I'll make hotel reservations for us."

David couldn't hide his pleasure at finally being on his way. "I've shipped my footlockers on ahead. There's not much left in the apartment for you to deal with."

"I'll take care of it while you're in Chicago."

"That's great, thanks, Annie." This time he didn't tell her to stay in the car. They stood on the platform locked in a long embrace until he had to sprint to board the train. She waved until she could no longer see him.

****

They had three days in New York. Annie knew it wasn't enough, especially if the worst happened. On the last night, David made love to her like he'd never done before. He didn't say that it might be the last time forever, but she knew he was thinking that, because the same thought was crowding everything else out of her mind, too.

Neither spoke as they held hands in the back of the taxi on the way to the pier the next morning. Annie was filled with too many emotions to sort into any kind of order. Guilt, regret, anger, hopelessness...all of them vied for a place in her heart.

"I'll cable you when we arrive," David said.

"Are you sure they'll let you in?"

"I have an American passport. It's not marked with a *J* the way the passports of the German Jews were. You've got my address, and I'll let you know if it changes."

"Don't get lost, David."

He kissed her cheek. "I don't plan to."

"You're really excited about going, aren't you?"

"I admit it."

"And you don't feel guilty about anything?"

"About leaving you behind?" he interrupted. "Would you be surprised if I said that I did?"

"A little."

"Well, I do. These last few months, we've had more of a marriage than we had in five years. I want you with me, Annie."

"But not enough to stay."

He caught her eyes and held them. "No, not enough to give up what I know I was born to do."

She nodded. "When will you come back?"

"Don't look for it to happen outside of a year."

"I'll be here." She leaned against him. "I'll be right here waiting, David." .

Chapter Twenty-One

May 14, 1947
Dear Annie,
Things are heating up over here. I'm working for the "cousin's" friend over whose store I'm living and also helping with military training at a nearby kibbutz for younger settlers. All the young people, girls included, have to be prepared to defend themselves when the time comes.

The climate here agrees with me. I miss Mrs. Swane's cooking, but I'm getting used to plainer fare. New settlers are arriving all the time despite the best efforts of the British to keep them out. It's not that the British really care, except that an increased Jewish population makes the Arabs nervous, so then it's harder for the British to keep the peace.

Someday, when things are settled, I'm going to have a business of my own. Meanwhile, I'm doing my bit to further the cause of Israel, and for now that's enough.

Love,
David

David's letters were so impersonal that Annie could read them aloud to Alan and Lenore. She didn't think he'd forgotten their time together in Canon City and more recently in New York, but he was, she suspected, ignoring it. She couldn't forget or ignore it, despite her determined attempts, and most nights she ached for David's warm, solid body next to hers.

Almost like a sulky child, she wrote equally impersonal letters, full of news about Ashley

Enterprises and its employees. Since the war, the business had expanded beyond Alan's wildest imagination, but he insisted on keeping his finger on its smallest pulse. To that end, she traveled as much for him as for Trent Young.

"Pa isn't thinking of retiring, is he?" she asked Lenore on one of her increasingly rare nights at home.

"He hasn't mentioned it to me."

"Sometimes I feel like he's grooming me to take over, and I'm just not ready."

"I think he's trying to give you every opportunity to be ready."

"Uncle Trent or Mr. Vannoy could..."

"Trent will likely retire before Alan does. Jerome is happy overseeing the fiscal aspects of the company, and I don't know who could do it better. I doubt he'd want to leave his position and take over the entire operation."

"Then that leaves me."

"You've always known that Alan plans to give you the opportunity to head Ashley Enterprises someday if it's what you want."

"I'm not ready."

"When it's time, you will be."

When it's time. Annie couldn't get Lenore's words out of her mind. If she stepped into Alan's position, the final decision regarding her marriage to David was a foregone conclusion. Any hope he harbored of her joining him in his chosen life would evaporate. He could, on the other hand, be a large help and support to her here. Maybe he would see that and come home.

****

January 2, 1948
Dear Annie,
You know by now that the British have given us a timetable for withdrawal. The State of Israel will

be a reality soon. So will armed conflict, but we are ready. Even if people don't openly support us, we're receiving support in money and materials every day.

I left my will with Mr. Ashley's attorney. Not that I have a great deal to leave, except for my trust fund, but it will make it simpler for you if and when the time comes to settle things.

Despite the political uncertainties, the country is blossoming in so many ways. I watch the young people here, many of whom spent their childhoods in Hitler's camps and left their entire families behind in mass graves, and am moved by how fully they've embraced this land, how willing they are to fight and die for it.

Keep up with the news on the radio. It will get to you faster than my letters. If you don't hear from me regularly, don't worry. Just wish me—wish Israel—well.

Love,
David

****

January 20, 1948
Dear David,
This is our sixth anniversary, in case you've forgotten. Last year we were together, and I hoped you were going to tell me, when you gave me the ring, that you'd changed your mind about returning to Palestine. But it didn't happen, and I'm not trying to make you feel guilty about it. I don't think I could anyway.

We listen to the radio every night after dinner. Sometimes there's no news about what's going on over there, and other times there's only enough to leave me wondering and worrying.

Gram is leaving us at the end of the month. Her sister needs her. We need her, too, but she's as determined to leave as you were. Pa told her to interview her own replacement and then let Mum decide if they could co-exist. Mum is worried that she'll have to take over the household accounts and make more decisions now. She says that no one knows the house, not to mention us, the way Gram does, and she's right.

I'm hardly home anymore, so it doesn't matter to me who comes in, I suppose. I'll miss Gram less if I'm not here.

I drove to Greenfield last week and put flowers at the cemetery. Pa suggests taking Mr. Ryan, our gardener, with me sometime and letting him plant some shrubs or something. I'll try to do that before summer. The County doesn't keep up the place. It's only a Potter's Field, after all.

Your letters are still coming every seven to ten days. I'll try not to worry if they don't.

Love,
Annie

****

"The real trouble will begin when the British withdraw," Alan said after dinner one evening. He lit his pipe while Lenore fiddled with the tuning knob on the new radio. "If the Arab nations attack in force, and that seems likely, the Israeli army will stand alone."

"Can they win?" Annie asked.

"I hope so."

"The United Nations voted for the partition plan," Annie said. "Why doesn't that just end it?"

"Palestine isn't just a Jewish homeland, you know."

"Yes, but…"

"Perhaps when things are settled, David will come home." Lenore's cheerful voice made Alan smile.

"Is Pollyanna back?" he asked.

Annie frowned. "Who's Pollyanna?"

"A character in a very old children's book. My

brother Teddy used to call me Pollyanna when I was a little girl," Lenore said. "He said I looked for the bright side of everything."

"She was still Pollyanna when I first met her in 1921," Alan said.

"There's nothing wrong with a positive outlook," Lenore defended herself.

"Not in the least, darling Lenore, as long as it's also realistic." Alan reached across the short space between their chairs, and she met his hand with hers.

"David said he'd come home for a visit when he could," Annie offered.

"But this isn't really home to him, is it?" asked Alan.

"Maybe it will be someday," Lenore began.

"No, Mum, Pa's right. I've tried to be positive about this whole thing, but thinking that David is going to come home to stay *is* unrealistic. You've heard his letters. You know how he feels about where he is and what he's doing."

Lenore sighed. "There's no chance of your joining him?"

"I don't belong there."

"Why not?" Alan drew on his pipe as he waited for her answer.

It was a long time coming. The mantel clock ticked steadily, and no one spoke until Annie said, "There's Ashley Enterprises to be considered."

Alan's eyebrows went up. "You can't use that as an excuse, Annie."

"You've always expected me to step in someday."

"I've always expected that you'd have the opportunity."

"Pa, I love the business. You've created more than just a business. It's a family."

"We've been fortunate with the caliber of our employees."

"The hiring practices and employee standards are yours."

"I've had good people to share the responsibility with me."

"Annie's right, Alan," Lenore said. "You've made Ashley Enterprises what it is."

"Well, it is what it is, and it will go on with or without an Ashley at the helm."

"How can you say that, Pa?"

"Because those on the board of directors share my vision and want to see it continue. No, Annie, you can't use Ashley Enterprises as an excuse not to follow your husband and share his dreams."

"I don't belong in Palestine or Israel or whatever they're calling it. I belong here. This is my home."

She squirmed as Alan turned his eyes in her direction. "There's something in the scriptures that speaks of married people forsaking all others, isn't there?"

"Do you think I'm wrong?"

"I think you're trying to live a very fragmented life that, in the end, will destroy who you are."

"Alan!" Lenore recoiled at the harsh judgment.

"No, it's okay, Mum. He's probably right. He usually is." Annie rose. "I'm going up for a few minutes, but I'll be back to hear the late news."

****

"Alan, you're too hard on her," Lenore said when Annie was gone.

"I don't think so. Do you remember how you kept vacillating between marrying me and running away to Canada?"

"That was a different situation altogether."

"Not really. You didn't feel you really belonged with me, but you took the help I provided in order to keep Annie safe from Robert Harcourt. That last day when you told me you were going, I really thought I'd lost you, Lenore."

"I didn't go."

"You might have, and for the same reason that Annie is risking her marriage and ultimate happiness. You simply couldn't accept the risk involved with a long-term commitment. In your case, you risked losing Annie."

"What is it in Annie's case?"

"I'm not entirely sure. At the same time I know that it's easier for Annie to retreat from her feelings of abandonment into her safe childhood room."

"She *was* abandoned by everyone but the two of us."

"Possibly, but for her own good."

"David might have stayed and been happy here. In a way, he abandoned her, too."

"She'd like to think that, certainly. It gives credibility to her choice to retreat from life rather than meet it head on. If you'd run to Canada, you'd have been retreating, too."

Lenore rose and curled herself into Alan's lap. "Do you think she truly loves David?"

"I think she's using him for her own purposes. She has a certain status as a married woman, and...she has the physical needs of any young woman. I don't think either one of them love each other the way that we do." He toyed with the pins in her hair. "But, I think they could."

"I do love you, Alan. I think I love you more with every year that passes."

"You're my heart, darling Lenore. When you came back into my life that day..."

"I know. Out of breath and smelling of damp talcum."

He brushed her lips. "Yes. After that, I don't think I ever questioned the reason why I survived the war. You were in my life, and I wanted to live again, really live, not just exist."

"I want what we have for Annie."

"She'll have to want it for herself, my love, and then go out and find it, just as we did."

****

By the middle of February, the new housekeeper, Mrs. Ford, occupied the apartment off the kitchen. Annie conceded that she was pleasant enough and certainly an expert cook. Lenore simply felt relieved that the woman showed definite expertise in managing the household accounts and dealing with the regular cleaners, the gardener, and the various people who made deliveries to the house.

David's letters continued to come regularly through April, but Annie hadn't heard from him in two weeks when, on May 14, Prime Minister Ben-Gurion declared Israel an independent state. The British announced their withdrawal for the same day.

After listening to the news, Annie went upstairs and sat down at her desk, gazing at the picture of herself and David taken in Canon City shortly before David's departure. She sat in a wing chair, and he stood behind her, his hands resting affectionately, though not possessively, on her shoulders.

The memory of that day had ingrained itself in her mind. The idea for the picture had been David's. He came home the night before with a box from a department store. "I saw this in the window," he said. "I hope it's the right size." He didn't say he hoped she liked it.

She did like the plaid skirt and forest green sweater twin set, though they were more casual than most of her wardrobe. David whistled when she modeled for him.

"I want you to wear that for our picture tomorrow."

"Is that why you bought the outfit?"

"It makes you look sort of, well, soft, Annie.

Most of the time you're all business."

"And you don't like that?"

"Don't put words in my mouth. This is how I want to remember you."

Now she picked up the framed photograph and studied David's face. His smile was genuine, while hers was forced. That was the difference between them, she mused. David was real. He knew who he was. She didn't.

What was it that Pa said? That my fragmented life would destroy who I am? The whole problem is that I don't know who I am. David was right...Bobbie is hiding inside Annie...and I don't want to let her out.

She set the frame down and picked up her pen.

May 14, 1948

Dear David,

We listened to the news broadcast tonight. Finally, Israel exists. I'm happy for you and for all of the people there. Pa says the trouble begins now, and I'll admit that I'm afraid for you. Don't be a hero, David. I know you said you were born for this, but that doesn't mean you have to die for it.

On a lighter note, Mrs. Ford is settling in well, and we're all getting used to each other. I miss Gram. Pa misses her butter cookies. Mum is like a cat licking cream off its whiskers because Mrs. Ford has, so far, not forgotten to pay the household bills on time without going over her household budget, nor has she made enemies of the milkman or the grocery delivery boy, the gardener, or the two girls who come to clean once a week. The laundry and the dry cleaning go out and come in on time, and we're eating well. But she's not Gram.

Jack and Miriam are expecting a baby in November. She isn't going to work after the baby comes. Jack is strutting around like a man among men. When I said that the other day, he asked me how he could "strut" in his wheelchair. I said it could be done, and he grinned from ear to ear.

I'm away from home four nights out of five. There's a new subsidiary in Atlanta that Pa wants me to visit soon. While the company's worth has doubled since the war, with nine new companies, it's difficult to maintain the personal touch that Pa insists on.

I haven't heard from you in two weeks, and I know you said not to worry, but I do. Let me know that you're alive and well—sooner rather than later.

Love,
Annie

****

June 30, 1948
Dear Annie,

I've only got a few minutes to write this. If you're keeping up with the news, you know that the Arabs aren't taking this situation lying down, so we're kept pretty busy. We've had some casualties, including five people I know personally.

As to being a hero, I'm keeping my head down and my tail tucked, but I won't run from a fight. I'm all right for now, tired most of the time, hungry some of the time, and trying not to think of you when I'm doing night guard duty.

I need you, Annie, and I miss you. I wish I thought you needed me, too. Maybe you miss me occasionally.

Have to run.
Love,
David

After that, there were only six more letters before Christmas. Annie continued to write, but it was like writing to a ghost. Sometimes she felt sad, but most of the time she was angry with David for making her worry. Sometimes she considered that a divorce would finalize things and let her move on, though she wasn't sure exactly what she'd move toward. When she said as much to Alan and Lenore, Alan didn't respond as she'd hoped.

"I've considered that a divorce would be fairer to David," he said.

"What about being fair to me?"

"Are you really interested in the responsibility of a husband, Annie? Or children?"

"Alan, you can't mean that!" Lenore left her chair to sit beside Annie on the sofa.

"It's a fair question," Alan insisted.

"What kind of life would we have over there with everyone shooting at each other? What kind of a life would a child have?"

"What kind of life do you have here, Annie?"

"A very good one! I love what I'm doing."

"I'm afraid you love it too much."

Lenore made a disapproving noise. "Alan, please, let's talk about something else."

"What else would you have us talk about, darling Lenore? Annie has just presented us with the opinion that perhaps a divorce would allow her to move on. I'm merely agreeing with her and asking if she knows in which direction she wishes to move."

"You're criticizing her for staying here instead of going with David."

Alan reached for his pipe. "If the shoe fits."

"I'm sorry I brought it up," Annie said. "Please don't quarrel because of me."

"We're not quarreling," Lenore said.

"You're not billing and cooing, either, which is what the two of you usually do." Annie kissed Lenore's cheek as she rose. "I'm going up to finish packing for my trip tomorrow, and the two of you can kiss and make up."

Alan patted his knee as soon as he heard the door close behind Annie. "You heard what she said."

Lenore joined him. "I know you think I'm too

lenient where Annie is concerned."

"Yes, but you're just being a mother. I feel I have to play devil's advocate in order to balance things out."

Lenore removed his glasses, cleaned them, and laid them aside. "There seems to be no solution."

"I'm afraid there isn't, not unless one of them has a change of heart."

"And it's not going to be Annie's heart, is it?"

"I don't know, my love." He drew her head down against his shoulder. "A little billing and cooing is just the ticket, I believe."

Lenore laughed. "It makes us sound like a pair of doves."

"I shouldn't mind fluffing your feathers a bit."

Lenore lifted her face so that he could find her lips. "You're more scandalous with each passing year, Alan Ashley."

"I've created a scandal or two in my time."

"Is there something you haven't told me?"

"I'm not sure. Have I told you today that I love you?"

"I believe you told me this morning."

"Excellent."

Lenore put her lips against his eyelids. "I'm the luckiest woman in the world."

Chapter Twenty-Two

As 1949 began, David's letters became no more than brief notes dashed off whenever he had a spare moment. On their seventh anniversary, Annie wrote a lengthy letter filled with longing to see him again and wishes for his safety and well-being. Upon re-reading, it rang so false that she tore it up.

When he appeared the next day with a dozen roses, she was too shocked to be civil. "You might have given me some notice," she snapped as he tried to take her in his arms.

"I wanted to surprise you."

"It's been over a year! Thirteen months to be exact!"

He stepped away from her. "What did you need notice for, Annie? To get rid of another man?"

The stinging slap she delivered to his cheek shamed her and angered him. "David, I'm sorry." She reached to touch the crimson handprint, but he backed away.

"I'm sorry, too," he said with an iciness that chilled her to the bone. He tossed the roses on the table in the foyer and walked out.

She ran after him. "David! David, please, I'm sorry! Please come back!"

He kept walking down the private road.

"David!"

He stopped and turned around. "I'll be at the inn in town tonight. Then I'm going to Chicago to see Daniel."

She followed him a few steps before she realized that he was unmoved by her pleas. Covering her face with her hands, she stood in the waning daylight and sobbed.

****

Pleading a headache, she didn't come down to dinner. Lenore knocked on her door later. "I've brought you some tea, Annie."

"Come in, Mum."

Lenore winced at the sight of Annie's face swollen with crying. "I'm so sorry, Annie dear."

"He made me so angry, Mum! I reacted without thinking."

Lenore set the tea on Annie's desk. "I'm sure that David realizes that now."

"Is Pa furious with me?"

"He's disappointed that things didn't turn out differently."

"You must both be so ashamed of me."

"Of course not! We love you very much."

"I don't deserve it."

"Stop it, Annie."

"What should I do, Mum?"

"If you want your marriage to continue, the two of you must talk and arrive at some compromise."

"There isn't a compromise. Either I go, or he comes home. One of us is going to lose."

"If this isn't resolved, both of you have already lost. Now wash your face and come have your tea."

****

It was past ten when Annie heard Alan and Lenore come upstairs. After a few minutes, she let herself out of the house through the French doors to the porte-cochere where she'd parked her car earlier. At the inn, David answered the door almost before her first knock. She wondered if he'd hoped, even known, she would come.

Annie burst into tears and felt his arms go around her. "I'm sorry," she said, her voice muffled against his shoulder. "Please forgive me, David."

"What I said was mean and uncalled for. I deserved to be smacked." He closed the door and led her to the bed, where she hunched in a miserable heap. "Don't cry, Annie." He handed her a tissue.

"How long are you staying?"

"How long do you want me to stay?"

"Forever."

He kissed her lightly. "I've decided to start an import-export business. I'll be here long enough to get things set up on this side of the pond. My brother is going in with me."

"He's leaving the law?"

"No, just dabbling on the side."

"Is he thinking of moving to Israel in the future?"

"We're going to talk more about it."

"What does his wife think?"

"She's wavering." He brushed back her tousled hair and kissed her forehead. "I've missed you, Annie."

"I've missed you, too. Will you come back to the house with me?"

"Tomorrow." He slipped off her blouse and put his lips against her throat. "I'd as soon have some privacy tonight."

****

"We're good together," he murmured, stroking Annie's head pillowed on his chest. "We really are."

"What we're having is a legalized affair," Annie replied. "I'm not trying to pick a fight with you, but it's true."

"I won't argue the point."

Annie sat up, hugging the sheet around her. "David, why do you love me? Why do you want to stay married to me under the circumstances?"

He sat up, too, leaning back against the headboard. "I've asked myself that, but I told you a long time ago that you can't explain love. It just is."

"Are you sure it's love and not lust?"

He rubbed a strand of her hair between his thumb and forefinger. "I wanted you, there's no denying that. You presented an interesting challenge, I guess. But there was more to it, Annie. We're well-matched intellectually. We're alike in more ways than we're not."

"That's not enough to build a marriage on."

"No, you're right. We don't share a vision for our mutual future."

"In Israel."

"Yes."

She moved closer to him and leaned her head on his chest again. "I don't want you to go back, David."

"I have to."

"Why?"

"I've committed to it."

"I thought you'd committed to me."

He didn't reply.

"So nothing's changed."

"I guess not."

She sighed. "I love you, David, or at least, I think I do. Like you, I can't explain love, but there's something in me that doesn't want to look anywhere else for happiness."

"Are you happy, Annie?"

"Mostly. I like what I'm doing the same way you do."

"That's important. Do you ever think about children?"

"What kind of life would it be for a child over there?"

"There are plenty of children growing up healthy and happy in Israel. They're treasures, Annie, a new generation to replace the one that Hitler almost wiped out."

"I can't even imagine it."

"No, you'd have to see it." He scooted down again

and pulled her with him. "Do you have to work tomorrow?"

"I'll ask off a few days if you're going to be here."

"I'd like for you to go to Chicago with me and meet Daniel and Shelli."

"I'll see if I can work it out."

"Do you mean it?"

"I mean it." She yawned. "Is there an alarm in here that you can set? I'd hate to go in late and then ask for time off."

"I have one in my head. What time do you want to get up?"

"In plenty of time to go home and change."

"Early enough to sneak in without anyone knowing you've been out?"

Annie laughed. "We're married, David. I don't think we've created too much of a scandal by spending the night together at the inn."

He kissed her before he turned over. "Yeah, we *are* married, aren't we?"

****

Annie liked Daniel Levinson and found a sympathetic ear in her sister-in-law, Shelli. "I'll go with Daniel if that's what he decides to do," she said, "but I have reservations about it."

"What kind of reservations?"

"It's dangerous, for one thing. The fighting's not over. It could go on for the next fifty years."

"Surely not!"

"I don't mean an all-out war, but it only takes one shot to kill someone." Shelli handed Annie a cup of coffee. "Is that why you didn't go with David, because it was dangerous?"

Annie tried to formulate an answer as she sipped the coffee. "I don't think so. I just don't belong there, that's all."

"You don't belong with your husband?"

"Doesn't he belong with me?"

Shelli smiled. "I see what you mean."

****

Annie's unused vacation time allowed her to stay the full two weeks in Chicago with David. She wrote to Lenore and Alan that she enjoyed having a sister-in-law. *Bea talks about Patrick's family all the time, and now I understand what having extended family really means.*

On the first Saturday, just before sundown, she watched Shelli light two candles on the dining room table. The unfamiliar words that her sister-in-law spoke, after covering her eyes, both fascinated Annie and brought comfort to her soul.

"Barukh atah Adonai, Eloheinu, melekh ha'olam asher kidishanu b'mitz'votav v'tzivanu l'had'lik neir shel Shabbat. Amein."

"Blessed are you, Lord, our God, sovereign of the universe who has sanctified us with His commandments and commanded us to light the lights of Shabbat," David translated for her. "Now you can say you've experienced your first Jewish *Shabbat*."

"It's very nice," Annie said, knowing that she sounded trite, if not ignorant.

"My family was more traditional than Daniel's," Shelli said. "So when we married, I had to train him."

"She did," Daniel agreed. "My stepmother didn't go in for all this, and Father didn't insist on it."

"But Mom did, so you experienced it until you were twelve," David reminded him.

"Yes, I wasn't totally without some knowledge of tradition."

"Like I am," Annie said, feeling the heat creep up into her cheeks.

"Well, you hardly knew anything about your Jewish heritage," Shelli said, passing Annie the *matzoh*. "You can't know about something you weren't taught."

"My birth mother wasn't Jewish," Annie said. "And Papa always took me to Sunday School at the Methodist church."

"What is the religious persuasion of the Ashleys?" Daniel asked.

"Episcopalian. I was confirmed when I was fourteen." She glanced from Daniel to David. "But I remember my grandfather, Papa's father, wearing one of those caps like the two of you have on."

"Yarmulke," David filled in.

"And my grandmother always wore a scarf on her head." Annie squeezed her eyes shut, trying to recall the memory. "She made one for me and a little one for Alberta, but Mama took it away."

Shelli broke the uncomfortable silence. "Who is Alberta?"

"My china doll. Papa gave her to me just before Mama and I left. I still have her."

"I can attest to that," David said. "Her beady little eyes see everything that goes on in Annie's room."

"David!" Annie felt the heat in her face.

Daniel and Shelli laughed. "Maybe she needs another scarf that David can pull down over her eyes at the opportune time," Daniel suggested.

Everyone at the table, including a scarlet-faced Annie, exploded with laughter.

****

"You weren't uncomfortable tonight, were you?" David asked as they got ready for bed.

"A little, but I was interested, too."

"It's your heritage."

"Not really."

"Yes, it is, Annie, whether you want to acknowledge it or not. I'm not trying to convert you or take you away from your church, but you worship the God of Abraham just like I do."

"I suppose so."

"I know so." David slipped on his pajama trousers and got into bed.

"If we'd had children, would you have wanted them raised in the Jewish faith?"

"Yes."

"I see."

"I'd have wanted them introduced to it, anyway."

"There's a big difference between that and insisting on it."

"You should've been taught something as a child. Your father should have told you."

"I was only five, David. I expect he was the only Jew in Barnwell."

"I guess he was. My grandfather didn't live there, just opened the store and turned it over to Albert Rycroft."

"I've never understood why my mother married him. They fought all the time. I've forgotten a lot, but I remember the fighting."

"That's too bad. It's surprising, in a way, that they married, her being a *goy*."

"A what?"

"A non-Jew."

"Would you have married me if I wasn't half-Jewish?"

"At the time, yes."

"But you wouldn't marry a whatever-you-called-it now?"

"Probably not." David turned back the covers. "Come to bed, Annie."

She slid in beside him. "Actually, I enjoyed tonight. Watching Shelli light the candles...and all that food!"

"All kosher, too."

"Shelli explained that while she was cooking. She says she doesn't follow all the dietary laws during the week."

"A lot of Jews don't."

"Even in Israel?"

"Israel is a political entity, Annie. Just being a Jew in Israel doesn't mean that you subscribe to everything Judaism teaches."

"Do you think Daniel will join you over there?"

"It's beginning to look like it."

"Shelli isn't sure about going."

"But she'll go because she's Daniel's wife."

"Like I should go because I'm your wife."

"I didn't mean to imply that. Shelli will go for other reasons, too. I don't want you with me out of obligation alone." He turned over. "Goodnight."

Chapter Twenty-Three

Alan and Lenore welcomed them back to Rumers Crossing with dinner at Le Monde. "We've only been gone for two weeks," Annie said as she studied the menu. "And you're killing the fatted calf for us."

"Veal does sound good tonight," Alan remarked.

"Oh, Pa, that's a very bad joke."

His exaggerated sigh brought a laugh from the others at the table. "I suppose it's a good thing I don't have to earn my living as a comedian."

"We've missed you," Lenore replied. "Both of you."

"Did you get your business taken care of, David?" Alan asked.

"I think so. Daniel is the legal expert, and he says we're set."

"Has he made a decision on joining you?"

"It looks that way, but it may not be for awhile. He has to wind up his law practice." David closed the menu and laid it aside. "German and Hebrew aren't going to get me a meal here."

Alan laughed. "Would you like me to order for you?"

"Please. A nice big steak and all the trimmings."

"Does anyone want anything different?" Alan asked. When no one replied, he signaled the waiter that he knew was hovering nearby and placed the order in fluent French.

"Daniel's wife Shelli introduced me to kosher food," Annie said. "It was delicious."

"Annie had her first *Shabbat*," David explained.

"That's the Jewish Sabbath, is it not?" Alan unfolded his napkin and moved his hand toward the wine glass precisely placed by the waiter, who was familiar with the Ashley *largesse* for good service.

"Right. Not that I'm a regular, you understand, although if Daniel and Shelli locate near me, we'll probably make it a habit," David said.

Annie frowned. "I bought something for Jack's little girl when Shelli took me shopping."

Lenore picked up the abrupt change of subject. "Miriam brought her in just this week after their regular visit with Dr. Sims. She's growing every day."

"I'm sure Jack will bend my ear with every detail."

"Will you be in the office next week, Annie?" Alan asked.

"Yes, I think so." She glanced at David. "I can't be idle forever, you know."

If Annie missed David's slight sigh, Alan Ashley did not.

****

At the beginning of September, David told Annie that he had to go back. "It's time to get my business up and running."

"Did the letter you got yesterday have anything to do with this?"

"Actually, it did."

She waited, but he didn't offer more information.

"I've gotten used to having you around," she said, trying to sound casual.

"I'll miss you, too."

"But not enough to stay."

"Annie, we can't keep having this same conversation. Neither of us is going to give an inch, so that's that. Let's just enjoy what we have when we have it."

"Do you want to be free to marry again, David? Surely there's someone over there who'd be a better fit for you than I am. Someone who would give you the children you want."

"It's crossed my mind, Annie, but no, for now I'm willing to leave things as they are."

"Hoping I'll change my mind."

"I'm not holding my breath."

"Then why hold on?"

"I love you."

She went into the bathroom and closed the door.

****

They spent four days in New York City before David sailed for Israel. On their last night, David asked Annie what she wanted to do.

"Walk."

"That's all?"

"I like seeing the lights and watching people."

"All right, we'll walk. Broadway?"

"Yes. Don't you think it's exciting?"

They took the subway to Forty-Second Street, where they ate in one small café, walked awhile, then stopped for coffee and dessert at another.

"There's nothing like this in Israel, is there?" she asked.

"No, but there are other things."

"Have you thought more about going on an archaeological dig?"

"Maybe. When I have time."

"I...I might visit you if it happens."

"All right."

"I've always wanted to do that." Annie twirled the spoon in her coffee.

"It's an unforgettable experience, although it's pretty exhausting and usually dirty."

"I wouldn't mind."

"Well, I'll let you know."

"When do you think you'll come back again?"

She didn't look at him, but she could feel his eyes on her.

"I don't know, Annie. Six months, a year, I can't really say. It depends on a lot of things."

She pushed aside her unfinished pie. "I'll miss you, David."

"I'll miss you, too." He took out his wallet and picked up the check. "Are you ready to go back to the hotel?"

She met his eyes then. "Yes. Yes, I am."

****

She thought how their last lovemaking, before he left each time was, always different, a tender but desperate time with a hint of regret. "Sometimes I wake in the night and wish for you," Annie whispered as they lay tangled together afterwards.

"I keep busy," David said in a brusque voice that she'd never heard before. "I try to fall asleep in a hurry and not wake up until I have to get up and get busy again."

"I'm sorry, David."

"I know." He turned on his side, facing her. "I wish..."

"What?"

"Nothing."

"Tell me."

"I'd like to hear that you love me. You don't say it very often."

"You know I do, David."

"Sometimes I just need to hear it."

"I love you." The words tasted strange on her tongue. "I do love you."

"Thank you."

"David, I'll let you go if that's what you want...what you need."

He took a deep breath and blew it out. "I'll let you know."

****

223

Annie parked under the porte-cochere and let herself into the house through the French doors. Lenore met her in the foyer and folded Annie in her arms. "We didn't expect you until later."

"I was able to make the earlier train when I connected in Canon City."

"Run into the kitchen and tell Mrs. Ford that you're home, and set a place for yourself at the table."

Annie dropped her suitcase by the stairs and started for the kitchen. "Mum." She paused at the dining room door but didn't turn around. "Mum, you've never been separated from Pa, have you?"

"Never."

"Could you...I mean, what about a vacation by yourself or with Aunt Ellen?"

"I wouldn't enjoy myself without Alan."

"How do you know?"

"He's part of me, Annie, so I'd be leaving part of myself behind. Anything I did or saw, I wouldn't enjoy as much because I wasn't sharing it with him."

"You couldn't live the way David and I do."

"Not for a single moment."

"It was harder telling him goodbye this time."

"Do you wish you'd gone with him?" Lenore asked.

Without answering her, Annie hurried on through the dining room.

****

September 20, 1949

Dear Annie,

Sorry I haven't written sooner, but things have been happening in a hurry. I have a location for my business now, and stock is arriving daily. I've enlisted some help as far as arranging things for shopper-appeal, although most of my business is going to be by shipment for awhile.

Daniel is coming after Christmas. If their house

*doesn't sell before then, Shelli will stay until it does.
I'm looking for an apartment for them here in Tel
Aviv. Daniel is only a silent partner in the business,
because he doesn't want to give up the law. I think he
can easily find work in some civil service position.
He's studying Hebrew with a rabbi at night.*

I'll write again when there's more news.

Love,

David

****

October 1, 1949

Dear David,

*It sounds as if things are going well for you. I
know you'll be glad to have Daniel and Shelli there.*

*I'm traveling more than ever. We're gradually
getting a handle on the new companies, but some of
them are still holding out on adopting the policies
that Pa feels are essential for optimal business
performance. Some of their boards don't like it when
I show up at their meetings, mainly because I'm a
woman and also the "boss's daughter."*

*Lynda Shaw (Jack's and Miriam's little girl) will
be a year old next month. We're having a party for
her in the employee cafeteria at Ashley Enterprises.
Everyone seems to feel they have a stake in her. But
that's how it is at A-E. We're family.*

Love,

Annie

Annie re-read the letter and almost crumpled it
into a ball and tossed it in the basket beside the
desk. *I could be writing to a casual acquaintance
instead of the man I've been married to for almost
eight years. How did it come to this? Or was it
always like this? How long can it go on?*

She went to bed thinking about how she'd
offered David his freedom and wondering if and
when he'd finally accept her offer. Would she be
sorry or relieved?

****

"Annie, give Lenore her gift first, if you please." Alan gestured in the direction of the towering Christmas tree in the corner of the drawing room. "It's not a wrapped box, just a large envelope."

Annie retrieved the envelope and brought it to Lenore.

"Was my diamond necklace so expensive that you couldn't afford wrapping paper?" Lenore teased.

"The day you allow me to give you diamonds, I'll wrap them in gold, my love."

Annie smiled at their affectionate banter. "Just one day without all the billing and cooing," she said.

"What a wasted day!" Alan said. "Open your gift, darling Lenore."

Lenore removed a ticket folder from the envelope. "You're banishing me, Alan?"

"I'm banishing both of us to Europe for six weeks. We're long overdue for a real vacation. We'll sail on the *Queen Mary* from New York to Southampton and travel by train to London. A week later, we'll take a ferry across the Channel to Calais and see France, then tour assorted other places on the continent before returning home."

In a rare display of affection in Annie's presence, Lenore ensconced herself in her husband's lap. "Alan, it's wonderful! It's a dream come true. I've always wanted to see Europe."

"I'm sure many things have changed since I was there, but I know my history well enough to be an acceptable guide." He kissed her, then turned to Annie. "I know that Trent can't spare you for the full six weeks, but I thought you might sail with us and then fly back from Paris."

"I'd love to, Pa."

"And it occurred to me that David might meet us in London and go with us to Paris."

Annie's heart sped up at the thought of seeing

her husband. "I'll write and ask him tonight."

"Then our plans seem to be in order."

Lenore made no move to get up from her cozy quarters. "I've read that the *Queen Mary* is being refurbished for passengers after being used as a troopship during the war."

"According to the travel agent who handled the arrangements, she's a floating palace again."

"When are we going?"

"On the first of March. We'll celebrate our wedding anniversary on the Atlantic."

****

January 15, 1950
Dear Annie,

I'll plan to meet you in London on March 5th. I can arrange to take care of some business there at the same time. It sounds like a wonderful trip for the Ashleys and for you. Someday maybe we can make a similar one together.

Love,
David

****

Annie thought there was something unsettling in the brevity of David's note, but the very fact that he was willing to meet her in London dispelled her doubts. That he would be combining business with pleasure irritated her a little, but she determinedly put the thought aside. At least they'd be together.

Annie treated herself to a new wardrobe for the trip, including two expensive and somewhat daring peignoir sets which she didn't show even to Lenore.

As she packed, she reflected that it had been six months since she'd waved David off at the pier in New York. His letters had been irregular and brief, although she'd written to him twice a week out of a sudden urgent need to communicate. She wondered about the women with whom he came into contact professionally and socially. Was any one of them a serious rival for her position?

It wasn't the first time she'd wondered. As David regained his health, his handsome face contained a new element, a new strength of character forged in the fires of war and its aftermath. Not for the first time she considered how she might feel if David ever asked for his freedom, and if, despite what she'd said, she really wanted to give it to him.

Chapter Twenty-Four

David met them in the lobby of the Mayfair Hotel and immediately wrapped his arms around Annie. "You feel so good," he murmured in her ear.

"So do you," she whispered back.

Keeping one arm around her, he shook hands with Alan and Lenore. "I appreciate being included in your second honeymoon," he said.

"It's more like our eighteenth," Alan replied.

"If you ask me, they're always honeymooning," Annie said.

Lenore's face grew pink. "We've always gone back to the little place in the Catskills where we went after our wedding, but this year Alan surprised me with this grand trip."

David winked at Annie. "I won't be able to top this one for a few years."

"We'll need to register and go to our rooms," Alan said. "Then we'll meet for dinner."

"I might not be hungry," David said, pecking Annie's cheek.

"You've eaten?" Alan asked.

"I have my eye on a substantial snack," David said.

Annie reddened. "David, behave yourself!"

Alan laughed. "Ah, I see. Well, if you don't come down..."

"We'll be down for dinner, Pa," Annie said.

****

David tipped the bellman and closed the door. "I feel like I've been waiting for two days instead of two hours." He pulled Annie against him.

"You're glad to see me?"

"What do you think?"

"I'm glad to see you, too, David."

"Daniel sends his love."

"When will Shelli be joining him?"

"In June. He's practically pining away. Now about my snack." He slipped off her jacket and went to work on her sweater.

"David, we only have half an hour."

"That's enough time for me."

"Well, it isn't for me. I want to get showered and changed."

"Can I scrub your back?"

"Not even my foot." She took a key from her purse and unlocked her larger suitcase. "Wait until you see what I bought for tonight."

"I may not live that long." He came up behind her, encircling her waist with his arms, and nuzzled the back of her neck.

"It will be worth it."

"Promise?"

"Yes."

He heaved a mock sigh. "If you insist."

"I do."

He swept the room with his arm. "These are fancy digs."

"Pa wanted to go first class all the way."

"The Ashleys live very simply. This seems almost out of character for them."

"Nothing is ever too good for Mum as far as Pa is concerned."

"I've never seen her wear much jewelry and no fur at all."

"She doesn't like either one. I'm not much on it, either."

"I like what you're wearing now."

"Do you? I bought it with you in mind. In fact, I didn't bring a single business suit with me."

"Good for you."

She knew David was watching her as she went back and forth between her suitcase and the closet. "Has your wardrobe fallen into disrepair again?"

"I dress for the time and place," he said. "But I bought some new things for this trip. I won't look like the poor relation."

"I didn't mean that."

He leaned back in the chair and closed his eyes. "Hey, Annie."

"Hmmm?"

"Let's make it a short dinner, okay?"

****

"You did miss me," Annie said when David picked her up, carried her across the threshold of the room after dinner, not stopping until he dropped her on the bed.

"Sorry I forgot our anniversary."

"It's all right." She held out her arms. "We can celebrate now."

He tossed his coat and tie aside and joined her. "Your hair is different."

"I cut it a little. Putting it up every morning got to be too time-consuming. Women are going to short hair with permanent waves these days."

He grimaced. "I've seen the pictures. Don't do it."

"I won't if you don't like it." She removed his cufflinks and pushed up his sleeves. The tattooed number on his forearm always made her feel slightly sick, but tonight she made herself look at it without emotion. "If you'll let me up, I'll go change."

He rolled over. "Hurry up."

"I told you it would be worth waiting for."

He closed his eyes. "Just don't make me wait too long."

****

The Tower of London, the changing of the guard

231

at Buckingham Palace, the British Museum, Hyde Park, Parliament, Big Ben, Westminster Abbey— Alan made sure they saw it all and more. Annie and Lenore loved riding on the double-decker buses, while Alan suggested that the custom of afternoon tea should go home with them.

When David took himself off twice *on business,* Annie didn't comment and tried not to resent the time lost. He never told her what he was doing, and she didn't ask.

"I could stay here another week," Annie reflected over dinner on their last night.

"You'll be delighted with Paris, too," Alan assured her. "As a young man, I found it fascinating."

"Romantic?" David asked, winking at Annie.

"That, too, and it will be even more so shared with my particular love." He put out his hand and waited for Lenore to take it.

"Where will you go after Paris?" David asked.

"After Annie flies home, Lenore and I will continue on through France to Italy. Then we'll make our way north again through Austria and Switzerland."

"You're not going to Germany?"

"I think not this time," Alan replied.

"I understand that it's coming back from the war."

"I've heard that, too, but it's not on our itinerary. We're only taking six weeks this time, but I'd like to plan another trip in two or three years and stay longer. Perhaps after we retire."

David glanced at Annie. "Are you thinking of retiring, Mr. Ashley?"

"Lenore and I haven't discussed it thoroughly, but it's in our future plans."

Annie leaned across the table. "You haven't mentioned it to me, Pa."

"We'll all sit down and discuss it in more detail before any decision is made."

"It's only an idea for now, Annie dear," Lenore said.

"I can't run Ashley Enterprises," Annie said, trying to keep the panic out of her voice. "You know I can't, Pa. Not now."

"No one says that you're expected to. If you choose to step into my place, it will be just that, a choice." Alan placed his knife and fork across his plate with a precision that never failed to amaze Annie. "Now, shall we discuss dessert instead?"

****

"I don't want to talk about it, David." Annie began tossing clothes into her suitcase. "Not now anyway."

"Suit yourself, but we'll have to discuss it sometime. When you take over Ashley Enterprises, it will change things between us."

She sank down on the edge of the bed. "There's no chance that you'd come back and...help me?"

"You know the answer to that question."

She nodded, not looking at him.

"Mr. Ashley said it was your choice."

"It is. He says that Ashley Enterprises will go on with or without an Ashley in charge."

"I'm sure he's right."

"But I'm all he has, David. If he'd had a son, it would be different."

David walked to the window and pushed aside the drapes. "I could say that you're all I have, too."

"You have Daniel."

"A brother isn't a wife. Maybe we've been fooling ourselves, Annie. I was willing to go along with you on this long-distance marriage, hoping you'd change your mind and want to be with me all the time, not just occasionally."

"Would it really change things that much? You'd

233

still come back to the States like you do now."

"I come back because I have hope that someday…" He let the drapes fall back. "Well, never mind. It hasn't happened yet, and it's not going to happen tomorrow. So let's stop thinking about it, at least for the time we have left." He crossed the room and sat down by her. "I could give you something else to think about." He traced the outline of her jaw with one finger. "Hmmm?"

"We have to pack. The boat train leaves right after breakfast."

"Spoil-sport." He stood up and went to the closet. "Do you have business in Paris, too?"

"Nope. That week is all ours."

She rose and went back to her open suitcase. "I like the sound of that."

"So do I."

****

Lenore untied her robe and slipped into bed beside her husband. "I was watching Annie tonight when you spoke about our retirement. She looked rather like a little rabbit with a fox at its heels."

Alan opened his arms. "I've always thought in terms of Annie taking over Ashley Enterprises, but as I told her, the choice is hers. Trent and I have been discussing the fact that Jack Shaw is also a good candidate."

"Annie might feel less panicked now if she knew that you weren't depending entirely on her."

"I don't think she's as concerned about taking over Ashley Enterprises as she is about what that would mean for her marriage."

"It would effectively end it, you mean."

"I think so. David comes back because he hopes she'll change her mind and go with him."

"He comes back on business, too."

"Not altogether."

"They seem to be enjoying themselves right now.

I'm glad you invited her along and suggested that she ask him to meet us."

"Are you enjoying the trip so far?"

"You know I am. It's wonderful being here with you."

"I had that in mind." Alan slipped the straps of Lenore's gown from her shoulders. "I'm enjoying myself quite well, too."

"We needed this time together away from business."

"Yes, we did." His lips traveled from her shoulder to her throat. "I do adore you, you know."

"I've been so proud to be your wife, Alan. I don't mean proud of your status and position but that you chose me to share your life."

"You've shared it completely, both personally and professionally." He laced his fingers through her hair and drew it across his face, inhaling its fresh scent. "Before you came, I'd sit alone and think about how much I wanted to say, but there was no one to listen."

"You and Sam were always close."

"Yes, and we shared many things, but there were other things, intimate thoughts and feelings that could only be shared in the closest relationship. Perhaps it was because I was denied that closeness as a child. There was no one to talk to except those hired to look after me."

"Your parents only denied themselves by ignoring you."

"They didn't see it that way. Sometimes I wonder about their last thoughts that night on the *Titanic*. Were they of me, their son? Did they know they were going to die and have any regrets that they'd shared themselves so little with their flesh and blood?"

Lenore put her hand against his cheek. "We've shared so much, Alan dearest."

"When we first married, I felt as though my words were water pouring unchecked over a dam. I sometimes wondered if you were bored."

"Never."

"We don't lack for conversation even after all these years." Alan's lips traveled down from her throat.

"I don't think we ever will, do you?"

"Sometimes I listen to you move about the office, doing everything so precisely, and I think how surprised people would be to know that the perfect administrative assistant is, by night, a passionate and satisfying lover."

"Well, my goodness, Alan, they shouldn't know!"

He chuckled. "I wonder what they'd think, though."

"They shouldn't think about my personal life."

"No, you're right. That belongs strictly to me."

"All of me belongs to you, Alan. My heart, my soul…"

"Your lovely body."

She slithered out of her gown and kicked it away. "Always and forever," she murmured. "For eternity."

Chapter Twenty-Five

Annie thought there would never be another day so long or so cold as the one she spent huddled on the pier at Calais. The day which had begun with so much joy and anticipation had ended abruptly in a shuddering moment of smoke and flame.

The four of them had just strolled out onto the second-level deck when the tremors of an explosion deep within the ferry billowed upward. Helpless as feathers in the wind, their bodies skidded on the buckling planks. Annie thought she heard someone call her name. Her last glimpse of Lenore was of her clinging to Alan as they teetered against the shattered metal rail.

She would never forget the screams of terror, at least one of which was hers, or the way her body flailed about, weightless, until crashing painfully into the cold Channel water. She'd lost consciousness briefly, regaining it when someone hauled her upward into a smaller craft.

Not understanding the words spoken to her, shaking violently with the icy chill of the wind against her drenched body, she could only stare in horror as the ferry stood on end for a brief second before disappearing beneath the sparkling water.

When David found her among the survivors milling about the pier, he wrapped her first in a blanket, then in his arms, murmuring words that she comprehended no more than the ones from the men who had saved her.

Fortified by several mugs of steaming coffee, her body grew still. Only then could she manage to ask,

"Mum and Pa?"

"Not yet, sweetheart."

Later, when a French official approached and offered them transportation to a hospital, Annie refused. "I can't leave," she said. "I have to wait for my parents."

"They'll be brought to the hospital, too," David said. "They'd want you to be looked after."

"No!" The word echoed like a gunshot in the cavernous building. "No, I'm all right. I have to stay here."

****

Late in the afternoon, they began bringing in the tarp-wrapped bodies and laying them out in the warehouse next door. "I can't," Annie moaned when she understood that the man wearing a Red Cross armband was asking people to accompany him there and identify whom they could. "Oh, David, I can't do it! They're not...they can't be..."

"I'll go," he said, pressing a kiss on her forehead. "Will you be all right here by yourself?"

She nodded, pulling the damp blanket closer around her. "Please, David, don't find them. I couldn't stand it."

When he was gone for half an hour, she convinced herself that Alan and Lenore weren't among those shrouded forms she'd watched lifted from the boats. Unable to sit still any longer, she rose and walked over to another man wearing Red Cross insignia. "Have they brought in all the survivors?" she asked in English, hoping he understood.

"No more," he said, shaking his head. "No more." He caught her as she fell and half-carried her back to a bench against the wall. "*Je regrette, Madame...votre mari...*your husband?

She shook her head wordlessly and struggled to her feet as she saw David coming back. "David, you

238

didn't..." As he came closer, she saw the tears streaming down his cheeks.

****

Sam and Ellen Bernard met their train and drove them home. "Thomas Greer will be out tomorrow to help plan the service," Ellen said. "Bea will come when she knows a date."

"I've asked Rod to meet the train with the..." Sam's voice trailed off.

"Thank you, Mr. Bernard." David patted Annie's hand.

Sam passed an envelope across the back of the seat. "Alan gave me this a few years ago after you lost your baby, Annie. It should keep you from having to make too many decisions."

Ellen turned to look at Annie, who hadn't spoken since she got off the train. "Annie, maybe Dr. Sims should have a look at you."

David shook his head. "The doctor in Calais gave her some sleeping pills. She'll rest better in her own bed tonight." He leaned forward and touched Ellen's shoulder. "As awful and unbelievable as all this is, we're just going to have to get through it."

Sam parked in front of the house and opened the trunk so that David could take out the two small suitcases hastily purchased to replace those lost beneath the Channel waters. "We'll be by tomorrow." He reached to embrace Annie, but she pulled away and ran up the steps. Mrs. Swane opened the door.

"Oh, Gram, I'm so glad you're here!" Annie burst into tears and let the older woman lead her inside.

****

"I read the letter that Mr. Bernard gave me last night," David said as they sat in the drawing room with Thomas Greer. "Apparently, after Annie lost the baby and wanted him buried near the people from Greenfield, he bought five additional spaces from the County."

Annie's eyes widened. "But the Ashleys are all together in the cemetery here."

"Mr. Ashley explained in the letter than he and Mrs. Ashley felt a kinship with the children and staff of the Home." He took Annie's hand. "And with our baby. It's not so strange, is it?"

"That sounds like Alan Ashley," Thomas Greer said. "You know it does, Annie. Now, what about the service?"

"Does there have to be one?" she asked.

"There are hundreds of people who will want to pay their respects, and I know for a fact that the employees at Ashley Enterprises here in Rumers Crossing need to say goodbye. Alan said it so often...they're family."

"We could have something private afterwards in Greenfield," David suggested.

"All right." Annie twisted her handkerchief in her hands. "I don't care. I just want to get it over with."

"There's a standard burial service in the Book of Common Prayer," the rector said, "but I could personalize it any way you want."

"You knew them," Annie said. "Do whatever you want to."

The rector leaned forward, resting his elbows on his knees as if he were too weary to sit upright. "Their love for each other and their very lives in the community inspired me. I'll miss them more than I can tell you."

****

To the current housekeeper's relief, Mrs. Swane took charge, coordinating the receiving of callers and the food they brought, answering the telephone and giving the messages to David, who relayed them to Annie, although she didn't hear them.

As the tide of grief rolled in on top of denial, Annie realized that David had stepped in to do everything she should have done. With typical forethought, Alan had left Trent a limited power of attorney for all business decisions, and Sam Bernard put other things aside to go to the office daily and help make urgent decisions.

Annie left her room only to eat the few bites that Mrs. Swane all but forced down her. At night, refusing the sleeping pills, which she said left her feeling as if she couldn't put one foot in front of the other, she dozed fitfully in David's arms.

Though aware of David's deep, personal sorrow, she couldn't comfort him. "I appreciate everything you're doing, David," she said several times. "I'm sorry you had to be involved."

"I'm your husband, Annie. Of course I'm involved."

"If you hadn't been with me there, I don't think I could've managed."

He drew her down beside him on the window seat. "I've thanked God every day that I was."

****

Latecomers to the service found only standing room extending into the street in front of St. John's. On the front pew, so close to the gleaming bronze caskets that she felt they were crushing her, Annie sat with David, Mrs. Swane, and the Bernards. Behind them sat the Youngs and the Vannoys, Jack and Miriam Shaw, and every one of the other Ashley Enterprises employees. Even most of the retired workers were there.

It had been David's idea to limit the flowers, so only three arrangements, one from Ashley Enterprises, one from the Bernards, and one from Annie and David, graced the front of the church. Because the mortician recommended against even a private viewing, David placed the most recent picture of Alan and Lenore on a small table between the caskets.

David squeezed Annie's hand as the strains of "I Know That My Redeemer Liveth" died away. Thomas Greer rose to intone the words, "The Lord be with you."

"And with thy spirit," replied those in the congregation familiar with the service.

"Let us pray. O God, whose mercies cannot be numbered, accept our prayers on behalf of thy servants, Alan and Lenore Ashley, and grant them an entrance into the land of light and joy, in the fellowship of thy saints."

Annie jerked her hand from David's hand, digging her nails into her palms, as sudden rage replaced grief. She felt none of the comfort intended by the familiar words echoing in the sanctuary.

They left me, just like Papa. Everybody leaves me.

****

Rod had asked to drive the family to Greenfield for the private burial. Mrs. Swane declined to go, saying that she could do more good at the church, supervising the luncheon that had been organized for the mourners. The truth was, Annie knew, that the woman couldn't bear to witness the interment of the two people who were the only children she'd ever had.

Sam put Annie into the back seat of the car between David and Ellen, then got into the front with Rod. "Reverend Greer will ride in one of the hearses. Just follow them, Mr. Rodman."

In recent years, Alan had seen to more than minimal upkeep of the Greenfield Children's Home monument and the tiny grave nearby. In the newly-budded branches of the trees he'd had planted, a flock of birds perched in silence. Ellen held tightly to Annie who recoiled from the sight of the open graves, as Sam, Rod, and David helped the men from the mortuary carry the caskets to their final resting places.

"In sure and certain hope of the resurrection to eternal life through our Lord Jesus Christ, we commend to Almighty God, our beloved Alan and Lenore Ashley; and we commit their bodies to the ground. Earth to earth..." Without warning, Thomas Greer's voice broke.

After a moment, Sam Bernard, a communicant of the church since childhood, took up the words. "Earth to earth, ashes to ashes, dust to dust. The Lord bless them and keep them. The Lord make his face to shine upon them and be gracious to them. The Lord lift up His countenance upon them and give them peace. Amen."

The pastor cleared his throat. "The Lord be with you."

"And with thy spirit," replied everyone except Annie.

"Let us pray. Our Father which art in Heaven..."

Annie remained tight-lipped through the remainder of the committal and hurried back to the car as soon as it was over. No one spoke as Rod drove them back to Rumers Crossing.

****

Mrs. Ford handed David a slip of paper as soon as he came through the front door. "The man said it was urgent."

David helped Annie with her coat. "Would you mind if I made this call from Mr. Ashley's study?"

She shrugged. "I don't care. I'm going upstairs."

"Mrs. Levinson, you should eat something," Mrs. Ford said. "Let me bring you some tea and a sandwich."

Annie shrugged again. "I don't care."

****

She was curled on the bed, the tea and ham sandwich untouched on the table beside her, when

David came in. He sat down and took her hands. "Annie, I have to leave tonight."

"Tonight! David, why? Why do you have to leave at all? I thought you'd stay with me now."

"Annie, sweetheart, I'm so sorry, but I have to go. I can't explain."

Shoving aside his hands, she leaped from the bed and began to circle the room like a caged animal. "You're leaving me, too! Everyone leaves!"

"I'm not leaving you, Annie. I'd give my life if I could stay, but I can't. You'll just have to take my word that I don't have a choice."

"You have a choice! You've always had one, and it's been to leave me again and again."

"You had a choice, too, Annie."

Her pacing grew more frantic. "I need you, David. Of all times that I ever needed you, it's now."

"I'd stay if I could."

"You *could* stay. What's so important that you have to leave on the very day that I've buried my parents?"

"Annie, I can't explain."

She glanced up, then away, not wanting to see the pain in his eyes. "You couldn't explain before. It was just a bunch of words about Israel and a homeland and..."

"You don't know what you're talking about."

"I know exactly what I'm talking about." She whirled around and stood with her back to him. "Just go then."

"I'll be back as soon as..."

"No. No, David, if you leave now, don't come back. Not ever."

Chapter Twenty-Six

Annie spent two days sequestered in her room, opening the door only to accept a tray that usually found its way back into the corridor nearly untouched. On the third day, Mrs. Swane didn't bother to knock.

"You're not dressed, and look at this room!" The woman moved Annie out of the way and began to pick up the scattered clothes worn to the funeral days before. Books tumbled from the open glass doors of the built-in cases, and pieces of stationery littered the desk as well as the floor around it.

"Don't do that, Gram. I'll get to it."

"You always kept this room spotless."

"You made me."

"I didn't have to try too hard. You called it your *pretty pink room* and ran the carpet sweeper at least once a day."

"Gram, stop. Just sit down, and I'll pick things up." Annie took the woman's arm and led her to the window seat. "When do you have to go back to your sister's?"

"I spoke with the doctor this morning. She's not doing well at all."

"Then you should go today. I'll drive you to the station."

"I've already called for a reservation." Gladys Swane watched Annie begin to bring order from chaos. "She's dying, Annie. When she's gone, I'll take care of things there and come back."

"Oh, Gram, I'm sorry. Not that you're coming back..."

"I know."

"I'm not sure how soon a contractor can start work on the third floor, but I'll call tomorrow."

"Don't do that. I'll use the guest room at the end of the hall until you're settled."

"Settled?"

"Until you decide what you're going to do about everything. The house. David."

"I'm keeping the house, of course, and as for David, the marriage is over. It's been over for a long time. I'm not sure it ever got started."

"I'm sorry to hear that. Mr. Alan and Miss Lenore would be sorry, too."

"They're gone. I don't want to talk about them. Or David."

"Will you take Mr. Alan's place at the office?"

"I don't know."

"Mr. Bernard telephoned this morning. He'd like for you to call him this week."

"I'll go by his office after I take you to the train. Are you packed? Is there any way I can help you?"

The older woman took Annie in her arms. "Just help yourself, Annie. Don't shut out the people who love you."

"I have to, Gram, don't you see? If I let people get too close right now, I'll fly into a million pieces."

"There are other people hurting, too, you know. Rod came by this morning to ask about you and to see if we needed anything. He broke down and cried like a child."

"He loved Pa like a father."

"Yes, he did, and I loved Mr. Alan like a son."

Annie buried her face against the woman's shoulder and began to cry. "Oh, Gram, I can't stand it. I can't."

****

"I know it's almost too soon," Sam said as he ushered Annie to a chair in his office, "but you need to know the terms of Alan's will."

"Can you make it as brief as possible?" Annie sat on the edge of a chair, her hands clenched so tightly that she could feel her fingernails cutting into her palms.

"It's quite simple. Aside from two substantial bequests to Rod and Mrs. Swane, you inherit everything."

"Including the responsibility for Ashley Enterprises."

"I'm afraid so. Alan told me he felt you might be reluctant to take charge, but you don't have to do it immediately, Annie. Trent and Jerome are here, and you can ease in gradually."

"What if I don't want to do it at all?"

"In that case, Alan's will provides that the board of directors will meet and make a choice. You can continue in your present position or simply draw a share of the profits at the end of each quarter."

"Pa didn't take a salary."

"No, he had a large trust from his paternal grandmother, which was well-invested and provided a substantial income. Lenore continued to draw her salary, which by the way was, at her own request, never raised. She liked having it for her personal use."

"And mine."

"Yes, she insisted on paying all of your expenses except for school. Alan took care of your tuition at Arlington Hall and all your fees at Vassar." Sam hesitated, crossed to his desk and sat down behind it, folding his hands on top. "You're a very wealthy young woman, Annie. Alan's personal worth alone is three million dollars. That's a considerable amount in this day and age."

Annie covered her face with her hands. "I'd give it all to have them back."

"Of course, you would." He took off his glasses

247

and wiped his eyes. "Their loss is incalculable to Ellen and me. I can't begin to imagine what it's done to you."

"Mrs. Swane is coming back."

"When I spoke with her this morning, she said that her sister isn't expected to live more than a few days. She also said that David was called away unexpectedly."

"David isn't coming back."

"I see."

"I'm going to file for divorce."

"I'm sorry to hear that. Alan and Lenore were fond of him."

"I tried to let him live his life, but when I needed him most, he left me."

"I don't think he would have left at this time except under duress. Do you know what…"

"He wouldn't tell me."

"Did he say he'd be back?"

"I told him not to come back. Ever."

"You were speaking in the emotion of the moment."

Annie shook her head as she rose and started for the door. "Thank you for your time and concern, Uncle Sam."

Sam came from behind his desk to embrace her. "Ellen and I are here for you, Annie. And Bea also. Before she left, she suggested that you might like to visit them in Kentucky. Perhaps you need some time before you try to make any decision."

She pulled away from him. "No. I'll be in the office on Monday."

****

A letter from David, mailed from New York, lay on the table in the foyer. Annie glanced at it but didn't pick it up.

"Mrs. Levinson, would you like some lunch?" Mrs. Ford appeared in the door of the dining room. "I could serve it in the drawing room or upstairs, wherever you like."

"Thank you, Mrs. Ford. I'll come to the kitchen, if you don't mind."

"Mrs. Swane left me with strict instructions to get you to eat."

"Thank you," Annie said again. "I'll be there in a few minutes."

Annie reached for the letter and felt a sudden longing for David's arms around her. She held the envelope to her cheek, then thrust it away. *He's gone. Gone like Papa, like Mum and Pa. I'll never trust anyone again, never care for anyone, never let anyone hurt me, not ever again.* Crumpling the envelope in her fist, she stuffed it into the pocket of her skirt and fled upstairs.

****

On Monday morning, wearing her standard business attire, with her hair pulled back into an unflattering knot at the base of her neck, she presented herself at Ashley Enterprises and went directly to Alan Ashley's office.

Alan's long-time secretary, Mrs. Fenton, seemed surprised to see her. "Good morning, Mrs. Levinson."

"You've known me since I was in dresses with sashes. You needn't be formal."

"Perhaps in the office it would be more appropriate."

"Then I'd prefer you to call me Miss Ashley."

"Certainly. How can I help you this morning?"

"I'll need to see Mr. Young and Mr. Vannoy at their convenience, and if you could find some small boxes, I'd like to pack anything personal in the desks in there." She nodded toward the closed door of Alan's office.

"I'll get some from the mail room."

"Thank you. Mrs. Fenton, you aren't thinking of leaving, are you?"

"I gave my notice just before the Ashleys left for Europe. I've been here twenty-nine years, after all."

"Would you consider staying a little longer? Just until I can get used to things?" Annie bit her trembling lip.

"I'll stay as long as you need me, Annie...Miss Ashley."

"Thank you." Annie hurried past her into the office and closed the door before giving way to tears.

****

"I don't know if I can do this," she told Trent Young and Jerome Vannoy. "I don't know if I even want to do it, but somehow I think I owe it to my parents to try. Especially to Pa. He should have had a son to step in for him, but there was only me."

"You were his joy, Annie," Trent said.

"Be that as it may, I'm not really ready to fill his shoes, even if I could, and you both know it. But I'll give it six months. Then, as I understand the terms of his will, the board of directors can meet and choose my replacement."

"I've decided to delay my retirement by at least six months," Trent responded. "Jerome has a number of years before he'll even think about retiring."

Jerome Vannoy put the tips of his fingers together, appearing to consider his words. "I told Mr. Ashley that at no point in time would I be interested in assuming the directorship of Ashley Enterprises. I feel that I'm at my best in my current position of comptroller. So like Trent, I'm not in line for Mr. Ashley's position in the event that you decide not to take it."

"What about Jack Shaw?"

The two men exchanged glances. "He's an excellent candidate," Trent said. "I'm amazed at what he's learned in five years."

"Then perhaps he should be in on all our

meetings during this transition period," Annie suggested.

"I think that's a good idea," Jerome said, "but I think you should make it clear that you may choose to retain control."

"Jack and I have worked together since he came home after the war. I don't think we'll have a problem with the changed circumstances, but I'll discuss it with him today." Annie looked around the plainly-furnished office. "Somehow this always looked like an executive's office as long as Pa was behind the desk. It doesn't now."

Trent stood up and took her icy hands between his. "Make this your own place, Annie. Don't feel you must keep it the way he did. It suited him, and it suited Lenore, but you should feel free to change things to suit yourself."

Unable to speak, Annie nodded. "It's so empty," she managed finally. "Pa always said that a company was its employees, but he was Ashley Enterprises."

"Yes," Trent said, struggling with his own emotions, "yes, he was."

Chapter Twenty-Seven

"I found this in your pocket when I was getting the dry cleaning together." Mrs. Ford held out the crumpled letter from David.

Annie took it. "I must have put it in my pocket and forgotten it," she lied. "Thank you."

"Shall I bring you a tray?"

"No, just leave something for me. I'll be down in awhile."

In her room, Annie tossed the envelope on her desk and changed into her robe before going downstairs to the kitchen. Mrs. Ford was nowhere in sight, but there was a plate in the warming oven. Annie took it upstairs and sat down at her desk to eat.

I don't care what the letter says. He knew that I needed him, and he left anyway. It's over.

Even as her last thought completed itself, Annie reached for the envelope and tore it open.

March 30, 1950

Dearest Annie,

Maybe it's worth one more try to convince you that I didn't want to leave but couldn't help myself. I won't apologize for not being able to explain why. That's just the way it is.

What happened shouldn't have happened, either to the Ashleys or to you. I cared for them a lot, and I'm hurting, too, but I know that I can't even begin to feel what you're feeling. I want to be there to do whatever I can to ease your burden, and no matter what you said, I'll be back.

I'll write to you, and if you've re-thought what

you said, you can write to me at the same address as before.

I love you, Annie. I believe there's a future for us. I know the Ashleys wanted that. Maybe someday you'll come to believe it and want it as well.

All my love,
David

She flung the paper away from her and watched it drift to the floor. *It's too late, David. Maybe we could've worked things out if you'd stayed, but you didn't. I'm alone, and I'll stay that way. You've left me for the last time.*

****

In the night, she slipped out of bed and found the letter. Holding it against her cheek, she slept again and dreamed.

Take me with you, Papa. You promised. You promised we'd always be together...you promised, too, David, but you lied. Just like Papa, you let me believe in you, but it was all a lie.

I waited for you, Papa. I waited a lifetime, but I won't wait for David any longer.

****

Over the next month, Annie settled into Alan Ashley's office and position. At first she worked from Lenore's smaller desk, but as her confidence grew, she moved to the massive oak desk that had belonged to Alan's great-grandfather, the first Richard Alan Ashley.

Though she'd removed her parents' personal possessions, their comforting presence remained. She put pictures of Bea's little girl, Margaret Ann, on her desk, as well as some of Lynda Shaw. She bought a new coffeepot for the kitchenette but didn't replace the cups and saucers that Lenore had selected.

Trent Young always had a positive comment to make whenever he came to the office. Sam Bernard dropped by daily at first, usually with a folder of papers for Annie to sign. "Death is more complicated than life," he said. "Alan took care of things to ensure an easy transition for Lenore, if she survived him, and they both ordered things well for you. You need to think about doing the same thing."

"I'm only twenty-nine," she said. "And there's no one to leave anything to."

"As long as you're legally married to David, he stands to inherit everything. Either make a will leaving him a nominal amount, or divorce him with whatever settlement he requires."

"Then draw up a will for me, and I'll sign it."

"It's not that simple, Annie. You need to decide how you want things left and to whom."

"I'll make a list then."

"Do it soon."

"Why? I'm not going to die next week."

"Alan and Lenore didn't plan their deaths so soon either."

"I'll do it tonight."

"Excellent." He slid the latest folder into his attaché case. "I think this is all for now. Put next Tuesday at ten o'clock on your calendar for probate court and meet me at the courthouse a few minutes early. Once that's taken care of, I'll order letters testamentary and start getting things out of Alan's name into yours."

Annie brought him a cup of coffee. "I like what you've done with the office," he said.

"I made a few small changes."

"It looks enough the same to be comforting to me and different enough to be comfortable for you."

"I left Mum's desk in case I decide to hire an administrative assistant."

"Do you need one?"

"Uncle Trent and Mr. Vannoy have been wonderful, and Jack Shaw has hired someone to fill the position I had."

"Are you feeling more optimistic about heading Ashley Enterprises?"

"Maybe. I said I'd give it six months before I make a final decision."

"You need to make a decision about David, too."

"Are you recommending a divorce?"

"Far from it. Ellen and I hope you'll change your mind. Is there any hope of reconciliation?"

"David thinks so."

"Do you?"

Annie looked across Alan's desk at the man who had been his best friend, as well as his attorney. "I won't be hurt again."

"I'm sure that David didn't mean to hurt you. Even so, that doesn't answer my question."

"It's the only answer I have. The only one for the moment, anyway."

****

David's letters came regularly despite the fact that Annie never replied to them. She told herself that she would write when she finished all the notes acknowledging the flood of condolences. Then she told herself that she'd write when she could tell David that she had successfully taken the reins of Ashley Enterprises and was managing well without him.

She told herself that she'd write when she wasn't so angry with him, when she'd made a decision about the divorce, when she wasn't so dead inside that it took all her strength just to function at Ashley Enterprises.

But somehow she knew that she wouldn't write at all and that he'd come back anyway. *What will I do when he does? What is there to say? It's over...over...I don't want...*But she knew that she did.

****

Mrs. Swane returned in May and took up residence in the guest room beyond the rooms Alan and Lenore had occupied. When she offered to help go through and dispose of their things, Annie refused. "I'm not ready, Gram."

"It has to be done sooner or later."

"But it doesn't have to be done now." Annie wondered if the woman knew how often she slipped into their sitting room at night just to feel close to them and to remember the good years they'd shared as a family.

Gladys Swane became the liaison between Mrs. Ford and Annie, making sure the household money was deposited regularly and that the checks went out. She made herself available to listen and talk, but most nights Annie went upstairs after dinner and shut herself in her room. "I don't know what to do for her," Mrs. Swane confided one day when Ellen dropped by to check on things.

"At least you're here, Mrs. Swane. She's not alone."

"She's alone in the worst way. She needs her husband."

"Has she mentioned him at all?"

"She picks up his letters from the table where I put the mail. I don't know if she reads them, and there's never any outgoing mail for him."

"She's walled herself off from us, too. She doesn't even write to Bea. Maybe when David comes back..."

****

Emory Roth came to see Annie at the beginning of June. "I've let Albert Rycroft know about the Ashleys. Would you like to continue the communication with him through me?"

"Why does it have to be through you?"

"Alan initiated it that way, and Rycroft has accepted what I've sent, but there's been no response from him in eighteen years."

"But you know where he is. More than just somewhere in Palestine. I mean Israel."

"I know how to communicate with him."

"Would you tell me more if I asked?"

"No."

"Why not?"

"I have my reasons, Annie. Alan knew I didn't tell him everything I learned, and he understood it was better that way."

"What do you know about David?"

The man waved his hand as if to dismiss the question.

"More than I do? About why he left on the day I buried my parents?"

"Possibly."

"But you won't tell me."

"No."

"Why?"

"There are things better left alone, Annie. Alan Ashley trusted me. That should be enough reason for you to trust me, too."

"I guess I don't have anything to say to Papa. He didn't want me."

"On the contrary. He did everything for your benefit. He even killed for you. Twice."

Annie shivered. "I don't want to think about that."

"You should. He loves you that much, Annie. And so does David."

Annie threw out her hands. "Then why isn't he with me? Tell me that, Mr. Roth!"

Emory Roth shook his head. "You'll just have to trust him."

Her bottom lip thrust outward in a child's pout. "It hurts too much to trust. I won't do it again."

****

By the end of six months, Annie had stopped thinking about leaving Ashley Enterprises.

257

Inexperienced as she was in making executive decisions, the work as head of the enormous conglomerate was grueling, and it occupied her entire being. Mrs. Fenton left in September after choosing and training her successor from the secretarial pool. Trent Young retired, and Jack Shaw moved into the vice-president's position.

When Annie decided it was time to announce her decision to stay, she asked the employees to meet with her in the cafeteria one afternoon at closing time.

"I've known many of you since I was a little girl," she began, uncertain of how to present herself as being in charge and yet still one of them. "The summer I was fourteen, I begged to come to work with my parents, and I made it through every department before I graduated high school. I learned about Ashley Enterprises from those of you who were here then, and you need to know that I depend on you now.

"My father always said that a company was its employees, and I believed him. He said we were family. We care for each other and support each other. Whatever your job title, Ashley Enterprises couldn't function without any one of you.

"I told Mr. Young and Mr. Vannoy that I'd give it six months to see if I could really step into Alan Ashley's shoes. I'm still stumbling along, but I've decided to stay. Nothing will change. You have your own committees and representatives to handle problems and keep me aware of individual needs.

"I haven't seen any of you in my office, and I realize that you've been trying not to add anything extra to my load. But I'm there, and the door is open, just as it's always been. You knew you could come to my parents with anything, and I want you to come to me, too.

"Our profits are up this quarter, so you can

expect the raises set forth on your proposed pay scale increases for 1951. We've always had a low turnover in employees, and I hope that continues. If you're not happy with something, let your committee head know, and he or she will let me know, and we'll do whatever needs to be done."

Annie took a deep breath. "And that's all I have to say, except thank you for staying late for this meeting. Make it up by taking off a half hour early on Friday, and enjoy your weekend."

As she left, Jack Shaw wheeled himself into the elevator behind her. "You handled that very well."

"I tried to say what I think Pa would have said."

"I think you succeeded."

Annie let her mask drop. "I'm still scared, Jack." Instantly, she regretted exposing her vulnerability.

"I'm not full of confidence myself, but Mr. Young is only a phone call away if either one of us gets into trouble." The elevator stopped on the second floor, and Annie held the door while he rolled out. "I'm going to get some papers off my desk and go home. Miriam's probably fuming by now." He laughed and waited for Annie to join in. Instead, she let the doors close between them.

Judy Nickles

Chapter Twenty-Eight

On the last Saturday in October, Annie stood in the door of Alan's study, contemplating the necessity of going through his desk. Sam Bernard had offered to do it for her months ago, but she'd insisted she would do it herself. Now, perhaps, it was time.

She was alone in the house, and the silence wrapped itself around her like a shroud. Shivering, she stepped into the room and swept it with her eyes as if seeing it for the first time. The Monet seascape over the empty fireplace, with its stormy waves rolling out of the bleak ocean depths, reflected her own feelings of having no safe harbor.

Hurrying across the room, she yanked the cords that opened the drapes. As the sunlight poured in, she remembered how Alan never came into the room without inviting the light in also. "I can't see it," he told her when she first came, "but I can feel it. When I'm in a bright place, I feel happier and more energized."

Annie decided that she felt better, too, as she gazed out across the back lawn that sloped down to the river. More than a few red and yellow leaves, still clinging stubbornly to the branches, set the trees ablaze. Her eyes drifted to the spot under the maple where Prince rested. She hadn't been there in a long time, nor had she been back to Greenfield since Alan and Lenore were buried. Sam Bernard had seen to the setting of the monuments that she'd chosen only at his insistence. "You owe them the love and respect of making the choice yourself, Annie. I won't do it for you."

She recognized the familiar guilty discomfort swirling in the pit of her stomach. "Oh, Pa, this isn't the way you taught me, is it?" Did he whisper *no*? "You told me, when I came, that you and Mum wanted to give my childhood back to me, and you did. I soaked it all up, all the love and attention, and you meant to make me strong, but I'm not."

She hadn't realized she was speaking aloud until she heard, "Yes, Annie, you are."

She whirled at the sound of the voice behind her. "David!"

"Hello, sweetheart. The front door was unlocked. Is that a good idea?" He approached her, arms outstretched.

She stepped back. "I didn't expect you."

"I didn't tell you I was coming, because I wasn't sure until a few days ago." He reached for her. When she shrank farther away, he dropped his arms to his sides, and his smile faded. "You're still angry with me."

"What did you expect, David? You left me alone on the very day I buried my parents."

"I told you it wasn't my choice."

"You could have explained that."

"No, Annie, I couldn't."

"I don't believe you."

"Then don't. I brought you something."

"You can't gift your way out of this," she said, her anger spilling over. "Diamond rings and clothes..."

"It's nothing like that. Come on."

She frowned. "What?"

"Just come into the foyer." He walked out.

After a moment, she followed him. "What?" she asked again, impatiently.

He nodded in the direction of the stairs. "There."

Annie gasped at the sight of a small child sitting on the bottom step. She wore a faded pink dress too lightweight for the season and a pink sweater that had seen better days.

"David, what in the world...who is she?"

At the sound of Annie's voice, the little girl raised her head, and Annie found herself looking into a face so like her own that she couldn't take her eyes away. The room spun around her.

David caught her arm. "This is Chava, your cousin Rebekah's daughter. She's five years old, and you're all she has left in the world except for Albert Rycroft. He feels that you can take better care of her than he can."

Annie's anger steadied her and boiled into blinding fury. "And you expect me to do it? Just like that? Here she is, now take care of her. Is that what you expect, David?"

"She's part of you, Annie."

"No, she's not. I don't have anyone now. I don't want anyone!"

The look of disgust in David's eyes only fueled her rage. "Then I was wrong about you. You inherited everything from Alan Ashley except his strength of character. That's a pity."

"How dare you judge me!"

He shrugged. "I heard you say it yourself just a few minutes ago, that he tried to make you strong. Well, I tried to help you find that strength."

"By bringing me a child to be responsible for?"

"I thought we could raise her together, the way the Ashleys raised you, but I was wrong. We'll go to the inn for the night. Daniel has gone on to Chicago to sign the papers on their house. He said he'd talk to Shelli about taking her if you wouldn't."

Annie recoiled from his blunt words. "You don't have to go to the inn, David. There's plenty of room here." A sudden sound from the stairs drew her attention back to the child. Two large tears hung suspended halfway down the little girl's pale cheeks.

"I want my mommy," she said softly in English. "I want my mommy."

****

In the kitchen, Annie poured a glass of milk for Chava and made her some toast. The little girl fell asleep before she finished eating. Her head plopped onto the table, narrowly missing the plate, which Annie whisked away. "Put her in the room across from mine," Annie said. "Does she have anything except what she's wearing?"

"Not much."

"Take her upstairs and put her to bed, and then come down to the study. You have a lot of explaining to do."

Annie was on her knees in front of the fireplace, trying to coax a spark from the kindling under the logs, when David came back. "I'll do that," he said.

She retreated to the sofa. "So Rebekah is dead?"

"Yes, three weeks ago"

"How did she end up with a child?"

David replaced the fire screen as flames began to sputter around the logs. "Mr. Ashley could do that without even seeing it."

"I asked you about Rebekah. Who was Chava's father?"

"He was a brilliant Polish engineering student who lost his entire family during the war. Afterwards, he immigrated to Israel and went to work for the Hagganah, one of the Zionist organizations. He also trained as a pilot."

"Were they married?"

"Oh, yes. He worshipped her. Rebekah was beautiful, inside and out. Rycroft hired a British tutor for her. She was a slow learner, but one day something clicked, and she blossomed. Then, after she finished school, she went to work in a day nursery and also volunteered with a hospital auxiliary. Reuven saw her when he came into the clinic with a minor injury. It was, according to him, love at first sight."

"He's dead, too?"

"Unfortunately, yes. He was killed in the fighting after independence."

"Did they live with Papa?"

"Rebekah moved back home after her husband died."

"And what happened to her?"

"A random sniper picked her off on her way to work. She covered Chava with her body when she heard the firing. When they pulled Chava out, she was covered with her mother's blood."

Annie moaned. "How horrible."

"Yes, it was."

"What about Papa? Why didn't he want her?"

"His business requires a great deal of travel."

"He might have gotten a housekeeper."

"He wanted her brought up in a real home, Annie. He made that decision for you, and now he's made it for Chava."

"I suppose it's easier to give a child away when you've had some experience."

David grimaced. "That's unworthy of you, Annie. The man made a decision based on what was best for you at the time. It cost him more than you'll ever know."

"How do you know so much about it?"

"Because I know Albert Rycroft, and don't ask me to explain that, because I'm not going to."

"But you expect me to take the child."

"I told you that Daniel and Shelli will take her if you don't want her."

"It's not a question of wanting her, David."

"Isn't it?"

"I work, you know."

"You still have your housekeeper, and Mrs. Swane is back, isn't she? "

"How did you know that?"

"I had a letter from Mr. Bernard."

"Why would he be writing to you?"

"He was concerned because you mentioned filing for divorce and felt I should come back and try to work things out. Do you plan to divorce me?"

"I don't know yet."

"Then I'll take Chava to Daniel and Shelli. She deserves a home with two parents."

"She wouldn't have that with us, David. You're in Israel, and I'm here."

"That could change."

"How is it that she speaks English?"

"It was Rebekah's first language, you know. She was never able to master more than a smattering of Hebrew, although Chava is fluent. She'll forget it, though, if she stays here."

"I thought she was going to be with Daniel and Shelli."

"Is that what you really want, Annie? It seems to me, under the circumstances, that she's a gift straight from God. She's part of you in a way that no one else is. The same blood flows in your veins."

"Blood doesn't necessarily make a family."

"No, it doesn't, but we could, Annie. We could do the same thing for Chava that the Ashleys did for you."

"It isn't the same thing at all."

He shook his head. "No, you're right, it's not, because you're not remotely like Lenore Ashley. Mr. Ashley told me that she was willing to give up everything, including him, to take you to Canada, where she hoped you'd be safe."

"She didn't."

"But she was willing. What's wrong with you, Annie, that you can't have compassion for another little girl who's in the same situation you were in once? It's true she doesn't really remember her father, but she's been traumatized by her mother's death, and she misses *Poppy*—Albert Rycroft."

"I have compassion for her," Annie protested. "But I can't love her, David. I can't."

****

When Mrs. Swane came home later, Annie told her about Chava. "I just checked on her. She's still asleep, and David's in the study making some calls."

"I remember the day Mr. Alan walked through that front door with you."

"She's about in the same boat, I guess. I went through her things. They're all too lightweight for the weather here, but I don't have anything else. Mum gave all my things away as quickly as I outgrew them."

"It was hard times then, remember. She and Mrs. Bernard sponsored that thrift store for people who needed things they couldn't afford."

"Bea and I used to help out there. In fact, it's still open on Saturdays. Miriam Shaw is in charge now." Annie glanced at her watch. "I might be able to pick up a few things just to get her by. There's not time to drive over to the department store in Lowell."

"Do you want me to make dinner, since David is here?"

"Don't go to a lot of trouble, Gram. Whatever is easy."

"Mrs. Ford left a chicken in the refrigerator."

"That's good." Annie was already taking her coat from the closet. "Tell David I'm getting some things for Chava so she won't freeze to death before he can do something about her."

****

Chava was at the kitchen table with David and Mrs. Swane when Annie came in with two overflowing brown paper bags. "These will keep her covered, at least."

Mrs. Swane left the stove to inspect the clothes that Annie was taking out of the bags. "Are they clean?"

"Yes, Aunt Ellen donated a washing machine to the shop, and the coat has the dry-cleaning tag still on it." She held up a red wool coat with a hood. "There weren't any shoes that looked small enough, so her sandals will have to do until Monday. But I found plenty of socks."

"You had a coat almost like that," Mrs. Swane said. "You wore it to Greenfield when they dedicated the marker on Valentine's Day. Miss Lenore said you looked like a Valentine yourself."

Annie's face relaxed into a smile. "I remember, but it was Bea's coat first. Just about everything I had was hers first." Remembering made her happier, but only for a moment.

She pulled out a pair of tan corduroy pants and a yellow sweater. "Here, Chava, let's try these on you."

Chava looked startled, then shrank back in her chair.

"She doesn't bite, Puss," David said. He glanced up at Annie. "That's the first time you've spoken directly to her."

Annie flushed. "Come here, Chava. Look what's in the other bag." She brought out a small brown teddy bear. "I found it at the gift shop near the inn. She didn't seem to have any toys."

"She has a few things, but there wasn't room to bring them this trip."

Chava reached for the bear and held it to her cheek. "Thank you, Miss."

"It's Annie. Just Annie."

Chava's shy smile stirred something in Annie. "Thank you." She held the bear against her cheek again.

****

After dinner, Chava sat in front of the fire in the study looking at some of Annie's childhood picture books. She'd eaten well and seemed more comfortable in her new surroundings, but when Mrs. Swane mentioned a bubble bath, she frowned. "What is it?"

"It smells nice, and you'll float away in the bubbles," David explained.

"All the way home, Uncle David?"

"Well, not yet, Chava. Soon, but not yet." He lowered his voice. "I called Shelli this afternoon. She and Daniel will take Chava until I can find a place for her, hopefully in a home with other children."

"Why can't they keep her?" Annie watched the firelight dance off Chava's hair as she bent over *Cinderella.*

"Soon after they married, they made the decision not to have children. Both of them had good careers, which they didn't want to give up. They both feel that becoming parents at their age wouldn't be practical."

"Wouldn't it be better for her to be in the country she's always known?"

"I don't know, Annie. She needs a home and a family somewhere. I hoped you might see this as a way for us to start over."

"I have started over, David. I'm director of Ashley Enterprises and doing quite well."

"I never doubted that you would."

"I've had a great deal of help, but I've worked hard, too."

"Do you like it?"

"I'm doing it."

"That wasn't what I asked."

Annie shrugged. "I'm doing it for Pa more than for myself. Is that honest enough for you?"

"Yes. Do you want to do it the rest of your life?"

"I suppose I will."

"As opposed to doing what?"

"I don't know, David. Don't keep on at me."

"Sorry."

Mrs. Swane appeared to take Chava upstairs. "Time for your bubble bath."

Chava scrambled to her feet, her face wreathed in smiles. "Will I really float away on the bubbles?"

"All the way to Nid-Nod Land."

Chava put her book on the table in front of the sofa where Annie and David sat. "Thank you for letting me look at the book, Miss...Annie."

"You're welcome."

"Goodnight, Uncle David."

"Goodnight, Chava. Sleep tight. Do you have your bear?"

Chava retrieved the bear from the ottoman in front of the chair where Alan had always sat when he was alone in the room. "Here he is."

"Have you named him yet?"

"I'm going to call him Poppybear."

Annie caught her breath, but David nodded. "Very good, Chava. Poppy would like that."

"I don't understand why he didn't find some way to keep her," Annie said when Mrs. Swane and Chava were gone.

"You don't understand why he didn't keep you."

"No, I don't."

"Maybe you will someday."

"I doubt it."

"The name Chava comes from the Hebrew word for *life*, Annie. You can see what a sweet little girl she is. She could be a new life for you."

"I have a life."

"Not a very satisfying one, from what I can tell."

"You haven't been here in six months, David. How can you tell anything?"

"I still love you, Annie, but if you want a divorce, I won't contest it."

"I'll keep that in mind."

"Do you want me to go to the inn tonight?"

"There's another bed in Chava's room."

"I'd rather be in yours."

"That's the problem, David. We sleep in the same bed, but we don't have the same life. It doesn't make sense."

"It seems to me we always enjoyed that part of our marriage."

"I won't deny that, but it's not enough."

"It's better than nothing." He reached for her hand and felt her start to pull away. He tightened his fingers around hers. "I've learned to fight for what's important to me."

"I don't want to fight, not with you or anybody else."

"Just with life."

"Not with life, either."

"You're doing it."

Annie sighed, savoring his touch and knowing it was dangerous. "Why did you come back, David? Besides to bring Chava?"

"She was an afterthought. When I found out about Rebekah, I went to see Rycroft to express my condolences, and he asked me to bring her to you. I couldn't refuse."

"Why not?"

"He's not going to live forever."

"He's no older than Pa."

"Accidents happen."

"And you're not going to tell me how you know him?"

"No."

"I spoke with Mr. Roth. He said he'd facilitate communication with Papa like he did for Pa, but he wouldn't tell me how to get to him directly."

"He shouldn't, but he can keep Rycroft informed about Chava."

"And he said...well, he hinted at something very strange...that he knew more about you than I did, and that there were some things that just needed to be left alone. What did he mean?"

"He meant exactly that. Some things need to be left alone."

"Married people are supposed to share everything. Mum and Pa did."

"Our marriage is different, Annie."

"Too different. I don't like it."

The phone rang. "I think that's probably for me," David said.

Annie listened to his side of the conversation. "Yes. Where and when? I see. You're very sure? No, not yet. You can count on it." He hung up and returned to the sofa but didn't pick up Annie's hand again.

"All right, now I can tell you the rest of the reason I came back. The diamonds."

"The diamonds that disappeared from your grandfather's store?"

"I know where they are, and I have to get them and deliver them to a contact."

"Charlie Chan Levinson." Annie's lip curled.

"Close, but not quite. Go get Alberta."

"Alberta? What does she have to do with all this?"

"She has the diamonds. They're hidden inside her body."

Chapter Twenty-Nine

Annie winced as David used Lenore's embroidery scissors to make a delicate incision in Alberta's cloth body. "You don't understand what good care I've taken of her all these years," she murmured.

"She'll be as good as new, I promise." David put one finger inside the small cut and probed. "Aha! I feel them." He cut another quarter inch of cloth and tried again, finally drawing out a small paper packet, which he placed on the table.

"Your fingers are smaller than mine. See if you can feel anything else. Down the legs, maybe."

"I feel like a murderer," she mumbled as she placed her finger inside the doll. "Wait...there *is* another one. Two, in fact, one in each leg." She drew out one packet, then another.

David unfolded the papers to reveal a small pile of sparkling diamonds in each. "On today's market, they'll bring close to a million dollars."

"How do you know?"

"I don't, but that's what I'm told."

"Where did they come from?"

"I don't know exactly, just what I told you—that my grandfather was responsible for bringing them out of Russia after the first war. He was always vague about how he ended up with them, but he intended to use them for their specified purpose, which was to get more Jews out of Russia."

"So if they're in Alberta, does that mean that Papa really did steal them?"

"He heard about the intended robbery, so he

took them out of the safe and put them into Alberta. He told me that he bought the body of the doll separately so that he could hide the diamonds, before a neighbor woman attached the head. He couldn't know that your mother would take you out of Barnwell before he could recover them."

"Why didn't he take them before? He had to know that my grandfather was trying to use me to get them."

"He meant to take them the night of the fire in Greenfield, but you didn't have her with you."

Annie's head snapped back. "I remember. He asked me where Alberta was, and I told him that Mum had taken her when she left after Christmas."

"Then he intended to get them the night Robert Harcourt broke into the house, but he ran short of time. It was more important to get you to safety."

"In the secret room."

"Right. There wasn't time to get the diamonds out of Alberta."

"He could've just taken her."

"He couldn't get back into the bedroom without being seen. Besides, he wanted to finish off his ex-father-in-law once and for all."

"I can't believe that Papa deliberately killed him. Maybe he didn't have any choice in that alley in Canon City, but he could've just knocked Grandfather out and left him for the police here."

"I don't know, Annie. The man had cost him everything—his job, his home, his reputation." David's eyes locked with Annie's. "His shining star."

Tears filled Annie's eyes. "I never thought about it that way."

David's arms went around her. "Sometimes a man has to make decisions that he doesn't want to make. Sometimes it takes more courage to do the right thing."

Annie clung to him, but only for a moment.

273

"Why did Papa tell you all this? Did he know that you were supposed to..."

"That's one of those things best left alone, Annie."

"He'll talk to you but not to me?"

"He has his reasons."

"That's not good enough." She went to the door. "How long are you staying?" she asked without looking at him.

"I'm not sure."

"But you're not staying permanently."

"No."

Annie stood up. "Goodnight, David. I'll see you at breakfast."

****

Chava came to breakfast the next morning wearing a gray wool jumper with a long-sleeved pink blouse. "She picked it out herself," David said. "Mrs. Swane had hung everything in the closet, and she got right out of bed, went over there, opened the door and started pawing through her new wardrobe." He laughed. "Just like a woman. They start early."

Annie helped herself to coffee from the sideboard. "What would you like for breakfast, Chava?"

The little girl appeared confused. "Bread and cheese?"

"What's Mrs. Swane preparing?" David asked.

Annie shrugged. "I don't know. She'll make anything Chava wants."

"Don't you eat?"

"Toast."

"You've lost weight."

"That's none of your concern." Annie looked at Chava. "Go into the kitchen and tell Mrs. Swane what you'd like to eat."

"You could be kinder to her while she's here," David observed, picking up a cup.

"I went out and got her some clothes and toys, didn't I?"

"She's five years old, Annie, and she's just lost her mother and come thousands of miles to a strange place."

"Well, she'll be going home soon."

"You haven't changed your mind? You don't want to even try?"

"No."

"All right. I have that business to take care of, and then I'll take her to Chicago. Shelli will see that she gets back to Israel and look after her there until I can make other arrangements."

"I've been thinking about what you told me last night. Is Papa involved in some sort of spy business?" Annie sat down in what had always been her place. Alan's and Lenore's chairs remained pushed tightly under the table. "Are you?"

"Do you think Dr. Sims could take a look at Chava before we go?" David asked.

Annie started to say that he hadn't answered her question but decided not to press him. "This is Sunday, but he might come out to the house if I called him. Do you think she's sick?"

"She's been through a lot in the last month."

"He's not a psychiatrist."

"She doesn't need a psychiatrist, Annie, just someone to love and care for her the way Rebekah and her Poppy did. I have her immunization records with me. Dr. Sims might look those over and see if they're up to date."

"Her health card had to be current in order for her to travel, didn't it?"

"Not the way we came. Would you mind calling him?"

"I'll do it after breakfast. I think he still goes to early mass, so he should be free after that."

Chava followed Mrs. Swane through the

swinging door. "Cinnamon buns," she announced with a broad smile that showed her mother's deep dimples. David boosted her into the chair beside his. Mrs. Swane set a plate in front of her and handed her a fork.

"You loved those when you first came," the woman said to Annie.

"I still do. Mrs. Ford doesn't make them."

"I'll bring in the rest. What about you, David?"

"I could do with a few."

Chava's eyes mirrored adoration as she watched Mrs. Swane go back into the kitchen.

****

"She's healthy enough as far as I can tell," Rolf Sims told David and Annie while Chava occupied herself in front of the fire with more books from Annie's shelves. "If she's going to be here awhile, I could do some blood work to be sure. Meanwhile, a good tonic might not hurt." He scribbled something on his pad, tore it off, and handed it to David.

"She has nightmares about what happened," David said, lowering his voice.

"I can't help you there," Dr. Sims said. "She'll likely forget in time."

"You didn't tell me about the nightmares," Annie interrupted.

"You didn't ask."

"How would I know…"

"I told you what happened. You were traumatized as a child and were still having bad dreams after we married."

Dr. Sims patted Annie's knee to ward off the angry retort he saw forming on her lips. "We all react to stress in different ways." He put his stethoscope back into his bag. "She'll be all right, David. Lots of love and security will do the trick."

"I appreciate your coming out on a Sunday."

"I was glad to do it." The doctor turned to Annie.

"A tonic might not hurt you, either."

"I'm all right."

"If you say so. Call me if you need me."

****

Later, David buttoned Chava into her red coat and took her outside to play on the back lawn. Annie watched them from the window of the study. *Our child would be older than Chava. Our little boy. David would have loved a son.*

She stood transfixed as David picked up Chava and swung her around, then fell to the ground and rolled. She couldn't hear their laughter through the window, but the joy on their faces stirred resentment in her. How long had it been since she'd heard David laugh when they were together? Had she ever made him happy? Why did he stay married to her? Why did she stay married to him?

She turned Alan's swivel chair away from the window so that she couldn't see the two of them. Yesterday she'd made the decision to go through the desk, but David's arrival with Chava had sidetracked her good intentions. She would do it today without fail. Taking a deep breath, she pulled out a drawer and began to remove everything in it.

She was on the third drawer when David came in. "Mrs. Swane is giving Chava some hot cocoa in the kitchen. Anything I can help you with?"

"I'm going through Pa's desk."

"You haven't done that yet?"

"No, I haven't," she flared. "I had to take care of things at the office first."

She replaced the drawer and went to work on the ones on the right-hand side. They only contained office supplies, so she closed them. "I'm looking for the combination to the safe."

"I didn't know there was a safe."

"Behind the doors of the credenza." She nodded at the piece of furniture where a tray with six long-stemmed glasses and a crystal decanter had sat ready for guests as long as she could remember. "I doubt there's anything too important in it. Uncle Sam kept Pa's will in the vault at his office."

David opened the doors and stooped down to inspect the dial. "Do you think he even wrote down the combination? I could crack this if I had to, but I'd rather not."

"So you're a safecracker on top of being Charlie Chan and Jack the Ripper?"

David scowled. "I just said I could do it if I had to, and I didn't permanently damage Alberta. Feel around under the desk. Look under the drawers."

Annie's fingers skimmed the smooth underside of the middle drawer. "Here's something." She held up a piece of paper. "That's odd. It's in Braille."

"Mrs. Ashley read Braille, didn't she?"

"Almost as well as Pa. I learned it, too." She touched the raised dots. "Try this. Seven left. Twelve right. Forty-nine left."

David twirled the dial and pushed down the handle. The safe door swung open. "Good for you, Annie!" He rose and held out his hand. "It's all yours."

She sat on the floor and began to remove a stack of documents encased in thick covers tied with old-fashioned cords. "Here's the abstract of the house."

"That should make interesting reading. The house has quite a history."

"My adoption papers. Their marriage license. Here's something marked with Emory Roth's name and the date nineteen thirty-one. That's the year I came here."

"The results of his investigation, I'd guess."

"He knew about Papa, and so do you."

"I can't tell you anything, Annie, so don't ask."

"I don't like all this secrecy."

"That's just the way it is. What else is in there?"

"Some jewelry cases. I expect they belonged to Pa's mother and grandmother, although most of his mother's things went down with her on the *Titanic*." Annie set aside the worn velvet boxes. "And here's an envelope with my name on it."

She shook out some papers into her lap. "My original birth certificate from Texas. She held it up. Roberta Annette Rycroft. That was me."

"Why did you keep the name Annette?"

"It was Papa's sister's name. Actually, her name was Annika, but Annette was close enough."

"She'd have been Rebekah's mother, wouldn't she?"

"I guess so. Yes, that's right. And Chava's grandmother." Annie frowned, then went back to the box. "Here's a marriage license for Papa and my mother. Why would Pa have that?"

"Maybe he got everything he could, thinking you might want it someday."

Annie unfolded the paper and scanned it. "They were married in January nineteen-twenty-one. That can't be right. I was born in May of that same year."

"Sure it could be right."

"A forced marriage?"

"A belated one, anyway."

"They fought all the time."

"That was unpleasant for you."

"What you said once about marrying a non-Jew...Papa did that."

"There weren't any nice Jewish girls in Barnwell, I guess." David smiled. "So he didn't have much choice."

"Not if she was pregnant with me."

"He must have known he was responsible."

"She might have lied. I wouldn't put it past her."

"Well, speaking as a man, if a girl told me she was having my child, and I knew there was no way I could be the father, I sure wouldn't marry her."

"So they..." She felt the heat rising in her face.

"It happens, Annie. Don't judge him. He married her and gave you a name. You said he was a good father."

"He was wonderful—until he let her take me away."

"Maybe he didn't have any choice."

"We all have choices."

"I've been telling you that for years."

She returned the document to the envelope. "I don't have anything from that time except Alberta. No pictures, no keepsakes."

"You have your locket. Do you still wear it?"

Her hand went to her throat. "Yes."

David slid off the ottoman onto the carpet beside her and lifted the oval locket from beneath her blouse. "Was it new when he gave it to you?"

"I don't remember. I've had to replace the chain."

"I mean that it looks older than you are. Maybe it belonged to his mother."

"When he gave it to me for my fifth birthday, I remember promising him that I'd never take it off. I wear the other necklace, too, the one Pa and Mum gave me on their wedding day."

"This opens," he said.

"No, it doesn't. It's solid. Papa had the date and a little star engraved on the back."

"I see that, but there's a tiny spring catch at the top." He worked his thumbnail into the nearly-invisible opening and pressed. The locket flew open. "Look, Annie. Pictures." He unclasped the chain from around her neck and held the locket where she could see.

"Papa! It's Papa!"

"That's how you remember him?"

"And that must be me on the other side. The baby on the pillow."

"So now you have something besides Alberta."

Annie stared at the small faded faces, obviously cut from larger photographs. "I can't believe it. All these years, I never knew there were pictures inside."

"These lockets are meant to look like they don't open."

"How do you know?"

"Let's just say I've had some experience with similar objects that aren't what they seem to be."

Annie continued to stare at Albert Rycroft's face. "I'd forgotten what he looked like."

"He's still a handsome man."

"And he still doesn't want me." She snapped the locket shut and dropped it into the pocket of her skirt.

"He gave you the gift of a home with the Ashleys. Now he's given you Chava. Both gifts cost him a piece of his heart, Annie. That's love in its purest form." He gathered her in his arms. "And I love you, more than you know."

She let him hold her until Chava found them.

Chapter Thirty

The more Annie thought about it, the less she liked the idea of having the diamonds in the house. David was noncommittal about when he would deliver them to his contact, and when she pushed him for an answer, he simply shook his head.

"Those diamonds nearly cost me my life twice," she said. "They killed my baby. I don't want them around."

"No one knows they're here."

"Can you be sure of that?"

He admitted that he couldn't.

"And there's Chava to consider."

"Soon, Annie, that's all I can tell you."

"At least put them in the safe."

"They're already there."

"How did they get there?"

He laughed. "I slipped them in before you closed it on Sunday afternoon."

"It seems to me that you know how to do a lot of very strange things. You knew my locket opened."

"During the war, undercover agents were dropped into Europe with hidden messages and communication codes. Jewelry made a good place to smuggle things like that."

"You memorized the combination to the safe, I suppose."

He nodded. "But I'll show you how to change it later if you'll feel better."

"I trust you," she retorted, stung by the implication.

"Do you?"

****

The call came after dinner on Wednesday. "The diamonds will be history tomorrow night," David said. "I'll leave a contact number for you if I don't come back."

"If you don't...you didn't say it was dangerous."

"There are people out there who would kill for less than the diamonds are worth, and there are more people who would kill to keep them from financing anything that would benefit Israel." He hesitated. "I'm armed, Annie."

"You carry a gun?"

"Yes."

"I've never seen it."

"I don't make a habit of displaying it." He covered her hand with his. "Let's just say it's insurance."

"You're not in the import-export business at all, are you?"

"Certainly I am. I've built up a fair clientele in a short time."

"But that's not really what you do."

"It is as far as you're concerned."

"Didn't those years in a concentration camp make you value your life? Do you get a thrill out of taking risks?"

"There are things more valuable than life. Ideals, for instance." He searched her eyes. "Are you worried about me?"

"I don't want you to die. Not now. Not after everything you've been through."

"It's better to die for something than to live for nothing."

"That's a cliché, and if you intend to imply that I don't live for anything, I resent that."

"I didn't intend to imply anything of the sort, Annie. I was speaking for myself."

"You have something to live for. You have a

wife."

"It doesn't feel like it. Not really. Not sleeping in the guest room across the hall from you." Before she could reply, he waved his hand in front of her face. "I didn't say it."

"Chava is ready for bed." Mrs. Swane looked directly at Annie.

"David will go up," Annie said, retreating behind Alan's desk.

"I think you should know what she asked me while she was in her bath." Mrs. Swane took a step inside the room. "She wanted to know why you didn't like her."

Annie caught her breath. "Why I...did you tell her that I didn't dislike her?"

"It's not up to me to tell her anything. You're behaving like a spoiled child who lost the game and won't play anymore."

"Gram!"

Mrs. Swane left without replying.

"I'll go up," David said. "I'll explain things to her."

"What will you explain?" Annie's voice shook.

"I'll think of something."

When he'd gone, she sank down in Alan's chair and leaned her head in her hands. Her mind spun back to the night she'd arrived at Greenfield, terrified at being separated from Lenore. Even Miss Ervin's gentle reassurance that it was only temporary hadn't helped much. *And I was ten, old enough to understand. Chava's only five.* Shame sickened her.

What had David said? *Rebekah shielded her with her own body. Chava was covered in her mother's blood.*

Annie slapped the desk until her palms stung. Then she jumped from the chair and ran for the stairs.

On the landing, she heard the sound of singing coming from Chava's room. The strange, haunting melody wrapped around words in a language she didn't understand. David's deep voice and Chava's soft one blended seamlessly, shutting Annie out. The few steps to the open door of the room seemed like miles.

Hava nagila,
Hava nagila
Hava nagila ve nis'mecha.
Hava neranenah,
Hava neranenah,
Hava nerenah ve nis'mecha

As she reached the door, the voices switched to English.

Let's rejoice,
Let's rejoice,
Let's rejoice and be happy.
Let's sing,
Let's sing,
Let's sing and be happy.

She stood listening for a few minutes. Then, drawn by some unseen force, she went into her own room and removed Alberta from the glass cabinet. She'd stuffed the doll's ravaged body with fresh cotton and closed it so skillfully that the tiny stitches were almost invisible. For a long moment, she stood hugging the doll to her chest.

You're all I have left, Alberta, the only one who'll never leave me. But maybe Chava needs you more than I do right now. You guarded those diamonds for twenty-five years. Surely you can take care of one very little girl.

The singing stopped when Annie came into the room. She sat down on the bed beside Chava and held out the doll. "Your Poppy gave me this when I was just about your age, Chava. I think he'd like for her to be your friend, now."

Chava touched the painted face with one finger. "What's her name, Annie?"

"Alberta. Your Poppy's real name is Albert. She's named for him."

"She's very pretty."

"You're very pretty, too." Annie smoothed the child's dark wavy hair.

Chava's eyes sparkled in the light from the lamp. "My mommy was pretty. Did you know my mommy?"

"Yes, I did. We played together when we were little girls."

"My mommy's dead." The blunt words from the small pink lips cut into Annie's heart like a knife.

"Mine is dead, too, Chava."

"Do you wish she'd come back?"

"All the time."

Chava's eyes filled with tears. "I want my mommy back, Annie. Can't she ever come back? Who'll take care of me now?"

Annie tried and failed to stop the hot tears that streamed down her cheeks. "I'll take care of you, darling," she whispered, gathering the child in her arms. "I promise that I'll always take care of you."

David caught Annie's arm in the corridor after Chava had sobbed herself to sleep, still clutching Alberta and Poppybear. "That was a nice thing to do, giving her the doll."

"She needs her more than I do."

"Did you mean what you said?"

Annie nodded. "I'll do the best I can."

"I'll help you, Annie, if you'll let me." He slipped his arm around her waist and started for the door of her room. "I love you. I want to make love to you."

Annie nodded against his shoulder and led him

inside.

****

She wasn't sure what woke her, but the back of her neck prickled with the same terror she'd felt too many times before. "David?" She slid her hand across the bed and found it empty. "David?"

She was on her feet in seconds, grabbing her robe from the chair beside the bed. Trying to hold in her ragged breath, she leaned against the door and heard the faint sound of footsteps in the corridor.

"Mommy!" Chava's anguished cry propelled her across the dark hall into the child's room. "Be quiet!" The words came out more harshly than she intended, but the little girl stopped crying and clung to her.

"I want my mommy!"

"Shhh!" Annie strained to hear more movement. The footsteps on the stairs moved up and down as if someone couldn't decide which way to go.

Grabbing the quilt from the foot of the bed, she wrapped it around Chava and picked her up. "Don't make a sound," she whispered. "I'm going to take you to a secret place, and Uncle David will come find us there."

She hesitated before opening the door. Rage replaced terror at the words, "You get the kid. I'll take care of the woman." It was happening again, only this time she wasn't afraid. *No more. I won't be the victim again. They're not going to get me, and they're not going to get Chava, either.*

She turned the doorknob and slid out of the room. Hugging the opposite wall, she slipped past the landing and made a dash toward the far end of the hall. The attic stairs creaked beneath her bare feet, but she needed only another minute to reach the door of the deep closet.

Wrenching it open, she felt for the sliding panel against the back wall and eased it out of the way, stumbling a little as she stepped over the raised threshold. She set Chava down and moved the panel back into place, then fumbled in the pocket of her robe for a tissue to stuff around the catch so they wouldn't be locked in.

Finally, she sank down on the damp earthen floor and wrapped the quilt tighter around the child sobbing against her breast. "Shhhh. It's a game, darling. Uncle David will find us, and then we'll go down and have milk and some of Gram's butter cookies."

Gram. The commotion must have wakened her, too. Had the intruders hurt her? Would she have had time to use the telephone beside her bed to call the police? Where was David?

Chava was shivering. "I'm cold, Annie. I don't want to play anymore."

"Just a few more minutes." Annie heard heavy footsteps in the attic. *They won't find the panel, not in the dark. I closed it all the way, and they'd have to know about the cut in the edge.* The storage room door opened briefly, then slammed shut.

She could hear voices and decided there were at least two people, but their words were muffled through the walls. Finally, though she heard them leaving, she didn't move.

"I'm cold," Chava whimpered.

"Just a little while, Chava. Be a brave girl for just a little while longer."

"I don't want them to shoot me. Bad men shot Mommy."

"Shhhhh." She closed her eyes and tried to remember the night Papa had shoved her into the secret room and left her there. She'd been consumed with fear that night, but not now. Now she was only angry and determined to end the nightmare forever.

The moldy chill of the unfinished room began to penetrate the quilt. Snuggling Chava closer, Annie tried to think what she should do next. Gram would think of the secret room, if she was able to think, and David might remember it if he... She wouldn't think about that. Surely David would take care of the intruders once and for all. She strained to hear some sound, but only silence met her ears.

She was surprised when Chava fell asleep and tried to stay very still to keep her that way. How long had they been here? How long should she wait before venturing out to find David and Gram? What was happening downstairs? David had a gun, but maybe the others did, too.

She rested her cheek against Chava's silky hair and tried to think logically. Did the men know about Mrs. Ford in the apartment beyond the kitchen? Had she heard them and called the police? The musty odor emanating from the tunnel's earthen walls grew stronger, filled her nostrils, and settled in her throat, threatening to choke off her breath. Pa said he'd had the end of the tunnel sealed off, but the earthy smell and unbroken darkness of the chasm surrounded her like a hangman's hood.

She buried her face in Chava's hair again, inhaling the comforting scent of shampoo, and concentrated on her next move. They couldn't stay in the moldy chill much longer. Chava was still shivering a little, even in sleep. But they were safe here, at least for now, and if they left their hiding place...

She thought of Albert Rycroft again and saw the diamonds sparkling in the lamplight as David unwrapped them. *So small, so bright, so damning. What skewed reasoning caused Papa to hide them in Alberta before giving the doll to me? Didn't he know he was putting my life at risk? He gambled on my life. My baby died, and for what? Why couldn't he have hidden them somewhere else?*

Whatever his thinking, he'd left her vulnerable,

and now it was happening all over again. David was out there with desperate men bent on getting what they wanted. Chava was terrified, and she, Annie, was furious with the man who'd called her his *best little girl, his shining star.* All her life she'd been nothing but a pawn in a dangerous game, and it had to end. Now. Tonight. This minute.

The door opened again, and someone came inside the closet, heading straight for the panel. For a moment, she forgot to breathe. Her muscles tensed as she tightened her arms around Chava.

"It's right there. Look for the splintered wood." Mrs. Swane's voice came through the door. "I know that's where they are."

The panel slid back, and as the door opened, she blinked in the beam of a flashlight shining on her face. "Mrs. Levinson?" a man's voice said.

Annie's legs felt numb. "We're here," she said, her teeth beginning to chatter with the cold. "Where's David?"

One of the officers helped her to stand, but she refused to surrender Chava.

The little girl stirred but didn't open her eyes. "Mommy?"

"It's Annie, darling, and everything is all right," Annie murmured. "The game's over."

Mrs. Swane waited near the stairs. "I knew you'd come here," she said.

"Where is David?"

The older woman took her arm. "Let me take Chava and put her back to bed. You'll need to speak to the police."

As they reached the second floor, Annie heard the wail of sirens that she recognized as the newly-organized ambulance service. "David's hurt, isn't he?" Despite the burden of the child in her arms, she began to run toward the main staircase.

"Annie, don't!" Mrs. Swane called.

"Wait, Mrs. Levinson," barked one of the officers, reaching for her, but she eluded his grasp. She heard someone scream and realized that it was herself as she caught sight of the bloody body lying face down on the landing.

Mrs. Swane caught up with Annie and snatched Chava from her arms before Annie fell to her knees, cradling David in her arms. Though she called his name over and over, there was no response.

A heavy hand on her shoulder pulled her away. "Who is he?"

"My husband! David, don't die and leave me! Please don't die. If you die, I'll hate you forever. I swear I will. David...David..."

****

Scarcely taking time to wash the blood from her hands, Annie threw on the slacks and sweater David had so recently taken off her as they'd begun to make love. Snatching her coat from the closet near the front door but not stopping to put it on, she flung herself into the back of the police car. "Hurry! Please hurry!"

At the hospital emergency entrance, someone blocked her dash for the ambulance as the attendants unloaded David's body and rolled him inside. She pushed aside their restraining arms and ran alongside the gurney until a nurse stopped her at the door of the treatment room. "We'll let you know," she said. "There's a waiting room at the end of the hall."

By the time Rolf Sims arrived, she'd told her disjointed story twice to the police detective. "They've got him in one of the rooms," she told the doctor. "Please find out something for me. Please take care of him."

Dr. Sims embraced her briefly. "I'll do my best, Annie."

"Mrs. Levinson, are you sure you can't

remember anything else about what happened?" the detective asked again.

Annie shook her head. "All I could think of was hiding Chava before they got her."

"Why would they want her?"

"They..." She stopped, realizing that the police thought that a simple robbery was the motive for the break-in and that they probably didn't need to know about the diamonds..

"Well, if you think of something else, here's a number to call."

"All right." She sprinted toward Rolf Sims as she saw him coming out of the treatment room.

"It doesn't look good, Annie," he said, grasping her shoulders. "He took two bullets in the chest, and he's lost a great deal of blood. He's going to need surgery. I think he should be transferred to Canon City."

"Whatever he needs, anything. Just don't let him die."

"I don't operate anymore, but there's a top thoracic surgeon in Canon City. I'll call the hospital now."

"Will you go with him?" Annie leaned against the doctor. "Don't let him die, Dr. Sims. Please, please don't let him die."

The doctor nodded. "I'm not making any promises, Annie, but I'll be there."

****

Chava was asleep, Mrs. Swane reported, when Annie called to tell her that she was going to Canon City. "And the police are still here. They're going over the whole house."

"Just take care of Chava and let them do as they please," Annie said. "Is Mrs. Ford all right?"

"She didn't hear a thing until the police came."

"They left an officer here to drive me to Canon City. Pack a suitcase for me, and call Rod and see if

292

he can get it on the train tomorrow. And call the Bernards and the office and..."

"I'll take care of everything. Don't worry about Chava or the office."

"Thank you, Gram. Dr. Sims says it's really bad. I'll call you as soon as I know more."

****

The man who approached Annie as she paced the waiting room at the Canon City Hospital wore a rumpled business suit and spoke with an accent. "Mrs. Levinson?"

"I'm Annie Levinson." She looked him over. "You're not a doctor."

The man smiled. "No, definitely not. I wonder if we might speak privately. I've arranged to use one of the doctors' conference rooms."

"What is all this about?"

"I'll explain everything." He stood back and waited for her to precede him.

In the conference room, another man rose from the table as Annie entered. "Mrs. Levinson, I'm George Conroy of the FBI, and this is Loren Vail, a representative of the Israeli government."

Annie swayed. "I need to sit down."

The first man pulled out a chair for her. "You've had quite a shock."

"My husband may be dying," Annie flared.

"I'm very sorry about what happened," Loren Vail said. "I don't know David personally, but he's highly respected in Israel."

"Why? Because he's a spy?"

"Not quite." George Conroy sat down, too. "I'll let Mr. Vail explain."

"I was to be David's contact tonight in the transfer of the diamonds, but I was alerted to the plan to take them before we could meet. Unfortunately, I was unable to find out where the attempt would be made. It surprised me to learn that your house had been broken into."

Annie tried to decipher the man's accent. "I'm German-born," he said, reading her mind. "I immigrated to Palestine after the war. All my family died in the camps."

"I'm sorry," Annie said, warming her hands around the mug of coffee that George Conroy set in front of her.

"As I said, David and I never met, but I knew about him." He leaned forward. "David was instructed to leave a letter introducing me as *Levi* and giving a representative a series of questions and answers to prove my identity so that I could take possession of the diamonds if he wasn't able to deliver them."

"I don't have a letter."

"No, he was told not to leave it with you. You shouldn't have been involved at all. He gave the initials *SB* over the telephone."

"That could be Sam Bernard, my attorney."

"Can you get in touch with him?"

"At this hour?" She glanced up at the wall clock. "It's four in the morning."

George Conroy slid a telephone across the table. "Mrs. Levinson, I know this is difficult for you, but your cooperation is critical."

She nodded. "Does the doctor know I'm in here so that he can tell me about David?"

"I have someone waiting outside the treatment room," Loren said.

No one answered at the Bernard home. "I don't know where they are," Annie said.

Almost as the same moment that she hung up, Sam and Ellen Bernard burst through the door. "Mrs. Swane called us. Annie, what's going on?"

The two officials insisted, with polite apologies, that Ellen leave the room, and then they provided Sam with several pieces of identification. He produced the envelope, opened it, and went through the series of questions David had formulated. When they were answered correctly, he turned to Annie. "Do you know where the diamonds are?"

"In the safe in Pa's study. David said that he slipped them in there when I had it open the other day, but I didn't see him do it."

"And the safe is locked?" the FBI agent asked.

The combination is in Braille, but I wrote the numbers under the dots and put it inside the middle drawer under some papers."

"Do you want me to get them?" Sam asked.

Loren Vail shook his head. "Not with the police in the house. Which brings me to the question as to what you told them, Mrs. Levinson."

"I didn't tell them anything except that someone broke in, and that I hid with Chava in the secret room."

"You didn't mention the diamonds?" Loren asked.

"I had the feeling I shouldn't."

Loren Vail sat back smiling. "You were exactly right."

"Who is Chava?" Sam asked.

"It's a long story." Annie closed her eyes. "Please...I need to know about David."

"We'll have someone speak with the police chief and ask him to discontinue the investigation," George Conroy said. "Nothing should be said about the diamonds or the proposed transfer."

"What is all this about?" Sam asked. "I think Annie has a right to know. Is David involved in some sort of undercover work?"

The two men exchanged glances. Loren Vail seemed to be considering his words. "Do you know what the Mossad is?"

Annie and Sam shook their heads.

"It's the intelligence service of the Israeli

government."

"David's part of that?" A tremor ran through Annie's body. Sam slipped his arm around her.

"Unfortunately, he isn't now, because his cover, as we say in the vernacular, has been blown."

Annie winced. "That's what he couldn't tell me." She bit her lip. "Is my father...is Albert Rycroft part of it, too?"

"I can't give you any more information than that," Loren said. "I'm sorry."

"Do you want me to get the diamonds?" Sam repeated his question with obvious impatience.

Loren Vail shook his head. "No, although I'd like to go with you to the house as soon as the police are withdrawn. It's probably being watched, and when I'm seen coming and going, it will appear that I've taken the diamonds. For now, however, they'll remain where they are."

"I want them out." Annie spoke with a harsh urgency that surprised everyone. "They've cost me enough, maybe even my husband!"

"We'll get them out as soon as possible," Loren assured her.

"What if the men come back before you get them? They could hurt someone. Chava and Gram. Mrs. Ford."

"As soon as the police are gone, I'll have two agents inside your house until the diamonds are removed," Conroy said.

"That's not good enough! There's a five-year-old child who's seen her mother murdered and who thinks that David is dead, too!"

"Annie, they know what they're doing," Sam murmured.

"Nobody knows anything." She jumped up and ran out the door, almost knocking down a nurse.

"They've taken your husband to surgery, Mrs. Levinson. Dr. Sims said to tell you that he's gone in as an observer."

Annie slumped against the wall, slid to the floor, and began to sob.

****

Ellen stayed at the hospital with Annie while Sam accompanied Conroy and Vail back to Rumers Crossing. Annie explained about Chava and made another telephone call to Mrs. Swane to check on her.

David was still in surgery at noon when Sam returned. "I had no idea that the letter David left with me was any more than a statement that he would make no claim on you in case of a divorce. He just said not to open it until you asked me to. But when Mrs. Swane called, I had the feeling that I needed to bring it with me."

"I didn't know any of this, either," Annie said. "Did those men take care of everything?"

"I hope so."

"But the ones who broke in could do it again."

"Vail says if they saw him leave, they'll go after him. I get the idea he's acting as a decoy."

"He'll get himself killed like David." She stopped as Dr. Sims and another doctor, still in surgical scrubs, entered the room. "Is David all right?"

Rolf Sims took hold of Annie's arm before he answered. "There was a lot of damage, Annie. It's going to be touch and go for awhile."

"But he's alive?"

The other doctor nodded. "It took a long time to repair everything."

"Can I see him?"

"He's been taken to intensive care. I'll let Dr. Sims go up with you."

****

Annie barely recognized David in the tangle of wires and tubes running from his body. She recoiled from their chill as she tried to find a place on his

297

body to touch. "Don't die, David," she whispered when she finally worked her face as close to his as she could. "Please don't die and leave me." She put her lips against his colorless cheek. "I love you. I was wrong to let you go off to Israel alone. Maybe if I'd gone with you and had children for you, you wouldn't have gotten mixed up in all this."

She kissed him again. "And I *will* go with you this time. We'll raise Chava together and give her some brothers and sisters and...oh, please, David, don't die! I can't stand losing you, too!"

Chapter Thirty-One

For three days, Annie never strayed far from the room in which David lay fighting for his life. Rod brought her suitcase and stayed with her long enough to assure her that Chava and Mrs. Swane were all right and to collect directives for various people at the office. A sympathetic nurse let her shower and change clothes in the nurses' lounge. She slept on the waiting room sofa, wrapped in a blanket brought by another nurse, and asked to be waked through the night, every hour on the hour, to spend her allotted ten minutes with David.

Twice a day she spoke to Chava by phone, assuring her that David was going to get well and come home soon. That she might be telling the largest lie of her life weighed heavily on her conscience, but she couldn't admit the possibility of another outcome.

Loren Vail never came back, but George Conroy did. "We convinced the police to drop the investigation, and the diamonds are out of your house and on their way to their intended destination."

"What about the men who broke in?"

"They did try to get back into the house that night, but we caught them."

"Who..."

"It's better you don't know more, Mrs. Levinson, but I will tell you that they had nothing to do with Barnwell, Texas."

"You know about Barnwell?"

"Yes, and that's all I can say."

"Mr. Vail said that David wasn't part of the intelligence operation now. What will happen to him?"

"He can't be used for undercover work, but I'm sure he'll be offered a position in another division."

"Where he'll be safe?"

George Conroy smiled. "Mrs. Levinson, nothing is completely safe anymore, especially not in Israel at the moment. He might even choose not to return."

"He'll go back," she said. "I'm sure of that."

****

On the fourth afternoon, David woke up. With a tube down his throat, he couldn't speak, but his eyes told Annie that he recognized her.

"Chava is safe," she said. "And I've been here with you all along. I won't leave until you can go with me." She worked her face in among the tubes to kiss his cheek. "I love you, David."

****

Only later, when David was moved to a private room, did Annie make a quick trip home. Hearing her come in, Chava hurtled from the kitchen and into her arms. "Did you bring Uncle David? Is he coming home?"

Annie picked her up. "Not just yet, darling, but soon."

"Can I go see him?"

"The hospital doesn't allow children, but I'll try to get a telephone in his room so that you can talk to him."

"Gram says the bad men are all gone, Annie."

"They're all gone forever."

"I was scared."

"So was I."

Chava snuggled closer. "Mrs. Ford let me make biscuits. I got to cut them."

"Did you?"

"And Gram says I've been good."

Mrs. Swane came through the dining room door. "She's been good as gold." She put her arms around Annie. "You need a night's sleep and some decent food."

"I'll get a room at a hotel when I go back, but I couldn't leave the hospital until I knew that David was going to be all right."

"Are you going to the office at all?"

"According to Uncle Trent, Jack Shaw is handling everything as well as I could."

"He sent Rod over with some papers for you to sign. They're on the desk in the study."

Annie set Chava on her feet. "I'll go upstairs and shower before dinner."

Chava grabbed her hand. "Can I come, too?"

"She's missed you, Annie," Mrs. Swane murmured.

Annie nodded. "I've missed her, too."

****

"Stop fussing over me," David snapped two nights later. "Go back to the hotel."

"I'm just making sure you're comfortable before I go."

"That's what the nurses are for."

Annie refolded the blanket over his feet.

"I want you to go home, Annie. You need to get back to work, and Chava needs you."

"Jack is taking care of work, and Gram is taking care of Chava."

"But that's your job."

"I want to be here with you."

"You're smothering me. I need some time to myself. Time to think."

"About what?"

"About the future. It's going to be different for me now."

"And safer."

He scowled at her.

301

"David, I had no idea you were involved in all that."

"You didn't need to know."

"I understand that, but it's over now."

"Its all so simple for you, isn't it? This was my work, Annie. Now it's gone."

"At least your life isn't gone."

"No, but it's changed, and I need time to sort things out and make some decisions."

"Those wretched diamonds! How could Papa have done that to me?"

David ignored her question. "I didn't like leaving them in the house, but I couldn't do anything until I was contacted."

"I know that. I don't blame *you* for what happened."

"I'd never have forgiven myself if you and Chava had been hurt."

"I wasn't going to let that happen. I was so angry that I forgot to be afraid."

"That was pretty quick thinking, to hide in the secret room."

"It saved me before."

"So you said."

"Do you want something to eat? A banana? Some milk? The nurses have been wonderful about letting me keep things in the refrigerator at the nurses' station."

"I'm fine, Annie. I just want you to go."

"All right. I'll see you in the morning."

"No, I want you to check out of the hotel and go home."

"You can't mean that!"

"Look, you've been here for almost three weeks, and I appreciate it. But you need some time to think, too. I have to decide about my future, and you have to decide about yours."

"I'll do anything you want me to."

"Why? Because you feel guilty that I almost died? Because you didn't want to share my life in Israel?"

She turned her back. "I love you, David."

"I love you, too, Annie, but that's not enough, not anymore. And that's what we've got to decide, both of us. We have to decide what we want for the rest of our lives. I already know that I'm no longer satisfied with a part-time marriage."

"I told you I'd go back with you this time."

"Playing the martyr isn't your best role."

"That's not what I'm doing. I..."

"Look, Annie, go home," he interrupted. "Go to work. Take care of Chava. Let me think, and you think, too. Then we'll talk about it."

****

Annie spent the weekend with Chava, trying to make up for weeks of neglect. "I'm sorry I've had to leave you by yourself with Gram and Mrs. Ford."

"It's okay. Gram said you had to take care of Uncle David."

"That's right."

"It's okay, Annie."

"It's almost Christmas. Do you know about Christmas?"

"Santa Claus? Mommy told me about him."

"Did he come to see you when you were at home?"

Chava's head bobbed up and down. "He brought me candy in my stocking, only I wasn't supposed to tell."

"And toys?"

"A baby doll."

"What would you like for him to bring you this year?"

"I don't know."

"Then next Saturday we'll go to the store so you can look at the toys."

303

"Does Santa bring toys from the store?"

Annie thought quickly. "Only if his elves can't make enough before Christmas."

"Oh."

"How is Alberta?"

"Gram made her a bed in a basket. Now I can carry her around and she won't get broken."

"She needs some clothes, doesn't she?"

"Maybe a nightgown."

"She had one once, and a lot of other things, too."

"What happened to them?"

"They got burned up in a fire."

Chava's eyes widened.

Annie lifted the little girl onto her lap. "I lived in a place for children who didn't have anyone to take care of them. My mother was sick."

"Did she die like my mommy?"

"No, but she couldn't take care of me for a long time, so I lived in a big house with other children, and one night it burned down."

"But you saved Alberta."

"Yes."

"I'm sorry about her clothes, Annie."

Annie put her lips against the child's hair. "Yes, so am I." *And a lot of other things, too. If David doesn't want me anymore, I'll deserve it, but...but I can't believe it's too late for us...and for Chava.*

****

Annie called David every night. He didn't have much to say, always chatting with Chava longer than he talked to Annie. When she suggested coming to see him on Sunday, he said no.

On the following Saturday, she took Chava to the new department store in Lowell to shop for more clothes and to let her look at the toys, making a mental note of everything in which the little girl expressed any interest. On Sunday, while Chava was taking a nap, Annie telephoned David.

"Do you object to Chava having Santa Claus?"

"Why would I?"

"I just thought I'd ask. I really don't know how she's been brought up, so I wondered..."

"Rebekah and Reuven weren't orthodox, if that's what you mean, and neither is Albert Rycroft."

"Oh. Well, I took her to look at toys yesterday."

"What did she like?"

"A dollhouse, very like the one I had in Barnwell. And I'm trying to find clothes for Alberta."

"The doctor was in this morning and said he'd release me early next week."

"Oh, David, that's wonderful! You'll be here for Christmas. Chava will be so excited."

"We need to talk first."

"We'll talk when you get home."

"Not around Chava. I assume you're going to keep her?"

"We've become very attached to each other. David, I was thinking. Why don't we invite Daniel and Shelli for the holidays?"

"They're going back to Israel in January."

"But they could be here for Christmas. I know it's not a Jewish holiday, but apparently Rebekah kept some of her American traditions for Chava." When David didn't answer, she hurried on. "I don't want to offend them or anything."

"You don't have to worry about that, Annie."

"Then it will be all right if I invite them?"

"I'll call them tomorrow. You and I still have to talk, though."

"Do you want me to come to the hospital?"

"Sure, tomorrow, I guess. And Annie, before you come, be sure you know what you want and why you want it. Be very sure."

****

David was wearing slacks and a sweater when

305

she arrived the next morning. "The doctor said I could leave today, since you were coming. I can follow up with Dr. Sims."

Annie put her arms around him, being careful not to press too hard against his chest. "You look wonderful." She waited for his embrace, but his arms remained at his sides. She backed away.

"We can sit in here and talk," he said, motioning to the chair. He eased himself down on the edge of the lowered bed.

David's unsmiling face made her feel edgy. "All right, let's talk."

"What I said before about not wanting your attention out of guilt—I meant it."

"I can't help feeling guilty about what happened. It was Papa who started the whole thing."

"It had nothing to do with you."

"All right, it didn't, but I've been involved in it my whole life."

"That's unfortunate. You didn't deserve what happened to you anymore than Chava did."

Annie shuddered. "I've had a hard time trying not to think about what happened to Rebekah."

"You have to think about it. It happened. Chava's memories may dim over time, but she won't forget something like that. Whoever takes responsibility for her will have to help her through the bad times."

"I said that I'd take her, David, and I'll be good to her."

"Because you want her, or because you feel guilty for resenting Rebekah all these years?"

"I didn't...all right, maybe I *did* resent Rebekah. Papa chose her over me, and while I understood why, it didn't really make me feel any better."

"So why are you taking Chava?"

"I told you, David, we've become attached."

"Can you love her?"

"I already do. It would be hard not to."

"So now let's talk about us. Exactly what do you have in mind for our future?"

"Whatever you want."

"You'll go to Israel with me and live there?"

"Yes."

"As a wife who wants to be with her husband? Or as a martyr?"

"You're casting me in a very unflattering light, and I don't think I deserve it. Not all of it, anyway."

"I don't mean to judge you, Annie. I just want you to be honest with yourself, for both our sakes."

"I don't know anything about Israel, so I don't know if I'll be happy there. And I don't know anything about being a Jew, but maybe you're right that it's part of my heritage."

"Not all of it, Annie. You spent more time with the Ashleys. It was unfair of me to expect you to embrace a part of yourself you never knew about, just because it was important to me."

"I can learn, David. I'm willing to try. And I do know that I love you and don't want to be apart from you ever again."

"How did you come to that conclusion?"

"Do you know what it was like for me to see you lying on the stairs in a pool of your own blood? Do you know what it was like to wait for days before I knew that you were going to live? I think I paid my dues, David."

"We never fully pay our dues in this life. We always owe something."

"Then tell me what you want me to say."

"We've been married eight years and lived together less than one."

"I offered you your freedom more than once."

"I almost took you up on it the last time."

"Maybe you should have."

"Maybe so."

A long, uncomfortable silence fell between them. Finally Annie said, "I'm sorry for not trusting you, but I need for you to understand why."

"I've been trying to understand, but two people can't be married and not trust each other."

"Then consider it from my standpoint. I've lost everyone I ever loved, and I almost lost you. If we go back to Israel, I could still lose you. I could lose Chava. Even the possibility terrifies me."

"I can't work in intelligence again. Not in the field. I might work in administration."

"Do you want to?"

"Sit behind a desk? No. But my export-import business is interesting, even if I did start it as a cover for what I was really doing."

"Is Daniel with the Mossad?"

"No. And he won't be. He promised Shelli. He's going to stay with the law."

"What do you want to do, David? What would make you happy?"

"It's just an idea, Annie, but what if I tied my business into Ashley Enterprises? I'd still travel, though not as much. Shelli could manage the store in Tel Aviv."

"You'd actually consider that? You'd stay here?"

"I love Israel, Annie. I've been part of her birth, and I want to be part of her life. But I realize now that I don't have to live there all the time to do that. I can work for her here just as well. And I've been thinking about Chava. Maybe she doesn't need to go back there right away, not after what happened. Someday, if she wants to live there, she can make the choice for herself."

"So we'd stay here."

"That's right, except for visits."

"For business?"

"Maybe we can finally go on that dig one of these days. When you can get away from work."

"Jack Shaw stepped in and took over at a moment's notice while I was here with you, and he's done an exceptional job. I realized something, too, David. I love the Ashley Enterprises family because it was important to my parents, but I can be involved with it in a different way. I can stay on the board of directors, and Jack can run Ashley Enterprises."

"That's what you really want?"

"I've already talked to him. He's willing to give it a try. Besides, I want to be a real mother to Chava and all her brothers and sisters."

"All her...I see." A slow smile spread over David's face. "Then we'd better get home and get started. Neither of us is getting any younger, you know."

Annie went to his outstretched arms. "Not until after Christmas. You've got to save your strength to assemble that dollhouse I ordered. It was the biggest one in the store."

Epilogue

On New Year's Day, Thomas Greer stood under the *huppah* erected in the drawing room, a silent but smiling presence, while the rabbi from Lowell performed the Jewish marriage rites for David and Annie. At the conclusion, Greer extracted the napkin-wrapped wine glass from his vestments and placed it on the floor in front of David, who smashed the glass with his foot to the cheers of "*Mazeltov!*"

Mrs. Swane and Mrs. Ford presided over the wedding supper, which included some traditional dishes prepared with Shelli's help. Afterwards, the guests danced in the empty foyer until almost midnight.

"Rabbi Steiner and I agree that two ceremonies in two separate religious faiths are enough to make this marriage last forever," Thomas Greer joked as he said his goodbyes.

"It will," David said. "Thanks for helping out again."

"Just name your firstborn after me, and we'll call it square." The rector winked at Annie. "You blush exactly like Lenore."

****

"Are you sorry we're not taking off on a honeymoon?" David asked as they went upstairs after the last guest had gone.

"We've had a honeymoon...several of them. And we agreed that Chava didn't need to be left alone right now."

They checked on her before going to their own room. Tucked between Alberta and Poppybear, she slept peacefully. "I'm going to move her into my room as soon as I clear out Mum's and Pa's sitting room and bedroom for us," Annie said.

"Are you sure you're ready to do that?"

"It's been almost a year, David. I'll grieve for them forever, but I have to let them go."

He sat down on the window seat and motioned for her to join him. "I have something for you. Not a wedding gift exactly, and don't ask me how I got it." He handed her an envelope.

Annie hesitated before she took it. "From Papa?"

"I think probably so."

"I don't know if I want to read it tonight."

"I think tonight is exactly the right time. Would you like to be alone?"

"No, I want you to stay. Please." She tore off one end of the envelope and tapped the single sheet of paper into her palm.

Bobbie, my best little girl, my shining star,

You have never been far from my thoughts since that terrible day I knew I was losing you, probably forever. In the end, it was the best thing for you. The Ashleys gave you all the love and security, not to mention the opportunities, that I wanted for you.

Now you have Chava, Rebekah's daughter, and I know you will see that she has the boundless love and devotion that you were given. David is a good man who loves you very much. From fear and sorrow has come a second chance at happiness for you both.

All these years, I have harbored a hope for reunion with you, but now my heart tells me that it will never be. This decision, too, is best for both of us.

I have always loved you, Bobbie, and I'm proud of the woman you have become. Raise Chava to be a strong, good woman, too.

Shalom.

Papa

Annie lifted her eyes to meet David's. "Will I

ever know more about him?"

"I don't know, but the important thing is that he knows about you."

"I really was his shining star...once...a long time ago."

"And now you're the light of my life, Annie."

"You were right, you know. Bobbie isn't gone. I'm still her."

"And still Annie, too?"

"Yes. I loved Pa and Mum so much. Part of me will always belong to them."

David stood up, lifting her with him. "You'll always belong to me, too."

Annie laid her face against his chest and felt his heart beating beneath her cheek. Glancing toward the bank of windows where the moonlight streamed through the sheers, she noticed a single star glowing brighter than the rest.

Thank you, Papa. And goodbye.

A word about the author...

Judy is a retired teacher who has written stories and poems since she could hold a pencil, always promising herself that someday she would pursue publication.

Grandparents and older friends gave her a passionate interest in history and genealogical research, from which she draws many of her characters and plot ideas.

Widowed for many years, she has two grown sons and a granddaughter whose smile lights up her life.

Thank you for purchasing
this Wild Rose Press publication.
For other wonderful stories of romance,
please visit our on-line bookstore at
www.thewildrosepress.com

For questions or more information,
contact us at
info@thewildrosepress.com

The Wild Rose Press
www.TheWildRosePress.com